Love Finds You™

IN

Carmel

by-the-Sea

CALIFORNIA

Love Finds You™
IN
Carmel
by-the-Sea
CALIFORNIA

BY SANDRA D. BRICKER

summerside
PRESS™

Summerside Press™
Minneapolis 55438
www.summersidepress.com

Love Finds You in Carmel-by-the-Sea, California
© 2010 by Sandra D. Bricker

ISBN 978-1-60936-027-6

Scripture references are from the following sources: The Holy Bible, New International Version®, NIV®. Copyright © 1973, 1978, 1984 by Biblica, Inc.™ Used by permission of Zondervan. All rights reserved worldwide. The New King James Version (NKJV). Copyright © 1982 by Thomas Nelson, Inc. Used by permission.

The town depicted in this book is a real place, but all characters are fictional. Any resemblances to actual people or events are purely coincidental.

Cover Design by Koechel Peterson & Associates | www.kpadesign.com

Interior Design by Müllerhaus Publishing Group | www.mullerhaus.net

Photos of Carmel by Stephen Brown, www.flickr.com/photos/sjb4photos. Used by permission.

Published in association with the literary agency of WordServe Literary Group, Ltd., 10152 S. Knoll Circle, Highlands Ranch, CO 80130, www.wordserveliterary.com.

Summerside Press™ is an inspirational publisher offering fresh, irresistible books to uplift the heart and engage the mind.

Printed in USA.

Dedication

······················

For Jemelle and Alberto,
the real-life parents of Sherman and Murphy,
the cutest and most personable beagle rescues *EVER!*
May both puppies rest in peace
and find lots of lettuce leaves where they are now.

And for Rachelle Gardner
with sincere thanks
for her humor, guidance, grace,
and a shoulder that is *much stronger than it looks!*

Acknowledgments
....

Deepest thanks to my Summerside editors,
Rachel and Connie.
I love you both so much.
And Carlton, thank you for wanting me to tell the story
when you fell for Carmel-by-the-Sea.

Wonky, goofy gratitude to Tom Merino,
my favorite FilmGypsy.
I love you more than my thesaurus.
Tommy, Don, and Evelyn,
you all made awesome Carmel tour guides,
showing me the spirit of one of
the most extraordinary places on earth.

Then a great and powerful wind tore the mountains apart
*and shattered the rocks before the L*ORD,
*but the L*ORD *was not in the wind.*
After the wind there was an earthquake,
*but the L*ORD *was not in the earthquake.*
*After the earthquake came a fire, but the L*ORD *was not in the fire.*
And after the fire came a gentle whisper.

~1 KINGS 19:11–12 NIV

Carmel-by-the-Sea, California

LET'S BE HONEST. I'M A CALIFORNIA GIRL. I WAS BORN IN OCEANSIDE, lived in the area several different times as the child of a Marine Corps officer, and spent most of my adult life in Los Angeles. So it goes without saying that I'm partial to the blue waters of the Pacific, and I'm programmed to believe that "There's no place like home." But scenic Carmel-by-the-Sea is the absolute ultimate among the countless unique villages that garnish the Californian shores.

Carmel's foundation consists of the spirit of the artists, poets, and writers that built it. As early as 1910, it was reported that over half the houses built there belonged to residents connected to the arts, and it shows. Over three hundred miles north of Hollywood, Carmel oozes the charm and nostalgic glamour of a classic movie set without the bells and whistles, as well as the European influence of its earliest beginnings.

The city's plans for a simple "village in a forest overlooking a white-sand beach" are spot-on. The beaches are pristine, the neighborhoods enthralling—and Carmel Village hosts locals and tourists alike (right along with their dogs!) with an inviting ambiance that makes a visitor think twice about whether they *ever* want to leave.

Sandra D. Bricker

Chapter One

....

Fade in.

"So did you ask him to make your day?"

"Of course," Annie replied, mock-serious. "I stared him down with my steely *Zoolander* glare and said, 'Look here, Eastwood. The question is whether or not you feel lucky. Do ya, Clint? Well, do ya?'"

Zoey crackled with laughter as Annie put on her best *Dirty Harry* face.

" 'Go ahead, Clint,' I told him. 'Make my day.' "

Annie's grandmother shook her head as she left the parlor, making a clicking sound with her tongue.

"I can't believe your gram knows Clint Eastwood!" Zoey whispered.

Annie picked up the scrapbooks scattered on the sofa next to Zoey and stacked them on the coffee table before she sat down beside her friend.

"I know! And get this. *He calls her Dori.*"

Zoey grinned as Dot reappeared with a silver tray holding two tall, crystal glasses of lemonade. Annie's dog, Sherman, a rounder-than-he-should-be beagle with soulful brown eyes, followed close at her heels, his paws clickety-clacking on the mahogany floorboards.

"Dot," Zoey marveled, "Clint Eastwood calls you *Dori*?"

"That's what everyone called me back then, before the dinosaurs were extinct," she replied, setting the tray on the table in front of them. "Honestly, Annabelle. Are you dragging out those old scrapbooks again? Get out of the past, or you'll get cobwebs all over everything."

Annie grinned and slid one of the leather-bound albums to her lap and turned over a page. "These books are impeccable, Gram. There's no dust or webs anywhere near them."

"I was speaking metaphorically."

Annie sighed as she gingerly ran her finger over a black-and-white head shot of classic film star Dorothy Gray. "You were such a hottie, Gram."

Dot sat down in the wingback chair beside the brick fireplace and smoothed the front of her floral cotton dress as she glanced in the direction of the photograph.

"Perfect skin, perfect hair," Annie remarked. She gave Zoey a gentle poke in the side with her elbow. "Gram was quite a looker."

"You were exquisite," Zoey said on a sigh.

"A lifetime ago," Dot remarked. "That girl looks like another person to me now."

"It's still you, Gram," Annie assured her. "The same sparkling eyes…and those amazing legs!"

Dot chuckled. Raising the hem of her skirt, she bent one leg and pointed the toe of her slippered foot as she shot them both a twinkling smile. "I do still have quite the gams."

"Yes, you do!" Zoey cried.

"I don't know why you couldn't have shared the love a little bit, with the silky hair and porcelain skin," Annie pointed out.

"You're stunning anyway," Dot declared, and Zoey gently

twisted a section of Annie's long, gold ringlets around her fist and tugged playfully.

"I don't look like anyone in our family."

"This is true," Dot stated. Her crystal blue eyes glistened as she added, "But you do bear a striking resemblance to that very nice man who used to deliver the milk."

Zoey snorted as Annie exclaimed, "Gram!"

"He had curly hair and very nice bone structure. That's all I'm saying."

Annie closed the album on her lap and plunked it on top of the other ones before placing them next to a dozen others on one of the floor-to-ceiling bookshelves flanking the bay window. She sat down on the arm of Dot's chair and touched her grandmother's soft linen hand.

"Are you all settled in?" Dot asked her.

Annie nodded as Zoey replied, "We've carried the last of her boxes upstairs."

"Is there anything you need up there? Helen helped me put on clean sheets, but I'm afraid we might need to get a new box spring and mattress if it's too lumpy for you. Try it out for a couple of nights and see what you think."

"Gram," she half whispered, "it's fine." Accepting her grand-mother's hand, Annie's hazel eyes misted over with emotion. "I'm just so grateful to you."

"For what?" Dot dismissed the notion. "You're family."

Annie sniffed. "Yeah. The kind you avoid at reunions."

"Don't say such a thing. You just landed on hard times, Anna-belle. It happens to every one of us at one time or another. It's God's way of telling us it's time to reorganize."

Zoey shot her a nod of encouragement as Dot continued to reassure her. "You know you're welcome to stay here for as long as you need. You're doing me as much a favor as I'm doing for you."

"What I really need," Annie groaned, falling into the adjacent over-cushioned chair, "is a plan."

"That's a very good place to start!" Dot exclaimed. She tugged open the drawer of the end table. "There's a pad and pen in there. Why don't we make a list?"

Annie grinned at Zoey. "My gram is a list-maker, like me."

"There's nothing wrong with a good list," Zoey said on a chuckle.

"That's right," Dot declared. "We'll start with what you want to do about a new job."

"Now that my demeaning call-center job has gone up in flames?"

"There are no demeaning jobs," Dot corrected.

"Only demeaned employees," Annie finished. Zoey chuckled.

"Zoey, there are snickerdoodles in the cupboard. Why don't you arrange some on a plate, and Annie will take the pad and pen so that we can start to make a plan."

Zoey hopped to her feet as Annie remarked, "A plan is much easier to devise when there are cookies."

"Not just any cookie either," Zoey said, her arm raised and her index finger pointed toward the ceiling. "Snickerdoodles!"

"Mock if you must," Dot told them. "But by the time we've finished our cookies, my granddaughter will have the plan that she needs."

Annie thought they must all look very serious, like a convening political summit, as they gathered around the red laminate-and-chrome kitchen table. But when a twenty-six-year-old floundered, a very serious plan was in order.

"First order of business," Dot suggested, "is a job. What would you like to do with your life from here, Annabelle? Sky's the limit."

"Does Charlie need any more 'Angels' these days?" she asked in jest. Then her thoughts skipped across the peninsula, up to Monterey, where she'd just left behind an apartment and the call-center job at Equity Now that had gone kaput after four tedious years. "Seriously," she told them, "I'd like something interesting, maybe even exciting; something that doesn't involve being tethered to a desk with an umbilical-cord headset."

"All right," Dot said with a nod. "Write that down."

Annie sounded it out as she wrote: "A much cooler job."

"Good! What next?"

"I would like to get some great hair." She stated it with all the seriousness of a reverend giving a eulogy.

"You *have* great hair," Zoey pointed out.

"I have curls," Annie corrected her, "and they have a mind of their own. I'd like some sleek Jennifer Aniston hair."

"Fine." The one syllable emerged as a sort of groan, which told Annie that Zoey had only let go for the moment.

"What else?" Dot asked her. "A really good plan needs at least five points to it."

"Oh." Annie wasn't sure she had five solid ideas about what to do with the mess that was her life. "Well, I want to eventually get back to Monterey."

"Why? Carmel is—"

Dot touched Zoey on the hand, and she pressed her lips together for a moment. "Sorry. It's your plan. Go ahead."

"It's not that I don't appreciate you letting me crash here, Gram. I just…I want a place of my own. Something that's just mine, you know? I want to know what it's like to really feel *at home*. Does that make sense?"

"Of course it does."

"I don't think I've ever felt that. I've always lived in my parents' home, your house…. Even my apartments have been rented from someone else."

"Home doesn't have to be about a house," Zoey told her. "It's really more about a feeling. Mateo is home for me, not the place where we live."

"Well, I don't have a Mateo either," Annie cracked. "So I'd like a place of my own, back in Monterey where I belong."

"You belong there?" Dot asked.

Annie shrugged. She wasn't sure she actually belonged anywhere, if she told the truth.

"And you know, I was thinking when I was looking through your scrapbooks again, Gram—I need to work on smiling more. You have such a movie-star smile."

Dot chuckled just as Sherman yawned from beneath the table and released a little high-pitched squeal at the end of it.

"No, really. You almost glitter when you smile. You light up the whole place. I'd like to have a smile like that."

"All right. Add that to your list, sweetheart."

Annie wrote it down. SMILE MORE. Then she paused and said, "I wouldn't mind finding a real boyfriend."

"As opposed to a fake one."

"Well, Evan is the person I spend most of my time with, but we're more like friends than anything else. I'd like a real boyfriend, one that I can take home to my family and show off a little."

Dot and Zoey exchanged glances.

"What?" Annie asked them, looking from one to the other and back again.

"Well, I was just wondering if you wanted to mess everything up by taking him home to meet...*your parents*?"

Annie's eyes darted to Dot, who only shrugged.

"Still. A little romance might be nice, don't you think?" Annie persisted.

"It certainly can be nice," Dot replied. Then she picked up a cookie and took a bite. "Now, what do we have on the list so far?"

"First, a new job," Annie read from the page. "Something fun and exciting. Two, some great hair. Three, move back to Monterey. And four, smile more often." She paused for a moment and then scribbled a note next to point number four before reading it out loud. "Get teeth whitened."

Zoey and Dot both giggled as Sherman dropped his head to the top of Annie's foot and sighed.

"I guess I'll save the new boyfriend for later, so I still need a fifth point."

"What about a new wardrobe?" Zoey suggested, and Annie frowned at her.

"I like my wardrobe," she objected, looking down at her cropped white pants, bright pink blouse with the sleeves rolled to the elbows, and black-and-white-checkered vest. "It showcases my personal style."

"And you have loads of that," Zoey retorted with a grin. "I just meant, since you're going to be looking for a new job, you'll want to...you know... I mean, it couldn't hurt to get something a little more conservative for interviews."

"Conservative? I want something exciting, maybe with a little intrigue to it. What's that got to do with a conservative wardrobe?"

Zoey leaned on her elbows and propped her chin atop both hands.

"I would like a new car, though," Annie continued. "Something sporty. Maybe a convertible."

"Job first? Convertible later?" Zoey suggested.

Annie nodded, filled in point number five, then circled point number one and drew a large exclamation point beside it.

Staring down at the words on the page before her, she whispered an awkward little prayer over them. "I don't want to be just one of the background players anymore. I want to star in my own life story. I want to really *do something* with my life."

For some reason, she couldn't find the words to continue. She just tapped her fingers on the pad of paper and sighed.

"Amen," Zoey said.

"And amen," added Gram.

* * * * *

"Nick Benchley, you are a saint, that's what you are. What would this community do without you?"

"Okay, Mrs. Ferguson. You have a good day now."

Nick waited until the station's elevator door clanked shut before allowing the smile to drop from his face. Heading back down the corridor toward his desk, he noticed Greg Thorton eyeing him with a grin.

"I see your fan club president paid you a visit."

Nick grunted as he passed by.

"What is it this week, Detective?" Thorton called out. "Saved her cat from the tree, did you? Nailed the bad guy stealing her newspaper in the morning?"

Shaking his head, Nick dropped to his chair and snatched up the phone in the middle of its first ring.

"Benchley."

"Bench, it's Deke."

"Deacon Heffley. What can I do ya for?"

"Wondered if you had a chance to run that check for me."

Nick cringed. He'd forgotten all about calling Deke that morning amid the paperwork on yesterday's corpse found in the parking lot at Ralph's and the subsequent curiosity visit from Mrs. Ferguson that morning. He riffled through the paperwork spread across his desk.

"Kingston, right?"

"Lawrence Kingston," Deke confirmed.

"Yeah, here it is." Nick flicked the first few pages and turned them over. "No record of his being employed at all over the last four years, much less for Monterey County. No taxes filed, no personnel records with the city. He was brought in for petty burglary last year, but the charges were dropped when he worked out restitution with the victim. Sorry I don't have more."

"That's plenty," Deke said. "Thanks for the help. I'll see you tomorrow night?"

"Pick you up at seven."

Nick thought about Deke for several minutes after he hung up the phone. He wondered what it must be like to deal with jealous husbands and insurance fraud all day long. Not that beautiful Monterey constituted a hotbed of crime or anything—not in comparison to his hometown of Chicago, anyway. But if a murder occurred or drug traffickers passed through on their way up north, they always seemed to land on Nick's desk.

He couldn't really complain, though. At the end of every day, he still got to climb into his Jeep and take the Cabrillo toward home. Almost without fail, the second he made that turn onto Ocean Avenue, the pressures of the job blew away with the Pacific breeze.

Home.

Carmel-by-the-Sea embodied the idea of home for Nick, even after only a few years as a resident. It was located fewer than fifteen minutes from Monterey and yet felt like a whole world apart, as far as Nick was concerned. Something about the place just soothed his soul.

"Bench. Coroner on line three."

Further thoughts of soul-soothing would have to wait until the sun went down.

"Nick Benchley... Yeah, Barnes. Whaddya got?"

* * * * *

Annie pushed her bicycle through the lattice gate and stood in front of the ivy-covered fence, surveying Casanova Street as she waited for Sherman to catch up to her. She clipped the leash to his bright blue collar and climbed onto the bike.

The dog seemed to realize just at that moment what was taking shape for this unexpected outing. With his big velvet ears pinned back and the appearance of an arched eyebrow, he regarded her with one part surprise and equal part disgust.

"Oh, don't give me that look, Shermie," she told him lovingly. "The exercise will do you good. And I promise to pedal as slowly as you need me to. Okay?"

He didn't look convinced, but he obediently trotted along beside her as she rode with her arm extended to keep the leash a safe distance from the bicycle. It was a short couple of blocks up to

Ocean Avenue, but when Annie navigated the corner to the right, Sherman stopped in his tracks and plopped down on his considerable fanny. She jammed the brakes and balanced the bike against her left leg.

"Sherman, come on, boy. It's just up there. Look! You can do it."

He apparently disagreed. Sherman clearly had no intention of moving from his spot, so Annie climbed off the bike and crouched down beside him.

"Listen to reason. It's just a couple more blocks, buddy."

He shook his head so swiftly that his tags jingled out the punctuation to his refusal.

"Are you kidding me with this?"

Sherman looked up at her without a trace of amusement, and their gazes locked.

"Seriously?"

The beagle sniffed the air and turned his head, tracing the path of a car turning down Ocean as it headed into Carmel Village.

Annie sighed. Sometimes it was just the better part of wisdom to admit defeat and march on. Wrapping his leash around her wrist, Annie pushed her bicycle forward. After a few steps, Sherman got up and followed suit, and the two of them ambled down the sidewalk toward the village without further incident.

There was something about Carmel, something unique and otherworldly. The village just oozed casual European sophistication, lightly dusted with the glamour of a classic Hollywood movie set and nestled into one of the most beautiful and scenic landscapes along the Pacific Coast. Annie remembered reading somewhere that when Carmel was originally created, the lots had been sold for one hundred dollars each. But over time, roads were built to curve around trees to ensure the maintenance of the natural beauty, and development evolved to where some of the property values rocketed into the millions. When Gram had retired from Hollywood in the 1960s, she'd purchased her two-story, sunny-yellow storybook house for a fraction of the one million dollars it was now worth.

"Morning, Annie. Morning, Sherman." Greetings from her favorite barista rang out the moment Annie crossed the threshold at the propped-open, weathered front door.

This particular coffeehouse had been a longtime favorite of Annie's even before she took up residence in Gram's nearby home. Like so many establishments within Carmel Village, the shop's owners were dog-friendly and allowed her to bring Sherman right inside with her. Despite the fact that she wasn't a big fan of coffee, Annie knew the place would surely become her regular spot for morning coffee because of their high regard for Sherman and his kind. And also because her friend Evan worked as a chef at the bistro next door.

"Hey, Kayla."

"The usual?"

"Please."

Annie took her latte and cinnamon Danish and grabbed a newspaper as she led Sherman up the rounded tile stairs and across the oak-slatted floor to the empty table by the window. As Sherman settled in at her feet, Annie pulled on the paper tucked under her arm and spread it out across the cherry tabletop.

The *Monterey Herald*'s classified section didn't appear to have a whole lot to offer beyond a few secretarial gigs, some restaurant work, and the need for a high school math and science tutor. Annie chuckled at the thought. The closest she'd ever come to utilizing her math skills was in her last position as a mortgage counselor for Equity Now, and they'd provided a very reliable calculator for people like Annie.

She'd dropped out of college less than a year from completing her degree when she began to realize how different a person needed to be from *herself* in order to make a good therapist. Consequently, she jumped into the first paycheck-generating position she could find, and *voila!* A mortgage acceleration counselor was born.

She was pretty good at the job too. She enjoyed working with people; she was dependable and trustworthy, always going the extra mile for her customers. But Annie thought that if she had to explain one more time why a mortgage would not accelerate if the extra principle payments were consistently skipped in deference to a trip to the mall or a newer model car, she might just pull out all the springy curls from her throbbing head and set them on fire. When the layoff news came, Annie's relief might have been colored by panic—if not for her dead aunt Henri.

She used to spend her summers in Ohio with Uncle Frank and Aunt Henri on their farm. When Frank died, Aunt Henri continued to live there for many years, running the place with the help of two hired hands who made a sort of bunkhouse out of the garage, and they lived right there next to the barn.

Aunt Henri shopped with coupons and reused the bags that the bread came in. She insisted on lights-out by eight thirty in order to conserve electricity, and she kept the thermostat down as low as a body could stand, even in those cold Ohio winters. So imagine Annie's astonishment when, upon her death, Henrietta left her a tidy little nest egg! She'd thought her mother, Henri's sister-in-law, might have a coronary over the news.

"You're my favorite niece," Aunt Henri wrote in the letter she left behind.

Annie was her only niece, but Henri was always saying things like that.

"You know why you're my favorite niece, Annie? Because you're not afraid to wear hats." Or "…because you sink a mean little white ball in putt-putt."

Aunt Henri's nest egg had been hidden away, weaving a catch-you-if-you-fall net for the nearly three years since her death. Rather than making the wrong decision on how to use it, Annie had unofficially decided not to use it at all and tied it up with a five-year bow when she purchased a certificate of deposit at her father's suggestion. But when she saw the classified ad in the *Herald* just then, right on the fold of the second column, the nest egg sprang to her mind. Along with Gram's hospitality of putting a roof over her head for the time being, she would at least have a few dollars to fall back on in case she'd made a colossal error in judgment by dialing the number listed in the advertisement.

"Yes. I'm calling about the job listed today in the *Herald*? Private investigator's assistant, no experience necessary?"

Chapter Two

....

"The stuff that dreams are made of."
Humphrey Bogart, *The Maltese Falcon,* 1941

Annie wore her crocheted Goorin baker boy hat in Aunt Henri's honor when she met with Deacon Heffley, the proprietor of Heffley Investigations. And when he told her the starting salary for the entry-level position, she tossed a quick thank-you upward for the financial backup. Twenty minutes later, she'd taken the job without another conflicting thought.

She sailed through the front door of the house, and Sherman greeted her with a stump of a bark and a frantic tail that wagged so hard it looked as if the force of it might knock him over.

"Gram?"

Annie bounced into the empty kitchen and picked up a folded note from the table.

Gone to see a man about some green beans.
Love, Gram

Annie dropped the note to the tabletop and scurried across the black-and-white-checkerboard linoleum. Taking hold of the pen hanging from a string on the front of the refrigerator, she squealed as she tried to cross off item number one from her "Five-Point Plan for Change" to-do list, which was stuck to the freezer with an out-of-season "Jesus is the Reason for the Season" magnet. When the pen wouldn't produce one streak of ink, she rummaged through the drawer next to the sink, pulled out a fat red Sharpie pen, and made a large X through the first item on the list.

"One down, four to go!" she announced to no one but Sherman. At least he had the heart to grin at her with enthusiasm.

Item number two on the list blinked at her.

Get some great hair.

And with that, she was off. She loaded Sherman into the Taurus and hit the road toward Monterey. Not until she reached the exit did she realize that she still held the red Sharpie pen.

Jake thought he could squeeze her in, but he had two people ahead of her: a quick cut and a blow-out. Annie picked up one of the entertainment rags from the table and led Sherman by his leash toward the seat in the corner that resembled a large orange bucket. She hadn't even made it all the way through the tell-all about John Travolta when Jake grinned at her from behind the counter.

"What are we thinking today?" he asked eagerly. "Highlights for the Shermster?"

"I want to go all the way," she exclaimed as she followed him toward his station, stopping long enough to fasten Sherman's leash to the empty receptionist's chair. "Cut. Straightening. Highlights. Whatever you think. Glam me up!"

Jake momentarily looked as if she'd handed him a blank check with his name on it.

"Cut it off," she declared boldly. "I'm a new woman, and I need to accessorize the change with new hair."

Two of the other stations were occupied, and they both looked on in anticipation, but Jake just clicked his tongue at her and shook his head at her reflection in the mirror.

"What?" she asked. "Isn't this the moment you've been waiting for?"

"First tell me what brought you here in such a hurry," he said with a pinch of suspicion, shifting his weight to one hip.

"I told you. I'm a new woman."

"And what was wrong with the old one?"

"You don't have that kind of time," she insisted. "But I could send you a copy of my five-point plan for change."

Jake gathered her curls into his fist the way Zoey often did, and he held them up over her head. Turning to the strangers filling the other chairs on the salon floor, he cocked his head. "If you had this Sarah Jessica Parker hair, would you want me to chop it all off for you on a whim?"

Annie groaned as every woman within earshot, including the stylists, expressed their displeasure and sincere warning against her triumph over point number two. Jake had been comparing her to SJP since the first time they'd met, but now he'd brought perfect strangers into it!

"Jake, you know Sarah Jessica has changed her hair numerous times over the years to reinvent herself, and her hairdresser has presumably allowed her to do it. She's been curly and straight, long and short. For goodness' sake, she even went Brown Sugar #67 for a while until she came to her senses. What is so wrong with me diving in for a great big old change? Maybe something silky and bouncy. What do you think?"

"Here's what we're going to do today," Jake declared, as much to his eager audience as to Annie. "We're going to give you a trim and a deep silk conditioning. And then, if you go home to your life, give it some serious thought, and decide to go Sarandon red or Aguilera experimental, you come back here and we'll talk."

Two hours later, Annie walked out of Jake's salon with her dog in tow, looking very much like a softer-edged version of the woman who walked in—her curls diffused and the ends less ragged, but pretty much the same girl, only seventy-five dollars poorer.

She'd called Zoey on her way to Jake's to announce her intention to see her afterward with a whole new head of hair. When Zoey opened her door to Annie now, her perfect features dropped a little, and she tilted her head slightly.

"Did you change your mind? I thought you were having your hair restyled."

"So did I. Jake is what happens when you're busy making other plans."

"Oh. Well, it looks nice anyway. It doesn't even look like it needs too much of a trim."

Annie didn't bother to tell her that she'd had the trim. The disappointment wasn't worth sharing.

"Come on in. Do you want a soda?"

"Something sugar free," Annie replied as she followed her inside. "With crushed ice...and maybe a cherry."

"As always, I have Diet Coke," she told her, deadpan. "With cubes. In a glass."

"Perfect."

The trek from front door to kitchen at Zoey's Monterey digs was farther than several laps around Annie's old apartment just a few miles away. A few years younger than Annie, Zoey had everything in life that Annie almost didn't dare dream about: a husband nearly as pretty as Zoey; a fabulous house with a gourmet kitchen, workout room, and pool; and a refrigerator that actually dispensed cubes of ice and filtered water right through the door. Although Annie did have an ice maker now that she lived with Gram, it was a small consolation.

"So tell me about the new job," Zoey said, setting a frosted glass in front of her. Annie thought it looked like a Super Bowl ad for diet soda.

They sat on barstools on opposite sides of the granite-topped counter, and Zoey arched her eyebrow eagerly. "Is there a 401(k)?"

"Uh, no. Well, I don't know, actually. I'll learn more about that once I start."

"Well, there are benefits, right?"

"Health benefits? Oh, I'm sure there are."

"Annie."

Zoey's face dropped into her hands and she shook her head vigorously. Her streaked gold-and-sandy blond hair rippled like an advertisement for shampoo.

"Tell me there's a paycheck involved," she added hopefully, peering up at Annie between her fingers.

"There is a paycheck involved."

"And we know this for certain."

"We do."

"Well, that's something, then."

Annie decided not to tell her that it was several hundred dollars less per month than her call-center job. But to be fair, Zoey didn't ask.

"I'm sorry," she said, reaching across the counter and squeezing Annie's hand. "Tell me. What will you be doing?"

Annie tried to put the kibosh on her overflowing enthusiasm, but there was nothing to be done. It bubbled up like the head on a carbonated drink. "I'm going to be a private investigator!"

The beginning of a smile dawned on Zoey's face, but it seemed to fizzle midway and kind of froze like that, as if it had been caught on its way to something.

"Oh," she said at last. "That's… Well…a private investigator?"

"Yes! I'm going to be a real, honest-to-goodness PI, Zo."

"Don't you have to have a license for that?"

"Well, I'm starting at entry level," she explained. "I'll learn the business from the ground up, working in the office and answering phones."

"So you'll be a receptionist."

"No," Annie corrected her, "a *PI assistant*. I'll sit in on client meetings and take notes for the files."

"Oh. More like a secretary, then."

"An assistant," Annie repeated. *Isn't she listening?* "After I get to know the business a little, I'll learn how to do research and gather important information for his cases. Then I'll start going with Deacon on stakeouts. And when I'm ready, he'll help me get my license!"

"Deacon is…?"

"Oh! Deacon Heffley of Heffley Investigations."

A couple of minutes ticked by while Zoey fussed with her soda. When she finally looked up at Annie, she sighed.

"Is it too late to give this some more thought?" she suggested.

"What?"

"Really think about this, Annie. Make sure it's, you know, a logical choice."

Between Zoey and Jake, Annie's enthusiasm was really taking

a beating! She suddenly felt a little like a piñata, once filled up with hope and excitement and energy but now being smacked to a pulp to expel what was inside.

"I'm not trying to be a bummer," Zoey apologized.

"No?"

"I just worry about you, Annie. I always kind of hoped you would use the tuition reimbursement plan at Equity Now to finish up your degree. You wanted to be a therapist, and you were so close. What did you have, another year?"

The look Annie gave her came right out of nowhere, and Zoey picked up on her irritation right away.

"Just promise me you'll take this one last night and really consider whether this is the right choice for you. Okay?"

Annie nodded.

"A little more thought can't hurt anything. Maybe pray about it, right?"

She nodded again, and it dissolved into a sort of shrug.

"And then if, tomorrow, you feel like this is the thing for you, we'll go out to dinner and celebrate your new job. Okay?"

Only about halfway up the wall toward encouragement, but it was something, and Annie snatched it while she could.

"Okay! We'll go to Turtle Bay for Mexican."

"But tonight you'll think about it a little more," she reiterated.

"Yes, Zoey."

"And maybe pray about it?"

"Yes, Zoey. I'll think about it. I promise. I'll think and think, and then I'll pray."

As Annie drove back to Carmel, her mother called on her cell phone. She sent her straight to voice mail. Why did she need a conversation with her mother when she'd already had all of her hopes dashed so effectively? She would save her mother for a fresh day of renewed hope and excitement just waiting to be dashed.

Funny thing about family, Annie realized as she drove right past the entrance to the highway, abandoning the idea of going straight home. *Their existence is something like the relationship between a moth and a flame. The moth should know from experience that getting too close can be dangerous. I mean, if not from the scorching demise of all their moth friends, then at the very least the increasing intensity of the searing heat should be a dead giveaway! But how many millions of moths have given their lives anyhow, by approaching the flame despite their own misgivings?*

Making what she knew would be a regrettable decision, Annie pulled into her parents' driveway, parked her car, and headed up the sidewalk toward the house.

"What have you done to your hair?"

These had been her mother's first words to her on nearly every one of Annie's entries into the house since 1991. But had it ever stopped her from going back?

Moth to a flame, I tell you. And all part of the intricate web of life's little mysteries.

Smoothing her daughter's wayward curls into submission with the palm of her hand, Annie's mother pecked her cheek with three quick kisses. It was a ritual for her, like approaching Annie on two different sides. One side said, "Your hair is the thorn in the side of our family's entire existence." And on the other, a sugary greeting certain to make her daughter feel welcome.

Is it any wonder I've spent such a large part of my life in utter confusion?

"What are you doing here in the middle of the week?" she asked. "You didn't get fired again, did you?"

"No, Mom. I wasn't fired the first time; I was laid off. And getting fired 'again' would imply that I'd started a new job since landing on Gram's doorstep this week."

"That's a relief. Have you found anything yet?"

"Well, actually—"

"Will you stay for dinner?"

"What are you having?"

"Stuffed peppers," she announced. "With fresh-baked bread sticks."

"I'll stay."

"Set the table, then. Oh, and your brother may stop by, so set it for four."

Annie shuffled across the kitchen obediently, menial labor being a small price to pay for her mother's stuffed peppers. But dinner with her brother? A horse of a different color.

"Look who's here," her mother announced as Annie's father strolled through the back door. "It's our little girl."

Their little girl.

Annie took a moment to ponder the dynamics of the mother-daughter relationship. Zoey and her mom, for instance, went shopping and took spa trips together. But the fleeting visual of Annie's roly-poly mother having a sea-kelp massage on the table next to her made Annie laugh right out loud.

"What's so funny?" her dad asked.

"Me. As a little girl."

"You're always our little girl, Annabelle. You know that," her mom tossed over her shoulder from the stove.

Her father tilted his shoulder in a shrug and kissed her forehead before heading to the living room toward his favorite chair.

"Let's wait awhile to dish up and see if Teddy arrives."

Or if Ted doesn't arrive, Annie thought hopefully. *We don't always have to be a glass-half-empty kind of family, do we?*

Annie nodded at her mother and then strolled into the living room as her father propped his feet onto the ottoman in front of his chair. "What's new and exciting, Annie?"

"Well, actually…" Annie bent down, lifted her father's feet, and dropped to the ottoman herself, putting his feet on her lap. "I do have some news."

"You have news?" her mother called out from the kitchen. "Wait! Wait a minute and let me dry my hands."

Sonar like a shark. They can sense a possible feeding frenzy from miles away, too.

"Oh, Nathan, for pity's sake. Don't put your filthy feet on Annabelle."

"They're not filthy," he returned. "They've been in socks and shoes ever since I stepped out of the shower this morning. Now let's hear Annie's big news."

All eyes on her, Annie's heart suddenly started to pound a little harder. Reminded of senior year when she'd backed her mom's Buick out of a space too fast and rammed into a cement post that popped up out of nowhere, Annie decided to follow Zoey's coaching advice from all those years ago: *A clean, honest statement is always the best way to go. Just come right out with it.*

"Mom, Dad, I've got a new job."

"Oh, honey, that's wonderful!" her mom exclaimed. "Why didn't you tell me?"

"Is it still in banking? You know how important it is to establish yourself in one industry."

"Well, no, it's not in banking. It's a whole new career, and I'm really excited about it."

"Annabelle, tell us. What is it?"

"I'm going to be…a private investigator."

Zoey must have phoned ahead. They had the same frozen expressions that she'd had.

"What do you mean—like Perry Mason?" her mom asked.

"Mason was a lawyer, Bess."

"Oh, that's right," she replied thoughtfully. "Like Barnaby Jones then."

"Is that it?" her father asked, somewhat sternly. "You're going to be like Barnaby Jones?"

Have these two turned on a television in the last two or three decades?

"Ooh, or Matt Houston!" her mother exclaimed. "Now, he was my kind of man. I like how he wore those big, silver belt buckles."

Guess not.

"I'll start out learning the ropes," she told them, hoping to fill the conversation void herself rather than letting them run amok. "After a little while, I'll get my own cases, and then I'll get my license."

"What does it pay?"

Her father always had been straight-out-forward like that.

"It pays okay, Dad. And it will pay more as I go along."

"Why would you want to leave the bank?" her mom asked. Annie didn't tell her that she'd never worked in a bank in her life. In the Equity Now call center, she was one of 112 other cubicles, and she had a headset, a battery-operated calculator, a computer, and, when no one made off with them, a couple of pens.

"Will the new place give you a retirement plan?" her father asked.

Now she felt pretty certain about it. Zoey must have phoned ahead.

"I didn't exactly choose to leave the old job, Mom. I was laid off. And I'd been thinking about making a change for a really long time anyway. It's something I'm excited about, and I'm looking forward to learning something completely new."

"What's completely new?" Ted asked from the doorway of the kitchen, and Annie's heart leaped right out of her chest and went *splat* on the floor.

Just what I want to do next: tell my overachiever lawyer brother that I'm—

"Teddy made it for supper!" Mom erupted as she hurried toward him for a hug.

"What's going on, sis? You moving again or something?"

"Annie's going to be a PI now. Like Barnaby Jones."

Ted's eyebrow arched right over the top of his conservative glasses, and one side of his mouth curled up into a spontaneous grin.

"Is that so?" he said before turning back toward their mother in the kitchen. "Need any help, Beautiful?"

Annie looked to her father with hope, silently pleading with him to say something encouraging. Anything. Just a trace of hope. *Come on, Dad. You can do it.*

"Annie, what'd you do a fool thing like that for?"

I'll call Gram on the drive back to Carmel. Surely she'll give me a little rah-rah.

* * * * *

"Well, isn't that just perfect," Nick said after a groan.

"Sorry," Thorton replied, giving Nick a casual shrug.

"I poured three months of effort into this guy, and he lawyers up ten minutes before I get the rest of the story?"

"Whaddya gonna do?"

Nick snagged a couple of quarters from his desk drawer and headed down the hall toward the vending machines for a bottle of OJ. On his way back, he diverted into his chief's office and plunked down in the chair across the desk.

"Smitty lawyered up," he stated, twisting the top off the bottle and guzzling the drink straight down.

"That's rough," his boss commented. "What are you gonna do about it?"

"What can I do? His lawyer isn't going to let him say another word to me."

"Guess you'll have to get some evidence without him leading you to it."

Nick stared him down for a long moment before letting out a cluck of a laugh. "Why didn't I think of that?"

"Look, Bench, I know you want Smitty."

"Like you can't believe."

"So it's frustrating. But you're a smart guy. You can still have him. Keep looking."

Nick turned his attention to the window. A couple of gulls sailed by and circled the tree before moving on.

"How's Jenny?" Chief Sheldon asked. "Getting settled in?"

Nick continued to follow the path of the gulls as he replied, "Yep."

"You going to Vinny's tonight?"

"Nah. Gotta head over to the center."

Sheldon nodded. "Good. That's good you do that—volunteer at the youth center, I mean."

Nick shrugged.

"So, anything else you want to discuss?"

Nick gave it a second's thought and replied, "Nah."

"Okay, then."

"Okay."

After a moment of silence, the chief leaned forward slightly. "This is where you get out."

"Right."

Nick waved halfheartedly as he vacated the office, entertaining thoughts of how to get around his perp's untimely sleight of hand.

"Thorton," he called as he moved across the squad room, "let's go interview Smitty's daughter again. Maybe we can get something out of her before they get a family rate on legal counsel."

Thorton nearly tore off the collar of his jacket when it caught on the hook as he snatched it and ran for the door behind Nick.

Chapter Three

....

"I think this is the beginning
of a beautiful friendship."
Humphrey Bogart, *Casablanca*, 1942

"Gram?"

"In here, sweetheart."

Annie unclipped the leash from Sherman's collar and the two of them moseyed into the kitchen to find Evan seated at the table with Dot, a pot of tea between them.

"You're drinking tea?" Annie asked him before leaning down and planting a kiss on her grandmother's cheek. Evan shrugged.

"Did you have something to eat?"

"Yeah. I stopped by Mom and Dad's."

"Uh-oh," Evan remarked. "How are the folks?"

"Would you like some tea too? Or maybe something a little stronger," Dot added, deadpan.

Annie grabbed a teacup from one of the hooks under the cabinet and brought it to the table, joining them.

"Let me recap," she said, pouring from the china pot. "I've accepted this perfectly wonderful, exciting new job. Then my hairdresser refuses to glam me up and my best friend does that 'Oh, Annie, please!' thing she does so well, only to be compounded by the frosting on the cake of having dinner with my parents and my perfect brother, all of whom think I'm wasting my life in a repeat of *Barnaby Jones*."

Evan snickered.

"I've just been telling Evan about your new job, Annie. And if it's any consolation at all, we both think you're going to make a fine private investigator's assistant."

"Very *Charlie's Angels*," Evan added with a nod.

Annie managed a thankful grin.

"Hey, look what came today!" he exclaimed, holding up a DVD case. "*Rear Window*."

"Just in the nick of time!" Annie cried happily. "Just when I can't go another ten minutes without some Hitchcock in my life."

Evan laughed, and Dot pushed to her feet. "You two fire up the television and I'll get the snacks," she said.

Evan Shaw never watched anything on television that wasn't shown on *The Cooking Channel* or *The Discovery Channel*. In fact, he and Annie had very little in common on paper, except for this one passion for classic films. Kicking off her shoes, Annie curled into one corner of Gram's sofa, and after queuing up the movie, Evan plopped down into the other corner. Sherman crawled up and stretched out between them with his chin resting on Evan's knee.

"Year?" Evan queried.

"Nineteen fifty-four. Studio?"

"Paramount. Screenwriter?"

"John Michael Hayes. Based on the Cornell Woolrich short story 'It Had to Be Murder.' "

"Show-off."

"I know." Annie grinned, stretched out her leg, and poked

Evan's shin with her sock-encased toe. "Riddle me this, Batman. Who plays the part of Miss Lonelyhearts?"

Evan thought it over. "Irene Winston?"

"Nope!" Dot exclaimed as she set a tray down on the coffee table—two cans of diet soda, large and small bowls of popcorn, and a glass dish brimming with peanut M&Ms.

"Gram, you're the best," Annie told her, grabbing a handful of the candies as Evan popped open her drink and passed it to her.

Dot sat down in the wingback chair and set her cup and saucer on the mahogany table beside it.

"So it's not Irene Winston," Evan stated. "Then who is it?"

"Irene Winston is the actress who played Mrs. Thorwald," Dot told him. "*Miss Lonelyhearts* is Judith Evelyn. Hitchcock liked her so much that she went on to play in two different episodes of his *Alfred Hitchcock Presents.*"

Evan glanced at Annie. "Definitely *your* grandmother."

"My appreciation for celluloid skipped a generation," Dot told them, "but Annie makes me proud."

They all fell immediately silent as bamboo shades rose slowly above four rectangular windows and a cat scampered up the stairs of a Lower East Side apartment building in sharp black-and-white images.

Evan's eyes fixed on the screen as he began mechanically raising kernels of popcorn to his mouth, and Annie couldn't help but watch him for a moment.

No Brad Pitt, Evan. In fact, he looked a lot to her like Jay Bush, the guy who made baked beans and traveled around with his traitorous family dog. Evan was a tall, husky guy who insisted upon referring to his baldness as being "follically challenged" and had spectacular eyes, which he shielded behind round, rimless glasses he called "specs." Thirty-four going on twenty-four going on sixty-four; consequently, a barrel of fun to be around but not much fun in those phases when the relationship morphed into something that could be more than friendship. He and Annie had taken that ride three times now, and it had become a little like an amusement-park roller-coaster ride to her. The coaster had lost its appeal, and she didn't plan on ever being coerced to ride it again.

He must have sensed her watching him. Evan turned toward her with a blink.

"What?" he mouthed. She smiled and turned her attention back to the screen.

"Hey," he whispered, tapping her knee with his soda can. When she looked back at him, he asked, "Did you change your hair? I like it."

Well, doesn't that just toast the big marshmallow! Nobody compliments or notices my hair all day long, but Evan is the one to notice.

Evan was like that. Whereas Annie's mother's sonar detected fresh blood, Evan's tended to hone in on every inclination Annie got to set out again on the search for a real relationship. Had she not been making all the changes in her life lately, she would have been willing to bet he'd never have noticed her hair.

"Thanks," she whispered. "Just a trim."

Just about the time that Grace Kelly slipped the accusatory note under Raymond Burr's apartment door, Dot leaned forward and asked, "How about a quick potty break?"

Annie paused the screen and took a sip from her soda as her grandmother left the room. Evan's face lit up suddenly, and he reached into the pocket of his jeans and produced a plastic baggie of lettuce leaves, dangling it in front of the beagle still resting on his leg.

"Look what I brought you," he said. "Your favorite snack, boy. Salad."

Sherman heaved to his feet and panted enthusiastically.

"It pays to know people in high places," Annie told Sherman. Evan often brought fresh lettuce leaves and other booty from his job as a lunch chef to his favorite dog.

"I'll take him for a quick walk, if you'd like."

"That would be great."

Annie watched them as Evan clipped the leash into place and they headed out the back door of the kitchen. They seemed like a cartoon to her just then, a man and his dog connected by a bright blue leash, both of them a little too chunky for their own bodies and neither of them caring about it in the least.

Annie glanced down at her cell phone and noticed the light blinking. Upon further investigation, she read the text from Zoey.

Sorry about today. Didn't mean to bring you down about the new job. Just remember to think about it tonight? I will too. In the a.m. we'll know if it's the right thing or not.

Subtle, Zoey. Very subtle.

Evan sauntered in and released Sherman from his leash just as Dot reappeared and folded into her chair. As Grace Kelly made her escape and returned to Jimmy Stewart's apartment, Annie found herself glancing at Evan again.

There was a time when she'd thought him to be her soul mate. But now, in the glow of her favorite Hitchcock film, Annie grinned as she realized that Sherman was Evan's match, not her.

He was an exceptional person, really. Funny and smart—and

Annie had never known a man in whose company she felt so completely comfortable. But at the same time, he was dangerous that way. One of those men who wooed a girl into a false sense of security with cups of coffee and blueberry scones, bags of lettuce for her salad-loving beagle, and long talks lasting for hours—talks about hopes and dreams and (of all things!) *feelings*. It could be very confusing.

She'd known him for almost five years, and their relationship had broken down, in Annie's mind anyway, into phases.

Phase I was still her favorite: *the Friendship Phase*. Getting to know one another, finding a larger connection out of a simple love of movies, discovering a few more ways in which they complemented one another. There were shared penchants for really good food, all dogs everywhere, jazz singer Stacey Kent, bluffs over the ocean, and, most of all, classic Hollywood films.

Naturally, there were conflicts discovered in the early stages of the friendship as well, such as his mistaken impression that Lakers basketball was inconsequential. But in Phase I, there had always existed the childlike hope that things could (and would) change.

They hadn't with Evan.

Rounds 1, 2, and 3 of Phase II were pretty much a blurry, bouncing ball of Evan's neurotic responses to the possibility of commitment and Annie's subsequent whiplash in trying to recover. Standing out in her mind—

Breaking her thoughts, Evan stuffed his mouth with popcorn and belted out a groan at Jimmy Stewart's panic, due to his broken leg preventing his escape from the wheelchair holding him prisoner.

Annie sighed softly and attempted to refocus. Standing out in her mind was the memory of a secret pact to avoid the equally unbearable idea of spending the day with their families. Evan and

Annie had concocted an Anti-Thanksgiving Plan a couple of years back. With Gram out of town for the holiday, there would be meat loaf and chocolate cake rather than turkey and pumpkin pie—and an entire day of old movies starring Humphrey Bogart (Evan's choice) and Cary Grant (Annie's). Just the three of them, counting Sherman. And it had been divine.

As Christmas began to roll out, they scheduled a day off from their jobs in order to shop for the perfect Christmas tree for Annie's apartment. Once they brought it home, they spent the morning decorating it with painted clay angel ornaments Annie and Gram had made a few years prior during Annie's let's-be-crafty stage. The stage didn't last long, but at least she had those ornaments to show for it.

Then later that evening they baked three different styles of holiday cookies while singing off-key to Bing Crosby and Nat King Cole Christmas carols, and they took pictures of Sherman in front of the tree wearing jingle-bell antlers and looking extremely disgruntled. On Christmas Day they had an early dinner with Annie's family and dessert with Evan's. Afterward, they went for a long walk through his Monterey neighborhood and enjoyed a balmy California breeze. It was ideal. They were settling into the niche of a relationship.

But the next day, when Annie offhandedly asked if he'd given any thought to what he wanted to do for New Year's Eve, one might have thought she'd greeted him at the door in a wedding dress with a shotgun in one hand and an open Bible in the other.

How dare she just *assume* they were doing something together?

Annie felt fairly certain that those were the last plans she would ever *assume* for anyone. After all, she didn't have to be smacked in the head with a steel beam more than once to get a message—which probably didn't explain why it took two more rounds to realize that Evan would never introduce her to anyone as his girlfriend.

Enter Phase III. *Can't live with him, can't shoot him.*

"Well, I'm going to bed," Dot announced, jolting Annie with the message that *Rear Window* had ended. "G'night, children."

"Good night, Dot."

"Night, Gram."

Evan looked at her over the top of his "specs," his eyebrows knit together and his lips pursed as if he'd just tasted something he couldn't define.

"Where are you tonight?"

"I don't know," she admitted. "Swimming around where the past meets the future, I guess."

He took a long pause and then stated, "A PI, huh?"

When his expression didn't evolve, Annie sighed.

"Does it pay well?"

"Not particularly."

"Benefits?"

"Probably."

"And you're taking this particular job because—"

"Because if I don't and I take another no-future call-center job instead, I'll wither up and die, Evan. There won't be anything left of me if I don't start making some changes."

"It's good to see you're not being overly dramatic."

Annie coughed out a laugh.

"Okay," he said with a nod, assessing her response. And finally, "Ben Franklin once said that it's okay to go nowhere as long as there's an interesting path to get there."

They both knew Ben Franklin never said such a thing. Evan had

told Annie long ago that people would much more readily accept
pearls of wisdom if they were told that Benjamin Franklin said
it first. It had become a private joke between them over the years.

"Wise man, Ben," she told him.

"He had a million of 'em."

Evan didn't say much more about the new job over the next
hour and Annie felt relieved when he stood up in preparation to
be on his way. *The true beauty of friendship, after all, stands not in
saying the right thing at the right time,* she decided, *but in leaving
unsaid the wrong thing at the most tempting moment.*

Surely Ben Franklin once said something close to that, right?

But at the door, he asked, "You're sure about this PI thing?" Annie
shrugged in response.

"That's my Annie," he said. "Always meandering to a different drummer."

And so my record stands, she thought as she watched him head
out the gate toward his car on the other side of the driveway. *Aside
from Gram, not one person has had anything good to say about my
new job since the moment I accepted it. I think I'll call it a day.*

* * * * *

It didn't occur to Annie until she sat in the drive-through in
Monterey, waiting for her medium Diet Coke, that fewer than
thirty minutes separated her from her new job. She began to
panic a little bit.

Deacon Heffley, or "Deke," as he had instructed her to call him,
appeared to be somewhere around fifty, maybe fifty-five, a light-
toned African-American man with short salt-and-pepper hair and

smooth skin. Somewhere around the eyes and nose, he reminded Annie a little of Morgan Freeman, which, for some inexplicable reason, made her feel comfortable with him.

"Read through these case files," he told her as he dropped several dozen messy folders onto her desk a bit later. "Familiarize yourself with the kind of work we do here and then file them in the drawers against the wall in the back."

Annie felt certain that getting them filed was the main part of the plan, but she felt eager to leaf through them anyway. By the time most of the morning had passed, she'd read over every sheet of paper in every one of the files.

Heffley Investigations appeared to specialize in exposing insurance fraud—at least in recent weeks, anyway. Case after case involved surveillance reports regarding supposedly injured workers. Supporting evidence included photographs, DVDs, and affidavits about people lifting groceries, tossing a football, even mowing the lawn. The second specialty of Deke's house looked to be infidelity. Then there were several background investigations into prospective employees, spouses, and child-care workers.

Annie neatly tucked the files into their drawers and rearranged some of the others already in the drawers. The phone rang at twelve thirty for the first time all day.

"Heffley Investigations."

She'd never actually been a receptionist, but Annie imagined this to be her best receptionist voice.

"Who's this?"

"Annie Gray," she replied. "And you?"

"Where's Becky?" the caller seemed to demand. "Don't tell me Deke's run another one off. You must be the third secretary this month."

Private investigator's assistant.

"Can I tell Mr. Heffley who's calling?" she asked instead.

"Mr. Heffley," he said. "Now that's a good one. Yeah, Annie Gray, you can. Tell Deke it's Nick Benchley. I'll be there in twenty to pick him up, and I don't have any time to spare today so we'd better make this quick. You got all that?"

"Yes, sir," she returned, relying on every bit of the customer service training she'd received at Equity Now. She *wanted* to tell Nick Benchley that he was a bit of an arrogant jerk and then hang up the phone just enthusiastically enough to make a cracking sound in his ear.

Benchley hung up without saying good-bye and the cracking sound ended up in Annie's ear instead. Grinding her teeth, she walked over to Deke's office.

"Who's on the phone?"

"That was Nick Benchley," she told him, as sweetly as she could muster. "He says he'll be here to pick you up in twenty minutes and he's on a tight schedule today."

"Ahh," he groaned, waving his hand, "Bench is always in a hurry."

"I've read through all of the files you gave me," Annie announced. "And they've all been placed alphabetically into the filing cabinets. Is there anything else you'd like me to work on?"

"Why don't you go get some lunch?" Deke suggested, leaning back in his chair until it creaked. "We've got adultery this afternoon."

"I beg your pardon?"

"Wife cheater," he clarified. "You can sit in and take notes…see how a case goes from start to finish."

"Great!"

It really did sound good to Annie, and she realized that, despite the bets people were no doubt taking, she hadn't once been sorry for accepting the job in the whole three and a half hours since she'd arrived. "Can I bring you something back? A sandwich—or some soup?"

"Nah, I'm grabbing something with Bench when he gets here. I'll see you in an hour."

Lunch consisted of an Asian chicken wrap from Jamba Juice, washed down with a Prickly Pear tea made with green tea and pear juice over crushed ice with a splash of lemonade and a wedge of orange. She'd never eaten there before, but it was close to the office. She hadn't realized until too late that she'd wandered into a foreign world of healthy eaters and caffeine haters. Back in the office with time to spare, she made fresh coffee and scrubbed the circle stains from the ceramic mugs stacked on the counter.

The 1:30 appointment was nothing like what Annie expected.

Adultery.

The word carried with it a certain visual, and Mrs. Armbrewster just wasn't it.

"Marion Armbrewster," she said when she stepped through the door. "I have a one-thirty meeting scheduled with Mr. Heffley."

Annie offered her some coffee, but she declined despite the fresh pot and the bright, shining mugs at her disposal. She folded neatly into one of the reception chairs and pressed the skirt of her very proper light blue suit with the palms of her hands. She was sixty-five, if a day.

Annie used the intercom to buzz Deke. Instead of answering it, he lumbered through the doorway.

"What was that?"

"The intercom buzzer," she told him, struggling to keep a serious expression. "I wanted to tell you that your one-thirty appointment has arrived. Marion Armbrewster, meet Deacon Heffley."

Mrs. Armbrewster moved slowly toward Deke and shook his hand with timid grace.

"Come on into my office," he told her. "Annie, I have a preliminary case sheet started. Why don't you come on in and take some notes?"

Annie followed them inside, and the two women flanked Deke's desk in chairs angled at each corner. Mrs. Armbrewster's smile rang tentative, and Annie noticed a slight quiver to it. Annie instinctively reached over and placed her hand on top of Mrs. Armbrewster's, squeezing it slightly, and the woman released a bumpy sigh.

"Now, you said on the phone that you think your husband is playing around," Deke stated, oblivious to the extreme effort it must have taken for Mrs. Armbrewster to have come to this meeting. "What makes you think that?"

She swallowed hard before peering up at him.

"Davis," she stated, and she looked to Annie to clarify. "That's my husband. Davis Armbrewster." Annie nodded, and the perfectly coiffed woman turned back toward Deke. "He retired three months ago. In the beginning, his days were filled with gardening and working in his wood shop, all the usual things a retired gentleman does with his new free time. But over the last month or so, he's taken to getting up early and leaving the house right around the same time, and he doesn't come home until just before supper."

Deke leaned back into his chair. "Forgive me for stating the obvious, but have you asked him where he's going?"

"Yes, of course," she replied. "He says he's playing golf."

"And?"

Mrs. Armbrewster turned back to Annie and sighed. "I suppose you'd have to know Davis to know how ridiculous that is. But my husband is not playing golf." She glanced toward Deke for a quick moment before she continued. "After forty-nine years of marriage, a woman knows if her husband plays golf. And my husband, I assure you, does not."

Deke asked her a barrage of questions about her husband's former career in retail, his general health, and the type of car he drove while Annie scribbled notes from the answers.

Leaning forward and grimacing, Deke said, "Pardon my candor, Mrs. Armbrewster." Annie's heart began to race as she wondered what horribly tactless thing might follow. "You said your husband is sixty-nine years old."

"Yes. That's correct."

"And he's in relatively good health."

"Oh yes."

"Then, aside from the obvious possibility that he's just decided to learn how to play golf, there are probably a dozen other explanations that don't necessarily lead to infidelity."

She considered that very carefully, smoothing her flawless silver hair as if it needed smoothing, and then reached into her leather handbag and produced a credit card statement.

"This is our MasterCard bill from last month," she said, sliding it across the desk toward Deke. "There are purchases for new clothing and shoes. Davis has bought more new clothes since his retirement than in most of our years of marriage. His gasoline budget has nearly doubled. And he bought four bouquets of flowers in just one month's time."

"Mmm," Deke rumbled as he inspected the statement. "Mm-hmm."

Turning to Annie, Marion added, "And they were beautiful flowers too. My favorite. Gladiolas."

"I'm sorry," she said, confounded. "I don't understand. The flowers were for you?"

"Oh, yes. Davis hasn't bought me flowers other than on Valentine's Day or our anniversary in nearly fifty years, Miss Gray. And now he's come home with gladiolas four times in a month."

Deke began to massage his temples, and Annie had to admit that she felt a bit of a headache coming on herself.

"I just want you to follow him for a day or so," Marion declared. "Tell me where he's going, who he's seeing. Can you do that?"

She looked so *hopelessly hopeful* to Annie. Such a dear, sweet woman should have been fretting over nothing more than the correct time for a garden party or a date with friends for tea. But the concern that colored her steel gray eyes instead cut Annie to the very core.

Deke quoted her his rates and showed Annie how to draw up the paperwork. She could see that he thought this would be a colossal waste of time, but Annie felt more certain of that fact than ever when he turned to her the moment Marion left and announced, "Your first case. This will be a good one for you to get your feet wet."

You mean a good one for me to take off your hands.

Chapter Four

....

> "Do women think it feminine to be so illogical,
> or can't they help it?"
> Cary Grant, *Charade,* 1963

Deke had prepped Annie for two straight days on the proper etiquette of surveillance, and as usual, she took very detailed notes.

Be unobtrusive. Look common and don't stand out. A memorable PI is an unemployed PI.

Keep your distance. This isn't the movies, where people are half blind and don't notice someone following them for any length of time.

Maintain your game face. Learn to pay attention without looking like you're paying attention. And remember: you're trying to remain undetected by the people around your marks as well as the marks themselves.

Take notes. Unremarkable details may play an important part in the case at a later time.

Wear comfortable clothes. You never know how long you'll be sitting in a car or what you'll have to hop over to maintain your surveillance.

First thing on Monday morning, Annie deemed herself ready. Donning her favorite pink Juicy Couture sweats, pale pink Keds with white laces, and a white *Shopaholic* baseball cap, she thought she looked pretty average.

Adding to her averageness: Sherman, everyday American beagle, age eight, just hanging out the passenger window and panting randomly at the passersby. Poor Sherman wasn't exactly in top form anymore, but Annie didn't figure he'd be chasing any bad guys that day. And what could look more average and unobtrusive than a woman and her dog?

She kept a couple of car-lengths between them as she followed Davis Armbrewster's dark blue Buick Regal straight to the Monterey Hills Golf Club. She pulled into a parking space two rows behind him and remained in the car as he made his way up the walk toward the clubhouse. She figured she'd amble inside in a few minutes' time and see him meeting up with a golf pro or the rest of a foursome, and the mystery would be solved—that alas, Davis Armbrewster really did play golf!

She took a moment to write the date at the top of the pad of paper Sherman had been standing on, and she made a few quick notes.

Davis Armbrewster. Full head of silver hair. Brown pants. Light blue shirt. Brown leather loafers.

Hey. Brown loafers. That's not something a man wears to play golf.

And now that she thought about it, he hadn't stopped to produce a set of clubs from his car before heading inside, either.

Annie looked up just as he disappeared through the double glass doors to the pro shop.

"Stay here, Sherman," she told her dog. "I'll be back in just a few minutes. Stay."

She rolled down both front-seat windows and patted Sherman's head before she left him. He'd been pretty dependable about staying put, especially as he'd gotten older. Annie's guess: he pretty much knew he wouldn't find a better situation than what he had with her, and he was too old and too tired to go looking anyway.

She walked casually across the parking lot, up the sidewalk, and through the pro shop doors, but Mr. Armbrewster was nowhere in sight. She scanned the racks inside and then informally searched the faces she found there.

She hadn't been inside the shop for thirty seconds when Armbrewster appeared from behind a light pine door, now wearing a square plastic badge with his name engraved above a sunny yellow smiley face and the words, How can I help you?

He greeted a few of the occupants of the shop as if he saw them often; then he set his sights on Annie.

Be unobtrusive and *Keep your distance* scampered across her mind. Maybe she could do better with note number three and keep her game face on.

"How can I help you today, young lady?" Mr. Armbrewster asked her, as his friendly smile practically radiated.

"Oh, I'm just looking around," she told him.

"Something for yourself or a gift?"

Oh boy.

"A gift?" she replied, and it popped out in the strange form of a question.

Over the next fifteen minutes or so, Davis Armbrewster proved helpful to the point of ridiculousness, showing Annie inexpensive possibilities for her father's birthday such as golf balls and tees and then the more pricy considerations like knit shirts and bags for the clubs he didn't own. As far as Annie knew, her father hadn't set foot on a golf course in his entire life.

"You're pretty good at this," Annie commented. "Have you been working here for a long time?"

"Not too long," he replied. "A few weeks."

Why retire from one job just to go and find another?

"You must love golf," she told him. "Working for greens fees?"

"Oh no, something much more important," Armbrewster confided in a hushed voice. "An affair of the heart."

Annie's disappointment danced a little jig across the inside of her stomach. This man just didn't strike her as a cheater!

"How's that?" she asked him, trying to mask her disillusionment.

"The wife doesn't even know I have this job," he said. Annie resisted the impulsive urge to take a swing at him with one of the golf clubs in the bag between them.

Old geezer!

"I'm saving every cent to surprise her for our fiftieth. She's dreamed all her life of going to Italy, and I'm going to take her."

Oh, good grief. Forgive the geezer remark.

"You're kidding," she said on a sigh. "Well, that's just... so romantic."

"She's put up with me for half a century," the geezer-turned-romantic-hero told her. "She deserves a big reward."

"I think that's a beautiful idea. I really do. Congratulations."

"What about your father?" he asked. "Decide on anything for him?"

"Maybe I'll just get him some slippers," she replied with a shrug. "Have a good day."

"You have a good one too, young lady."

Making her way back toward her Taurus, Annie's heart surged with relief for Marion Armbrewster. And she felt pretty good about solving the mystery too.

I'm a natural at this stuff. I mean, really. I went in, I got the information, and I'm out. Simple!

About ten yards from her car Annie whistled for Sherman, but his little head didn't pop up to the window as usual. She whistled again. Still nothing.

Closing the gap between herself and the car at a full sprint, she flung open the door and peered inside.

Oh, no!

Looking around frantically, Annie began to call his name. "Sherman! Sherman? Here, Sherman."

She headed across the parking lot at a full run, still calling his name, her heart pounding against her chest and all the worst scenarios running like movie trailers across her mind as she searched for him.

At the far end of the clubhouse, she heard someone yelling, and a group of others burst into laughter. Annie ran around the corner, hoping that her inclination to follow the raucousness proved on track.

A small delivery truck sat idle at the side entrance, and she noticed a half dozen club employees gathered around the back of it, peering inside curiously.

Something tells me…

"What's going on?" she asked as she joined them. She followed one of their nods into the back end of the produce truck.

And there sat her dog, an entire bin of lettuce leaves scattered on the truck bed around him, happily chowing down on his favorite treat.

Oh, good grief. He's in doggie heaven.

"Sherman!" she exclaimed, and he looked at her, appearing to grin.

"This is your dog?" an angry man in a dirty white apron bellowed at her. Sherman growled softly as one of the workers made a move toward him.

"Sherman!" she reprimanded. "That's enough!"

Annie climbed into the back of the truck and dragged him by the collar toward the edge until she could pick him up. All the while, her ridiculous dog resisted in one concerted effort to score a few more chunks of the lettuce near him.

"That's a thirty-two-dollar bin of produce your dog just ruined," the delivery man said with a groan as she lumbered off the truck with thirty pounds of disobedient beagle overflowing from her arms.

"I'll write you a check," she promised. "I really will. I'll pay for it as soon as I get him back to the car. I'm—I'm so sorry."

Annie hurried toward the parking lot, loaded Sherman into the front seat of her car like a sack of potatoes, and slid in beside him. Her heart raced as she bit her lip and closed her eyes briefly before reaching for her purse to dig out her checkbook.

After signing her name to the check, she glanced over at Sherman.

"You are a very bad dog," she told him sternly. But then she burst into a spontaneous and breathless stream of laughter as he panted at her, one eye covered diagonally with a pirate's patch of green leaf lettuce.

* * * * *

"You did what?!"

"I know you told me to keep my distance," she explained to Deke in a calm tone of voice, in direct opposition to the large vein vibrating erratically in his forehead. "But he went waltzing right in, no golf shoes, no clubs. I had to see what he was really doing in there, didn't I?"

"See what he's doing," Deke repeated, and he inhaled deeply through his nose before continuing. "Not make contact. You never make spontaneous contact!"

"But it worked out," she reasoned with him. "He's not cheating on Mrs. Armbrewster. He's working there to earn the money to take her to Italy for their fiftieth wedding—"

"You could have discovered that he worked there without having a conversation with him, Annie. You never—"

"—make spontaneous contact," she completed for him. "I know. I'm sorry."

Deke appeared to be having quite an intense dialogue with himself, looking straight through Annie. But then...something unexpected happened.

"It's my fault, really," he told her. "I should never have sent you out on a case in your first week. No matter how uncomplicated it was supposed to be, no one is ready that quickly."

Annie suddenly realized she'd positioned herself offensively on the other side of his desk.

"I'm sorry, Deke," she said, and she folded into the chair and looked him directly in the eyes. "You gave me a set of rules to follow, and I didn't. That was wrong. It won't happen again."

After a moment the corner of Deke's mouth twitched, and Annie saw the dawn of a smile.

"Let's call it part of a learning curve," he said. "For both of us."

Relief washed over her as he completed the foreshadowed smile.

"If it's all right with you, I'd like to keep Mr. Armbrewster's secret from his wife," she suggested—but the way Deke's eyebrows knit together and all traces of the smile disintegrated told Annie that he wasn't exactly onboard. "He's worked so hard to surprise her, Deke."

"Look. Marion Armbrewster is our client. She hired us to do a job, which was to find out what her husband was doing when he left the house. You have that information...not that I approve of the method."

"How about this," she offered, hope percolating as she slid to the edge of her chair and leaned toward him. "How about we tell her that we have the information, that he's not cheating as she thought, but that to tell her what he *is* doing would ruin a surprise he's been planning."

Deke cocked his head only slightly, enough to let Annie know that he was at least considering her plea. So she dove on it while she had the chance.

"Then she has the option. If she wants the information, I'll give her a full report. But if all she wants to know is whether her husband is faithful, I can tell her that without ruining the effort he's put into surprising her."

She paused. Deke's expression was a blank slate. She waited with no clear idea of how he would respond.

"All right, then."

"Yes?"

"Yes. Call the client, invite her in for a meeting, and explain it to her in that way. Let her choose."

Annie popped up from her chair, and it took all her resolve not to round the corner of the desk and hug the stuffing right out of him.

"That's the right choice, Deke. It really is. You won't be sorry."

"Going forward," he said, staring her down, "we follow the rules."

"Be unobtrusive," she recited, instinctively raising her right hand in a vow. "Keep my distance. Wear my game face."

"All right, all right," he interrupted. "Go on and call the client."

"Thank you," she sent back as she reached the doorway. "You're a man among men!"

"Yeah, yeah, yeah."

Mrs. Armbrewster said she could come to the office that

afternoon, and Annie made full use of the time until then by writing up a complete report on her findings. She felt so utterly *Maltese Falcon*-esque as she sat in front of the computer on the reception desk, typing out all the information about her first investigation. She could almost see herself there in black-and-white.

She planned to go over every paragraph and every letter with a fine-tooth comb to make it the best she could before showing it to Deke, but her concentration broke as the office door flew open and thumped against the wall. She nearly jumped to her feet on sheer instinct.

"You must be Annie Gray," said a rugged, dark-eyed man.

He looked dangerous. And a little wicked. He might have been the result if Colin Farrell and George Clooney had run into one another really hard. Her heart pounded harder when he met her gaze. Any other guy wearing a rumpled sport coat over a wrinkled denim shirt might not be noticed beneath it, but this particular jacket wore the guy. He was...*mesmerizing*.

"Yo. Are you mute?"

Huh?

"I–I'm sorry," she managed to sputter. "You are...?"

"Nick Benchley," he stated—and a flash flood of their phone conversation came barreling back at her.

"Oh."

"Deke around?" he asked, as he pushed the outer door shut behind him. Before she could respond, he swaggered straight past her desk and into Deke's office.

"He–e–ey!" Deke greeted him. "Take a load off."

"Why, yes," Annie announced softly to the four walls around her, "Mr. Heffley is in his office. Let me announce you."

* * * * *

Annie watched Mrs. Armbrewster pull her car into a space beyond the window. She gave a friendly wave that Annie returned, as she hoped against hope that she would find the right words to help the woman understand without actually hearing all the facts.

"Good afternoon, Miss Gray."

"Annie."

"All right, Annie. How are you today?" she asked, following her lead and sitting across from Annie's desk.

"Very well, thank you."

"You have some news about my Davis?" she asked. Annie could see the wariness in her eyes, so afraid of the answer she was desperate to hear. Mrs. Armbrewster's love for her husband of fifty years rocked something deep inside of Annie.

"Mrs. Armbrewster," she said, "I met your husband. And I can tell you that he loves you very, very much."

"You met him? I don't understand."

"Yes. It was completely innocent," she reassured her. "He had no idea I was working for you."

The tension drained slowly from Marion's face, like the last of the helium leaving a balloon.

"Now, I've prepared a full report on what we've discovered, Mrs. Armbrewster."

"Call me Marion." It came out almost as a whisper, her eyes fixed on Annie, expectation brewing.

"I'd like to begin, Marion, by telling you that your husband's activities have absolutely nothing to do with any other woman except you."

Marion released the air she'd been holding in her lungs, and she tried to smile. "Where is he going, then?"

"Before I tell you that," Annie replied delicately, "can I be so bold as to offer you an opinion?"

"Of course."

"Mr. Armbrewster is keeping a secret, but it's not the kind of secret you feared," she told her. "And since you're the client, I'll hand over every detail of this report to you, if that's what you want. But before you ask me to do that, you should know that you'll be disappointed in the long run. And you'll be interfering with what I think is going to be a really pleasant surprise."

Her eyes narrowed thoughtfully. "I'm afraid I don't understand."

"Your husband's activities are a result of something he wants very much to do for you. And if I hand you this file, all his efforts to surprise you will be ruined."

"A surprise?"

"And it's a good one," Annie said with a chuckle. "Believe me."

"Honestly?"

"Honestly," she replied tenderly. "Your husband loves you very much, Marion. Can you trust me on this? You came to us to find out if he's having an affair, and I can tell you unequivocally that he is not. Can you leave it at that for a while?"

"I…suppose."

"Just until after your wedding anniversary."

Marion considered Annie's words for a moment, and then she brightened so profoundly that Annie almost felt like she needed sunglasses.

"It's for our anniversary?" Marion exclaimed.

"Oh, don't make me say any more."

"You're sure about this?" The smile on her face broadened even before Annie replied. "That man! He's such a joy."

Annie's heart squeezed as she watched Marion. She could only imagine the elation—and the relief. She wondered for a moment what it would be like to be with the same man for fifty years, to know him inside and out, to know by heart everything about him: how he took his coffee, whether he freckled in the sun, if he liked shellfish, what he dreamed about as a little boy.

"Annie, you've put my mind at ease more than I can ever tell you. I can't thank you enough."

"No need to thank me," she told her. "Just take a deep breath and relax. You have the answer you really needed."

"Yes, I do."

Chapter Five

....

"Fasten your seatbelts.
It's going to be a bumpy night."
Bette Davis, *All About Eve,* 1950

Annie's Taurus made a bit of a whirring noise when she started it, reminding her about point number five on the list hanging on the refrigerator door in her gram's kitchen. Perhaps the time had come to go shopping for that convertible before Taurie, as she lovingly referred to the heap, began to exhibit some behavioral problems.

The girls had already scored a table, and cheese-laden potato skins had found their way to familiar shores by the time Annie made it to T.G.I. Friday's.

"Hey, Annie!" Tyra exclaimed, and she tossed her arms around Annie's neck and smacked a kiss against her cheek. One of the prettiest African-American women Annie had ever met, Tyra's dark brown eyes glistened as she smiled.

"I was kind of expecting you to call and cancel."

"Are you kidding?" Merideth cried. "She wouldn't dare!"

"I should hope not," Tyra said with a bob of her head. "I got a babysitter for this night out."

Zoey plopped half a sour cream–drenched potato on her plate and waved, then animatedly pointed to her very full mouth. Annie gave her best friend's shoulder a smack as she rounded the table and sat down between her and Merideth, across from Tyra.

Merideth always outdressed the rest of them, and this night was no exception. Zoey and Tyra had donned their usual casual outfits revolving around jeans; Annie topped off blue jeans and a black shirt with rhinestoned French cuffs by adding a simple black beret; but Merideth looked like a cover girl. Black Cambio velvet jeans and a chestnut-suede-and-woolen-piped UGG poncho that fell slightly off the shoulder to reveal a textured black shell underneath.

Big hair and big shoes. That was Merideth's motto on fashion. And the bigger the event, the bigger the streaked and sprayed hair.

"How's the new job?" Tyra asked as soon as the dinner order had been placed. "Better than mortgage acceleration?"

"If you can imagine that," Merideth teased.

"It's going great."

"What kind of cases do you work on?" Tyra wanted to know, shimmering with that mist of *I-still-work-in-the-call-center-you-left-behind.*

Annie regaled them with tales of missing persons over dinner, moving on to insurance fraud as they hiked up Alvarado Street. For some reason, she kept Marion Armbrewster all to herself, not ready to share her story just yet. It wasn't like any of her three friends would blow the surprise, but a certain energy pulsed around keeping Marion's secret, even from them.

"I'm surprised Dot didn't come along tonight," Zoey observed as they followed the crowd into the scarlet-red lobby of their favorite vintage theater.

"Prior engagement," Annie replied.

"Drinks with Lauren Bacall?" Zoey cracked. "High tea with Julie Andrews?"

"Dinner. Doris Day."

That yanked the attention of her friends, and Tyra's jaw dropped open slightly as she gasped. "Your granny's having dinner with Doris Day?"

Annie shrugged one shoulder and nodded. "I know."

As Merideth and Annie purchased their tickets at the window, Zoey leaned toward Tyra and nodded at the framed movie poster for the night's classic big-screen feature.

North by Northwest. Cary Grant ran from an airplane in front of Mount Rushmore atop the caption: *"Only Cary Grant and Alfred Hitchcock ever gave you so much suspense in so many directions."*

"Dot knew Cary Grant," Zoey whispered to Tyra.

"Are you joking?"

"We never joke about Dot's past," she said on a chuckle.

"Next in line."

Annie ordered a Diet Coke and a small popcorn; then she strolled around the lobby while her friends made their choices, glancing at several more versions of the *North by Northwest* movie poster displayed in glass cases on the wall leading to the theater. Two more posters announced the night's second feature, *Notorious.*

Zoey stepped up beside her and read one of the taglines with melodramatic flair. "Fateful fascination. Bold intrigue."

Annie chuckled and asked, "So what's the hubby doing tonight?"

Zoey sighed. "Working. What else? He's a permanent fixture at the warehouse these days. I'm lucky if I can catch up just to sort out his paperwork for him."

"Running a business of your own isn't all it's cracked up to be, I guess," Annie commented.

"It certainly is not."

Annie sensed something more in Zoey's tone, and it inspired

her to lean forward slightly to get a good look at her friend's eyes. As she suspected, they were misted with emotion, and Zoey cracked a lame attempt at a smile.

"Zo?"

"Ah, yeah," she replied with a wave of her hand. "I'm just a little overwhelmed lately. There's a lot going on—a lot of stress."

"Anything I can do?"

"Afraid not. But thanks."

They slipped into line behind Merideth and Tyra, following the crowd up the staircase to the balcony lobby. Inside, the theater glowed beneath the yellowish light of ornate chandeliers. A massive red velvet curtain shielded the movie screen, and a blue haze projected from behind it.

"I love this place," Annie breathed as they took their regular places in the first row of the balcony.

"I haven't been here since last spring," Tyra told them. "A bunch of us came to see Jeremy Camp then."

Annie had nearly forgotten that the theater was also a locale for concerts and large events. To her, the place propelled her into the past, a venue where she could see her favorite old films as they were meant to be seen, on the large silver screen. She'd seen all her favorites on that screen below over the years, from musicals to nail-biters, from *Cleopatra* to *That Touch of Mink*, but, as on most classic-film nights, there were far more vacant seats than filled ones.

The pleated curtains opened as the lights dimmed, and Annie curled into the corner of the padded velvet seat and leaned toward Zoey.

"Trains are very important to this movie, which is why the title sequence opens with those crisscrossing lines that look like railroad tracks," she whispered. Zoey nodded as she grabbed a few kernels of Annie's popcorn and tossed them into her mouth.

Bernard Herrmann's score swelled as the film's title and names of the featured actors moved up and down the screen like elevator cars over a New York skyscraper. Hitchcock's director's credit appeared, and Annie leaned forward to announce a key moment to her friends.

"Watch! Look, there he is!" she told them as Alfred Hitchcock appeared on the screen, racing after a bus—only to have the driver shut the doors before he could board. "He always gives himself a cameo in his films."

"Shh," someone a few rows behind them hissed, and Annie clicked her tongue as she leaned back into her seat.

Sensing the grin beaming from Zoey to her left, Annie tossed a kernel of popcorn at her without so much as a sideways glance. Zoey's snicker pushed a chuckle up and out of Annie, and next it was Tyra shushing them.

* * * * *

At the first sign of intermission, Nick ran downstairs to beat the crowd to the snack counter.

"Bag of Starburst and a large Coke, please."

Just as he paid the tab and gathered his things, streams of people emerged from the flapping doors to the first floor and the staircase that led from the balcony. As he reached the stairs, the same pair of giggling, golden-haired children he'd passed on his way down blocked his path. The fascination with running up and down a staircase had been lost on him years ago, but he grinned at their enthusiasm as he skirted them and headed up the stairs.

Just as he could almost see the top, something thudded into him and seemed to bounce right off again. *Thump-thump-thump*—and he realized it was a human being. Hair flew everywhere, and she screeched slightly with each bump. In an effort to stop the momentum, she tried to grab hold of Nick on her way down, but he didn't realize until too late that she'd miscalculated and missed him altogether. Finally she rolled to the landing with a groan.

"Oh, Annie! Are you all right?" The woman who raced down the steps and to the side of the fallen victim looked like someone he'd seen in a commercial for hair products, until she turned and glared at Nick with the accusatory sharpness of a fresh blade.

He took the stairs down to the landing as the woman on the floor began to sputter for air and grappled to indulge in it. He stuffed his candy into his pocket and set his Coke on the railing.

"Better?" he asked her, and when she peered up at him with greenish eyes poking through a nest of crazy hair, he realized…

Annie Gray.

"Can you stand?" he asked, reaching under her arms and lifting her to her feet. "Annie Gray, right?"

She looked at him oddly, and as she pushed her hair away from her face with both hands, she tilted her head and narrowed those glistening eyes of hers. He could almost hear her wheels turning as she seemed to try to figure out who he might be.

"Nick Benchley," he reminded her. "We met at Deke's office."

"Oh. Right."

He watched it take root as her friend stepped up next to her. "My gosh, Annie, you fell so hard. Are you all right? Did you hurt yourself?"

"She's fine," he answered for her.

The friend scowled at him for just a moment before charging. "Well, no thanks to you," she declared. "Why don't you look where you're going, huh? She could have been killed!"

Killed. Really?

"She's the one who wasn't looking where she was going," he countered. "And she fell down a couple of stairs, not off the side of the building."

As the woman opened her mouth, her intentions to rail at him fully understood, Nick just shook his head and dismissed them both, grabbing his drink and taking the stairs two at a time up toward the balcony.

"What a jerk!"

The words followed him like a wad of stiff paper hurled at his back. Then, more softly, "Are you sure you're okay?"

* * * * *

Zoey and Dot led with tied scores at the end of the first Scrabble game, and Annie and Evan were in the midst of mixing up the tiles for the start of another one when the doorbell chimed.

Annie glanced at the clock: 7:40 p.m.

"Who in the world could that be?" Zoey asked. Annie shrugged as she headed over to find out.

When she opened the front door, a large bouquet of assorted long-stemmed flowers greeted her, and a brown leather–jacketed arm extended them toward her. When he lowered the bouquet, Annie found Nick Benchley standing behind it on the doorstep.

"What…are you doing here?"

"I came to apologize," he said, and he tilted slightly, looking inside. "But it seems as if I've interrupted a party."

"No, not at all. More like an accidental gathering."

"The more the merrier?" he asked somewhat hopefully, and he handed her the flowers and moved past without waiting for so much as a nod from Annie.

"Nick Benchley," he said to Zoey, as he extended his hand.

The moment she reached up to take it, however, he quickly moved into a defensive stance, as if she might punch his lights out rather than shake his hand.

"When we last met, there seemed to be some question about whether you were going to deck me," Nick told her. "I come in peace. See? Flowers!"

"Nice start." Zoey grinned. She snatched his hand and gave it a vigorous shake. "Zoey Lopez."

Turning back toward Annie, half of Nick's mouth curved into a mischievous smile. "I'm sorry I recklessly got in your way on the stairs, Annie Gray. Can you ever forgive me?"

She sniffed at the flowers and turned her nose upward, as if to think it over.

"I suppose."

"Great. Now, do I—" Nick cut his own words in half as he caught sight of Gram through the arched doorway to the kitchen as she turned over tiles in the Scrabble box. "Dorothy Gray."

Still holding several wooden tiles, Dot glanced up at him and leaned back in her chair. "And you would be?"

"Nick Benchley, ma'am," he replied, rushing toward her with an extended hand. "I am such a fan."

"Really," Annie spouted, her hand on her hip.

Nick grasped Dot's hand with great care, as if it might be made of Tiffany glass. "I've seen all of your films."

Zoey pulled a face, and Annie shrugged.

Evan shifted from where he stood, wedged into the corner of the counter, and folded his arms across his chest. "Who is this?" he asked Annie.

"Nick, Evan. Evan, Nick."

Nick nodded then turned his attention back to Dot. "I saw you off Broadway when I was in high school," he told her. "You did *Love Letters* at the Promenade Theater."

"Oh." Dot chuckled. "That was great fun."

"Gram!" Annie exclaimed, taking the chair beside her. "I didn't know you did live theater."

"They enticed me with John Forsythe."

Evan's laughter seemed to bellow, and he leaned forward and rubbed Dot's shoulder tenderly.

"Do you like coffee, Mister Benchley?"

"Nick. Yes, very much."

"Then why don't you and Annie make some while we move the game out to the parlor?"

"Sounds like a plan." Nick smiled at her.

"No need," Annie interjected. "I'll make coffee. You join the others."

He didn't even have the good sense to object. He just wandered off with her gram, the two of them arm-in-arm like old knitting-club buddies or something.

A moment later, the doorbell chimed again and Sherman let out two halfhearted barks.

Annie chirped under her breath as she plunked the filter into the coffeepot. "You did *Love Letters* at the Promenade," she mimicked, snarling slightly as she did so. As she filled a vase with water and dropped the flowers into it, she heaved a rumbly sigh. "Flowers yet. He actually brought me flowers."

Chapter Six

. . . .

"Frankly, my dear…"
Clark Gable, *Gone With the Wind*, 1939

Annie pulled down the tray covered in beautiful, black metal grapevines dotted with amethyst grapes that Gram had bought in Lisbon while shooting a movie. Lining the tray with hand-painted coffee mugs, she continued to mutter Nick Benchley–inspired musings.

"Who are you talking to? Are we interrupting?"

She looked up to find Merideth standing in the doorway, flanked by a tall vision of a man that made Annie's heart sputter slightly.

"This is my friend Colby Barnes. We were on our way home from a meeting, and I thought we'd pop in and say hello."

Annie added two cups to the tray in one fluid motion and presented her hand to the vision. "Annie Gray," she said. "Pleased to meet you."

He returned a firm handshake, not overpowering.

Merideth made the introductions to the others while Annie doled out coffee, feeling very much like a server at a casual café.

"We're working on a charity thing in the village with a couple of the galleries," she volunteered. "It would have been a crime not to stop in."

Never mind that Annie might very likely have been hanging around in sweats and a ponytail at nearly eight thirty on a Friday night, and she might have met Colby Barnes for the first time looking like that!

Colby bordered on almost-too-pretty with a chiseled jaw and deep baby blue eyes. Not her usual type, but Annie could certainly appreciate the ease of looking at him. In fact, looking away proved to be almost painful.

"Any fake sugar?" Zoey asked, and Annie peeled her eyes from Colby with a jerk of a nod before heading into the kitchen.

"Can I help with anything?"

The vision had followed her.

"I don't really excel in the whole coffee-making arena," she admitted, pulling a box of sweetener packets from the pantry.

Colby took the box from her hands, pausing long enough to burn her slightly with a smile. "I'm an old hand," he commented, and she stood there watching him drop a handful of packets into a small crystal glass he'd produced from the dish rack.

Sherman waddled into the kitchen for a quick look at the newcomer then yawned and sacked out in the middle of the checkerboard floor.

"Careful," Annie said, pointing out her obstacle of a dog.

"Hello, boy," Colby said, but Sherman barely gave him a second glance.

"So you and Merideth are friends from work," she commented.

"We were assigned to the same fund-raising project, and it turns out I went to school with her sister."

"Small world."

Annie bit her lip. *Small world? Of all the dumb comebacks—*

"She's been talking about you nonstop," he told her, as he stood in front of her holding the bowl of pink packets. "I wondered how long it would be before she arranged a meeting."

"Really?"

Certain that her face had turned fifteen shades of crimson, Annie found herself doing that thing people sometimes did, looking at her feet and poking her toe into the ground, avoiding direct eye contact.

What am I, twelve?

She forced herself to look up at him, and when their eyes met, she swallowed around a huge lump in her throat.

"I can tell you now, I'm really glad she did. It's nice to meet you, Annie."

"You too, Colby."

He shot a curious glance at the doorway behind her, and she turned to find Evan filling it.

"Can I do anything to help?" he asked Annie without taking his eyes off Colby.

At first, Annie wondered if the power of Colby's hard-to-look-away factor might be gender nonspecific, but she quickly realized that she'd seen this look on Evan before. He was sizing up the opposition, checking Colby out, weighing his competition.

Competition for exactly what, Annie couldn't be entirely certain. It wasn't like Evan had been able to utter words anywhere in the vicinity of commitment. But always, when another male had come around in his presence, one might have thought he had Annie's ownership papers folded up neatly in his back pocket.

"I think we have the sweetener covered, Evan," Colby told him. "Thanks for offering, though."

Evan seemed to consider that for a moment; then he glanced down at the dog lump in the middle of the floor. "Sherman," he said with authority, "let's go for a walk."

WALK. The word held deep meaning for Annie's beagle friend, and he lumbered to his feet and shuffled toward the back door. Looking back at Evan over his bulky shoulder, the dog sighed. He seemed to be saying, "Well, come on. You offered. Let's go."

They didn't return until the first round of coffee had been consumed and a new Scrabble tournament had ensued. Annie wondered, as they came through the front door, whether Evan had been out there talking Sherman's velvety ears off about the unfairness of another man invading his territory. She hoped there would be no canine-like lifting of the legs to set things straight.

Zoey and Annie had tied scores at the end of the first Scrabble game, and in the midst of mixing up the tiles for the start of a third game, Annie noticed Nick grinning at her from his spot on the floor in front of the coffee table. Sherman was curled up next to him with his chin resting on Nick's leg. She looked to Evan immediately, and, sure enough, his face was crimped up as tight as a fist at Sherman's betrayal. Nick's smile irritated her for some reason, like sandpaper scraping the back of her neck.

Looking away from Nick, she assessed the diversity of the three men occupying the space nearby. Evan, brooding; Nick, annoying—and Colby looking almost elegant, the Cary Grant in the room, with one long, lean leg crossed over the other and balancing his coffee cup on his knee as he effortlessly soothed the scratch of Nick's smile with his silkier one.

Evan seemed to relax a little after Zoey and Dot chose a Tony Bennett CD from the music shelf. The group spent the next hour or so just chatting, sometimes a couple of conversations in play, crisp and easy like an amiable cross-breeze.

Once a lull rolled along, Annie got up and started clearing coffee cups from the table and floor. Nick grabbed what she couldn't carry and followed her into the kitchen.

"I appreciate the flowers," she told him. "But it wasn't necessary."

"Yes, it was," he replied, moving toward her.

She was deciding whether to set the cups on the counter or into the sink when he leaned forward, right out of nowhere, and planted a kiss on her lips. It was quick and somewhat tender, with a sort of electrical spark to it there at the last. Annie never saw it coming.

"What was that?" she asked when he pulled away. "You've got a lot of nerve."

"No one's ever accused me of being without nerve," he told her, and he took the cups from her hands, set them in the sink, and crossed the kitchen. At the doorway, he turned back and narrowed his eyes. With a somewhat mischievous lilt to his voice, he told her, "At least one of the three males in this house was going to do that tonight. I wanted to be the first. Now you have something to compare them to."

Annie stood there, speechless, as he returned to the living room and joined the conversation without ever missing a beat. Her lips tingled—and her fingers and toes as well, she noticed.

It had been such a long time since she'd been kissed like that, she didn't know how to respond. Part of her wanted to march right into the living room, pour the last of the coffee in his lap, and call him an arrogant jerk. The other part... Well, Annie didn't want to think about what that part of her wanted to do.

While she mulled that over, Zoey sauntered into the kitchen and slipped into a chair at the table. For a couple of moments, she just stared at Annie with curious, wide eyes. Finally she nodded, encouraging Annie to speak.

"What?"

"Oh, come on," she whispered. "There are three men in that room all bidding for your attention. This is, to say the least, a bit unusual, isn't it?"

Annie leaned back against the counter and stared at her briefly. "You think that's strange?" she said, still somewhat stunned by Nick's behavior. "Get this. That Nick Benchley? He kissed me."

"What do you mean? When?"

"Just now. He walked right up to me and kissed me, right on the lips."

"What did you say to him?"

"I said he had a lot of nerve."

"Good girl." After a moment, Zoey added, "How was it?"

Fortunately, they were interrupted by Colby's presence and Annie didn't have to respond.

"It was a pleasure meeting you, Annie," he said. "You too, Zoey."

"Are you leaving?" Annie questioned.

"We have a radio thing first thing in the morning up in San Jose."

"Oh. Well, I'm glad you stopped by."

"Listen," he said, moving a bit closer to her. "I was hoping you wouldn't mind if I called you sometime."

"Oh. That...would be great. I'd like that."

"Good. I'll get your number from Merideth, then."

"Okay."

Annie and Zoey exchanged facial contortions as he floated out of the room.

"He's gorgeous," Zoey mouthed.

"I know!" Annie returned without audio.

* * * * *

It seemed to Nick that everyone decided to sweep out of Annie's house at the same time. Except for Evan, who was still seated casually on the sofa and looking for all the world as if he lived there.

Annie walked toward the front door behind him, and he could feel her there. When he'd kissed her, he'd smelled that same distant scent of jasmine. He stopped and turned around, and she almost smacked right into him.

"Listen," she said softly. "Don't ever do that again."

"Do what?"

"You know what. That thing you did in the kitchen before," she said, her voice in a whisper but exaggerating the shape of the words with her mouth.

"Oh, you mean," he said, leaning closer, grinning at her, "when I kissed you."

"Yes."

"Never?"

She bit her lip, and he could almost watch the turning of her thoughts in her hazel green eyes. He made her crazy, and Nick loved it.

"I'm not kidding," she reiterated. "A kiss is a very private thing, and it should be agreed upon, not stolen."

"Well, when you put it that way," he began, falling silent for a long moment and mulling over the idea creeping up on him. "I'll tell you what, Annie Gray. The next time I kiss you, if I ever *do* kiss you again, it will be because you've asked me to. Deal?"

"I wouldn't hold your breath for that," she replied. "But do I have your word on it?"

"You have my word."

"Okay." She nodded. "Thank you for the flowers."

"And thank you. For the coffee, and for your grandmother!"

"I didn't give her to you, Nick."

"No, but thanks for letting me borrow her for a little while. Dorothy Gray! She's spectacular."

Nick meandered down the front steps before he turned around to face her once he reached the sidewalk. Despite the agreement they'd just made, he already recognized the inner struggle against breaking it. Nick really wanted to kiss Annie again.

Instead, he told her, "You have some very nice friends, Annie Gray."

"I know," she replied with a grin. "Good night."

"Sleep tight."

He opened the front gate, and she called after him, "By the way, Nick. How did you find my gram's house anyway?"

"I'm a cop," he told her. "I can find anyone's house."

"You're a...*cop*?"

* * * * *

Annie woke up at four o'clock the next morning because of a series of dreams straight out of a movie she'd once seen. Chased by hundreds of grooms down the middle of the Cabrillo Highway, Annie spotted Evan, Colby, and Nick at the front of the pack. When they backed her up against Exit 399B to Monterey, which was closed again for some new construction need, Nick emerged from the group, walked right up to her, and shoved her to the ground. He tossed a bunch of flowers at her before stalking away, and the petals fell upon her in colorful slow motion.

Three cups of coffee after sundown is not a good thing, she decided.

From now on, I'm sticking to something that won't betray me this way. Something that won't promote bad dreams of rebellious grooms.

Annie sat down at the kitchen table. The only light streamed gently through the doorway from the bay window at the front of the house. She'd never been a big proponent of herbal teas and the like, but it seemed like a really good night to try one. A few minutes later, she dunked a chamomile bag she found in the back of the cupboard into a cup of water made too hot in the microwave.

Sherman wobbled in, blinked several times, and made himself comfortable at her feet. His chin felt warm where it rested on her bare toes, and she wiggled them a little to give him a tickle that he was too tired to appreciate.

Nick's flowers seemed to wave at her from the vase on the counter. She figured the buzz on her brain could be attributed to an overdose of caffeine, but Nick Benchley seemed to be right there at the root of it as well. She found herself replaying his visit until her brain started to ache a little.

Two fingers flew to her lips, which were stinging again at the memory of his kiss.

It's been such a long time since... Why did it have to be Nick Benchley?

He did have very soft lips, though.

And very appealing dark eyes.

And the brash manners of a donkey to go with them.

Annie made a mental list of the overabundance of men currently floating through her life, omitting Evan's name before proceeding. Like the exit to Munras Avenue off the Cabrillo, that road had closed. Better to take an alternate route.

Colby might be a nice detour, though.

Annie giggled out loud at Merideth's straight-on matchmaking in bringing him right to her door, and Sherman shifted to his side, irritated at her lack of consideration. His beauty sleep was pending, after all.

Colby seemed almost too handsome to consider—and too handsome to dismiss, as well. But Nick Benchley?

His leather jacket with the suede inlays came to mind. With his force-of-nature entrances into a room and his *just-walk-right-up-to-you-and-kiss-you-whether-you-like-it-or-not*-ness, well, he had to go too. She crossed him off her mental list with a large, thick *X* and then scribbled over his name just for good measure.

Annie resolved to call Merideth in the morning and thank her, maybe suggest she give Colby a little nudge along with that phone number. Meanwhile, Annie would take care of one more pesky item on her list and find herself some really great hair.

I'm going to do something drastic. And if Jake won't help me, I'll find someone in the region who will.

Rubbing her front teeth with her index finger, she reminded herself to have them whitened then abandoned the drab cup of tea and headed upstairs to her bedroom. She'd already crawled beneath the covers when she heard Sherman's paws scamper-thumping up the stairs and down the hall. He landed on the bed with a thud, made a full circle, and tilted over sideways. He was snoring before she could turn off the light.

Clearly, Sherman hadn't had three cups of coffee to keep him awake. Perhaps a lesson could be found there.

Chapter Seven

"I don't have to show you any stinkin' badges."
Alfonso Bedoya, *Treasure of the Sierra Madre,* 1948

Important fact about undefined relationships: if you introduce someone to your gram, don't expect them not to love her.

Aside from the relationship questions, Annie had to admit that Evan had been an exceptional friend to her and her grandmother. The bistro where he worked in the village was just a few minutes' walk from Gram's house, and he'd been visiting Dot on a regular basis long before Annie gave up her Monterey apartment and came to live in the attic upstairs.

It seemed only natural that Gram had given him a key and asked him to look in on Sherman on days when Annie worked and she had one of her women's group meetings, luncheons, or yoga classes. Annie couldn't think of a kind way to revoke his privileges, but doling out keys was not indicative of where their relationship had finally landed. Still, why should Sherman suffer because of grown-up issues? Annie had begun to suspect over time that *that* relationship might be the real purpose in their association anyway. They were soul mates, Evan and Sherman.

But as she headed up the walk toward the front door on this particular evening, carrying a bag from the pharmacy containing a new teeth-whitening system, Annie questioned the wisdom of the whole key-giving thing.

The rattling of pots and pans drew her straight into the kitchen, where the back door sat propped open. As she stepped into the doorway, Evan and Sherman looked very much like housewife and child to her. She couldn't shake the comparison that she was the Ozzie to Evan's Harriet, and she stifled a hearty laugh.

"How about cucumbers?" Evan asked Sherman. "Do you like cucumbers as much as you like lettuce?" Standing happily at Evan's feet, the beagle wagged his tail hard in reply.

Evan tossed him a slice, and Sherman gave it mild consideration but ultimately rejected it. Annie picked up the slippery thing from the floor and deposited it into the garbage disposal.

"Welcome home!" Evan exclaimed.

"Thank you," she replied curiously, looking around at the obvious dinner preparations. "What's going on here?"

"Dot asked me to come over and check on Sherman so she could go out for dinner. So I had a brainstorm: why not make dinner for Annie tonight? So here I am."

"Here you are."

"Why don't you go and get cleaned up; change into something comfortable if you want. And I'll get dinner on the table."

So enthusiastic, so hopeful. So eager to please.

Annie glanced down at Sherman, still happily panting and wagging at Evan's feet, and the comparison just couldn't escape her. She didn't believe in reincarnation, but if she did...

They might have been brothers in another life.

Annie returned to the kitchen a few minutes later, having donned her favorite pair of jeans, an oversized chambray shirt, and flip-flops. It wouldn't be a formal evening, but no one would have known it from the spread Evan had prepared.

His wonderful potato soup graced Gram's stoneware bowls, and the creamy fragrance of onions, potatoes, and garlic served as a lovely greeting. Warm turkey sandwiches also waited, precisely placed on the edges of two small plates and piled on freshly baked whole grain bread. Nut stuffing and cranberry sauce peeked out from between the diagonally cut slices. Chilled grapes and chunks of watermelon formed a vibrant mound between them.

"Every meal with you is an event, Evan."

"Sit," he said with a warm smile. "And tell me about your new job. How do you like it?"

They covered general topics, such as Deke and current investigations, Evan's restaurant, and the amazing food he'd brought to her table. Not until they were just about finished eating did the real entrée come to light.

"So…which one of those pretty boys from the other night are you interested in?"

Annie dabbed at the corner of her mouth with a napkin and stared him down.

"I don't know that I'm interested in either of them," she told him. "I haven't learned enough about them to know if there's anything there. Why do you ask, Evan?"

"I don't know. You seemed very chummy with that Nick."

That Nick. Like "that dog" or "that pencil."

It occurred to Annie that men like Nick Benchley sort of forced "chummy" onto a person when he or she wasn't looking. Nick always seemed to know Annie far better than he actually did, and it drove her batty. But she chose not to share those observations with Evan.

"Does that bother you, Evan?"

There. It's out there. I've called you on it. What do you think of that?

"What do you mean?"

"Well, I can't help but notice. It seems to bother you."

"No," he managed, before immediately popping to his feet. He began clearing dishes as he added, "It's none of my business who you date anyway. I was just making conversation."

She considered pointing out to him that she wasn't dating either Nick or Colby—or Evan himself, for that matter.

"It just doesn't seem like either one of them is your type, that's all."

"I didn't know I had a type," she remarked, carrying her dishes to the sink.

"Dessert?"

She raised an eyebrow and smiled. "Tempt me."

"Oatmeal raisin cookies. Baked this afternoon."

"Sold!"

"I think I'll leave them with you and take off," he said, handing over a small white box tied with string in a perfect bow right at the top.

"You sure?"

"I have some things to do."

Evan didn't have things to do, and Annie felt confident that they both knew it. He also hadn't come over on a whim to cook her dinner, either. He came fishing. But the information he'd hooked with potato soup bait was definitely being thrown back.

* * * * *

Annie had been checking the newspaper often in search of a convertible she could afford. The newspaper ads referred to them as "pre-owned," which sounded much more hoity-toity, of course, but it really just meant "used."

Deke happened into the office just as she circled a good possibility: a 2005 blue Ford Mustang convertible. Great condition, low miles, one owner.

"I'm car shopping," she told him.

"Whatcha looking for?"

"I don't care about the make. I just want a convertible."

"Well, don't make it too flashy," he warned. "Private investigators need to blend in while on surveillance. Stay under the radar."

Deke looked over her shoulder at the newspaper and shook his head. "A Mustang?" he exclaimed with a chuckle. "Yeah, I guess you can't get more nondescript than that."

Oh well. Maybe I'll hang on to Taurie a little bit longer.

Deke headed back to his office but paused in the doorway. "Speaking of surveillance," he said, "are you up for a new assignment?"

Am I! Dialing down her enthusiasm a notch or two, Annie nodded. "Sure."

"Come on in. Bring a notepad."

Dr. Dwayne Biddle personified her next case, an orthopedic doctor specializing in performing unnecessary surgery in order to jack up the medical bills of arguably injured car-accident victims.

"These are the files from Northern California Life and Casualty where we've been able to link inconsistent behavior with injuries," Deke told her, handing over a stack of a half dozen folders. "It's going to make a tighter case for fraud if we can tie in the lawyer and the doctor with the claims and lawsuits filed."

Deke sparkled when he talked about his business. And if Annie wasn't already excited about this new career choice, she imagined he would play a great role in getting her there.

"I'm visiting the lawyer, a fellow named Zach Gleason, this afternoon, to see if he tries to hook me up with Biddle," he explained. "Meanwhile, you make an appointment with the good doctor and see if he returns the favor to Gleason. They'll probably make you wait a day or two for the appointment, but get one as soon as you can."

"I can fill the time by studying up on these other cases," she suggested.

"That should be a top priority," Deke agreed. "But how are you coming on that client database?"

"Another couple of hours to clean it up and it will be fit for human consumption."

Deke's astonishment sent Annie's heart soaring. "You got all that information into one place that quickly?"

"Yep."

"Okay, Speedy Gonzalez," he said, shaking his head. "I'm officially impressed."

Annie thought it almost ridiculous how happy that made her. Her work at Equity Now had been little more than a series of incoming calls, each of them pretty much the same as the last.

While still recovering from the euphoric haze of a job-well-done surge of adrenaline, Deke said something that almost choked her with it.

"I was expecting Bench sometime today."

Nick Benchley. The reference stopped traffic out on Alvarado Street.

"He's helping us out with a background check on Zach Gleason.

Doesn't look like he'll get here before I leave, so why don't you just go over the basics of his results with him and I'll take a look later on."

"O–kay."

"Oh, that's right. I hear you and Bench ran into one another at the movies the other night."

"You could say that," she replied on a chuckle. "We ran into each other with a definite thud."

"Bench is a very good guy."

"How do you know him?" she asked Deke.

"We volunteer with the same youth group," he said.

Annie resisted the rapid heartbeat she felt. *Nick Benchley? A do-gooder?*

"What group?"

"Community center, over in Santa Cruz."

She grinned curiously, realizing that it probably came off more as a disbelieving smirk.

"Bench came a couple of years ago with a boy he mentored through the police force, and he's been coming ever since."

A girl's brain could easily topple into "overload" from this new and unexpected information. *A nice guy? Nick Benchley?*

Once Deke left for his appointment with Zach Gleason, Annie grabbed a diet soda from the fridge and settled down at her desk with the insurance files. Deke had been working on the case for nearly six months, and he'd built a solid body of evidence linking car-accident clients of Gleason's to astronomical medical insurance claims, all routed through Dr. Dwayne Biddle. And then there were the incriminating photos, affidavits, and investigation reports.

Shara Himes, for instance, had injured her back so badly that she required intense physical therapy and had been out of work for over a year. But her file burgeoned with photo pages assembled by Deke that showed Himes playing volleyball, carrying boxes, and loading groceries into her car.

Randall Dillon had had knee surgery and nineteen months of physical therapy. He'd been collecting disability benefits for nearly two years, yet the photo pages in his file revealed activities as diverse as football and parasailing.

Every folder in the stack was chock-full of evidence that contradicted the associated medical reports. And the doctor for each of them was Dr. Dwayne Biddle.

Annie had just closed the last of the files when the office door burst open.

Does Nick Benchley ever *enter a room like a normal human being?*

"Afternoon, Annie Gray. How are you?"

"Very well, thank you. And you?"

He regarded her carefully for a moment, narrowing his eyes and looking so deeply into her that it felt a bit like the poke of an injection.

"My day has just gotten much better, seeing you," he replied—and his face tilted into one of those crooked dimpled smiles of his.

As hard as she fought against it, something about seeing Nick again brought with it an overwhelming urge to act like a girl.

Playing with her hair and batting her eyelashes at him, well, that was simply out of the question. And so she resisted.

* * * * *

"Deke around?"

"He had to leave," Annie told him, and Nick tapped the desktop several times with a large envelope.

"I have an update for him."

"On Zach Gleason. I know. He suggested I meet with you and discuss your results, and I can update him when he gets back."

"Well, that little matchmaker," he teased, and Nick made a mental note to pick up the check the next time he and Deke had lunch.

"It's all business, I can assure you," she insisted.

"Sure it is."

Nick grabbed a chair, scraped it up to the corner of her desk, and straddled it. As he opened the envelope, he noticed Annie looking at his hands. He hoped she thought how masculine and strong they appeared, but he grimaced, knowing full well she'd just noticed the nail on his right index finger, which was almost completely black.

"What happened?" she asked him. Wiggling her own index finger at him, she added, "Your nail."

"Misfire on a handgun a few years back."

"In the line of duty?"

Nick cracked a smile, and he felt the weight of the one she returned.

"Yes, actually. What's got you so nosy today, Annie Gray?"

She picked up her soda can and toasted him with it. "Caffeine high?"

And with that, she downed the last of it and tossed it past him. The can banked off the wall and bounced straight into the trash can.

"She shoots; she scores!" he said in his best announcer voice. "And the crowd goes wild."

Nick made applause noises while she bowed slightly and thanked the imaginary crowd.

"Next stop, Lakers," he declared. "Annie Gray, center court."

Her laughter resonated all the way to Nick's gut.

"Yeah, Kobe and me next to each other. That would be a sight, wouldn't it?"

The reference surprised Nick. "What do you know about Kobe?"

"Hey, now, what's that supposed to mean?"

"You just don't strike me as—"

"As what, Nick? A basketball fan? I didn't know that was gender-specific."

"No, it's just—"

"Mmm-hmmm. I see how you are."

He studied her for a moment and grinned. "What's his number, then?"

"You're calling me a liar?"

"Not straight out."

"All righty, then," she mocked. "I hope you have some crow handy."

"If it becomes necessary," he stated, "I'll eat a little crow for you." Giving her the come-on signal with both hands, he encouraged her. "All right now. No stalling. Let's go."

"Kobe's number twenty-four," she stated. "Six foot six, just over two hundred pounds."

Nick leaned into the backward chair and folded his arms across the top of it.

A woman that looks like this and a Lakers fan too? This is not possible.

"And then of course there's Andrew Bynum out of New Jersey. And the beautiful Spaniard, number sixteen, Pau Gasol. Shall I go on?"

"No!" he exclaimed with a full-on laugh. "Please stop."

"And would you like that crow sautéed or broiled?"

"What, you cook too, *Kobe*?"

"Well, no, actually. But I'm sure my friend Evan would take care of it for you. He's a chef."

"A chef, huh?" he repeated thoughtfully, remembering Evan from the other evening at Annie's house.

"How about we get to Zach Gleason?" Annie suggested. "What did you find out about him?"

"Deke felt pretty sure there was something there, but when he couldn't find it he asked me to look into it. The thing is, Gleason actually looks pretty clean." He unfolded several pages of printout and set it before her. "He went to college in Miami and then law school in Boston and joined a prestigious practice in L.A."

"No small list of accomplishments."

"Exactly. I don't find anything even slightly shady in his background. No complaints, not even a traffic ticket."

"Well…okay."

"Deke's instinct is usually dead-on," he told her. "I was a little surprised I didn't find anything to back it up."

"What about Biddle?"

"Who's Biddle?"

"He's the medical connection," she explained. "I wonder if we could find a link between them if we did the same kind of background check on him."

Nick produced a small notebook from his jacket pocket and then snatched the pen right out of Annie's hand.

"Biddle?"

"Dwayne Biddle," she replied, double-checking the information inside one of the files. "He has an office right here in Monterey."

"I'll find him," he promised, snapping the notebook shut and sliding it back into his pocket. "Tomorrow morning all right?"

"Great."

As he tucked the paperwork into the envelope, Nick let out a long, laborious sigh. Screwing up his resolve, he smiled.

"Now let's get to the heart of things, Annie Gray," he said, plopping the envelope down on the desk with a *smack*. "Where would you like to have dinner tonight?"

* * * * *

Standing in the doorway to her mother's kitchen, holding back the bloodcurdling scream rumbling within her, Annie wondered if counting might help.

One-hippopotamus. Two-hippopotamus. Three-hippopotamus.

"Isn't it wonderful news, Annie? I'm going to be a grandma!"

Leave it to her younger brother to not only marry before Annie, but to make their folks grandparents before she even found a solid marriageable prospect.

"I'd hoped you would be married by the time they started their family," her mother continued, and Annie was tempted to cover her ears with both hands and make some noise to drown her out.

La la la la la la.

"Oh, Annie, I hope it's a little boy. I've always wanted another boy in the family."

To make up for the defective girl, no doubt.

"Can you stay for supper, honey? We're having pot roast."

"No thanks, Mom. I really have to get home and walk Sherman."

"Carrots and onions," she sang. "And those little round potatoes you like so much."

"It sounds great, but I really—"

"Well, at least stay and say hello to your father."

Annie glanced at the clock. Her father wasn't due for another hour, and she wasn't sure she could endure an entire hour of "grandma" talk.

"Give him my love," she said, planting a kiss on her mom's cheek and then heading toward the door with determination. "I'll call you this weekend."

"Okay, sweetie. And I'll be sure to tell your brother how happy you are for him."

Annie knew it was unfair to feel the way she did. But she couldn't manage to see beyond how his happiness affected her.

I know. Selfish. Terrible and selfish.

But knowing this did not help one little bit in expelling the thoughts, despite how hard she tried to do so on the drive home. Her mind ruminated about weddings and babies, none of which she had in her near future. When she finally turned onto her gram's street, she realized she hardly remembered making the drive. She parked her car and turned off the engine, then tilted her head back to the headrest and closed her eyes.

What is wrong with me?

Her brother's wonderful news had her in a tailspin. Why couldn't she manage to just be happy for him? Why couldn't she rush into the house and call Linda and tell her how great it was that she would finally have the baby she and Ted had been hoping for?

I'm a sorry excuse for a sister.

When she really thought about it, Ted had never done anything to her except…be a little brother. It wasn't his fault that he excelled over her in every possible way, was it? Or that their mother thought the sun rose and set because of him. Why couldn't Annie be less competitive and more loving?

She nearly had to peel herself off the roof of the car when a knock on the window next to her came out of nowhere. She knew she must have looked like a startled deer as Colby smiled back at her from the other side of the glass.

"I'm sorry," he said as she lowered the window. "I didn't mean to scare you."

With her hand to her heart, she forced herself to breathe. "It's all right. I just didn't see you there."

"I should have called, but I was in the area for a walk-through at one of the galleries, and I saw your street. My car sort of steered itself over here. Have you had dinner yet?"

"No, actually, I haven't."

"What do you think of PortaBella?"

"Love the place. I have to check on Sherman first, though."

Colby offered his arm as she slid out from behind the wheel; then he closed and locked the door behind her.

"Why don't you go ahead and walk your dog? I can still make it to the printer before they close and pick you up in about thirty minutes."

"I'll see you then."

He smiled, warm and sincere. "I'm really looking forward to it."

"Me too."

While she let Sherman sniff around in the grass, Annie wondered why she'd agreed to have dinner with Colby Barnes so quickly when she'd turned Nick Benchley down flat just two days prior. She felt certain that Colby's timing had something to do with it, finding her in her car, lamenting over her unmarried, childless status. Looking up to find Colby on the other side of the window, all willing and eager and handsome, felt a bit like finding a warm appetizer on a silver platter.

With that, Annie decided to rush Sherman through his walk so she could go inside and change into something appropriate for a first date at an upscale restaurant in the village.

She applied first aid to the day's makeup and headed to her closet to change her attire. She decided on a frilly black skirt and a vintage pink angora sweater that had an iridescent, beaded leaf pattern cascading from the shoulders. She sat down on the stairs and slipped into a pair of clunky, strappy sandals just as Colby arrived to pick her up.

Perfect timing.

Annie had been to PortaBella many times, and she never tired of the storybook cottage. They were led to one of several dining rooms and seated in one with climbing vines and an exposed ceiling overhead. Colby started with crab bisque, and Annie eagerly ordered her favorite salad of baby spinach, red grapefruit sections, and sliced apples.

"I think I need to do something nice for Merideth," Colby remarked later over his paella. "What kind of flower best says, 'Thank you for introducing me to a dream'? Roses, maybe?"

Although Annie didn't really favor roses, she still thought they should be reserved for the angel herself.

"Merideth is a little like a hurricane," Annie told him instead. "When she gets a direction in her head, she's unstoppable."

"Well, this was one of her better ideas."

"I have to agree," Annie replied with a smile.

"Tell me about yourself, Annie," he said, as he folded his arms on the edge of table and leaned forward on them. "Did you grow up in Carmel?"

"Monterey, really. My gram retired in Carmel."

"Is it true she's an old, legendary film star?"

"Don't let her hear you call her *old*," Annie said on a chuckle. "But yes, she was a true Hollywood film star back in the day. What about you? Where are you from?"

"I never know how to answer when someone asks me that," he replied. "My father was a lifer in the military, and we moved eleven times by my eighteenth birthday."

"That's rough."

"It is, but it's also an adventure. You get very good at making friends quickly and adapting to change."

"I envy that. I hate change."

"Well, maybe I can help you with that," he suggested.

"I'd appreciate it. Until recently, I've been kind of stuck in a rut. Dull job, dull life."

Dull hair.

"Until recently?" he asked, leaning back in the chair and regarding her seriously.

"Yes. I've been all about changing my life these days. I have a new job already, and I've been car shopping and thinking about where I want to live. Maybe even a new 'do," she added, fluffing her curls. Then she let out a laugh and waved her hand in dismissal.

"You shouldn't change the hair," he commented. "It really works for you."

"Thanks. But I'm thinking of something completely different. Maybe having it straightened."

Colby grabbed his chest with both hands and fell backward, wounded by an unseen attacker. "You're going to straighten the life out of those curls? Why would you do such a heinous thing?"

"I've had this crazy hair my whole life," she explained to him. "I'd like to try something silky for a while. Something very Jennifer Aniston or Cameron Diaz."

He cringed. "No, don't do it."

Annie couldn't help but laugh at his animation, and Colby grinned broadly.

"You know, the fund-raiser Merideth and I have been working on is next Friday night," he told her. "It's going to be a lot of fun. Black tie, very elegant."

"It sounds lovely."

"Would you be interested in going with me?"

Her heart percolated. "That would be really nice, Colby. Thank you. I'd love to go."

Annie hoped Merideth hadn't gone shopping for her dress yet. It would be so much more fun to go shopping together.

And just like that, her fears and insecurities about Ted and Linda and their baby news flew gracefully through the window, bobbing their way through the village toward the ocean in the distance, replaced with thoughts of a new dress and killer shoes.

And Colby Barnes in a tuxedo. The picture was almost swoon-worthy.

Chapter Eight

....

"Round up the usual suspects."
Claude Rains, *Casablanca*, 1942

"Does this hurt?"

"A little."

"How about this?"

"No."

"Are you sure?"

Annie nearly screamed as Dr. Biddle pressed harder into her lower back with both of his thumbs. "Y–yes!" she exclaimed. "That hurts."

"I suspected as much," he stated. "Go ahead and sit up."

She gingerly pushed herself upright and perched on the edge of the examination table.

"When was your accident?" he asked, flipping through the paperwork in the file before him. "Oh, here. January. And you haven't seen any other doctors since then?"

"No."

"Have you spoken with an attorney?"

"No."

"Well, here's my suggestion to you, Miss Gray," he said, looking very trustworthy and *doctorly* in his white lab coat with the shiny stethoscope hanging loose around his neck. "The treatments I have in mind for your back pain are very expensive. I'm not going to lie to you. But I know an attorney who can set it up so you won't have to pay these costs out-of-pocket."

His name wouldn't be Gleason, *would it, Doc?*

"I think I have a card here somewhere," he said, rummaging through his pockets. "Ah, yes, here it is."

He handed her the card, and Annie read the name aloud. "Marcus Benjamin, attorney-at-law."

Annie had been so sure it would be Zach Gleason's card. When she arrived back at the office and showed it to Deke, so certain she'd failed, Deke's beaming white smile confounded her.

"I don't understand."

"What it means," he explained, "is that we're probably digging into a whole network, m'girl."

"A network of insurance fraud?"

"That's right. Get Bench on the line for me, will you?"

Annie hadn't given much thought to Nick Benchley over the last couple of days. Her thoughts had been devoted instead to Colby and their upcoming date. It was a tight squeeze, having Nick forced into her current frame of mind, leaving her feeling a little like she wanted to crawl out of her own skin.

"Benchley."

This is the way to answer a phone?

"Hi, Nick. It's Annie."

"Annie Gray!" he exclaimed. "I knew it was just a matter of time."

"Until?"

"Until you came searching for me, realizing the error of your ways."

"Well, I hate to deflate your ego any," she told him, "but I'm calling on behalf of Deke."

Silence.

"Hello?"

"You've injured me, Annie Gray. You've truly injured me."

"I have a feeling you'll recover," she stated offhandedly. "We've had a development in the insurance fraud case, and Deke was hoping to set up a meeting with you to discuss it."

"Will you be attending this meeting?"

"I don't think so, no. Why don't I put you on the line with Deke, and the two of you can hash it out."

Silence crackled for another few beats before he sighed. "All right, Annie Gray. Why don't you do that."

"Hold for just a moment, please."

As she passed off Nick's call to Deke, Annie had the oddest feeling. What was it about Nick Benchley? He always seemed to leave a strange remnant behind. Kind of like working with something very sticky that she couldn't wipe off her hands.

* * * * *

Her purse hiked over her shoulder, Annie stood on the street corner with a blank rental application in one hand and a bottle of Diet Coke in the other. She hadn't intended to leave her gram's hospitality quite so soon, but this Monterey apartment was available immediately at a great price for the location. Now that she counted herself among the gainfully employed once again, it seemed like finding the apartment was just meant to be. Still, standing there on that curb, preparing to fill out the paperwork and lay down a deposit check on a more-expensive, less-roomy apartment than the one she'd previously occupied, Annie couldn't help asking herself all of the key questions:

Is this really what I should do?

Is it worth giving up space simply to have a Monterey address?

And what about Gram? Oh, sure, she made it seem like she needed me to move in with her, but we both knew it was just her way of lending a hand when times got really tough. Wasn't it?

"Zoey, I need you. Can you meet me right now?"

Annie spent the next half hour filling out the paperwork, just in case, and polishing off her third Diet Coke for the day. She'd been vowing lately to cut down on the amount of caffeine she consumed, but she realized as she took the last swig from the bottle that she wouldn't be keeping that promise today. In the spirit of the great Scarlett O'Hara, she decided she would think about that tomorrow.

Relief pulsed through her as Zoey pulled up and waved. The most decisive person Annie knew would surely be crucial in helping her determine her next step.

"Great neighborhood," Zoey said as they met up on the sidewalk. "Is this it?"

"Yeah. What do you think?"

"Let's go in and look around."

Up the stairs and to the left, then through a heavy wooden door, the small apartment was pure old-Spanish with dark hardwood floors, arched doorways and windows, and low-dropping, curved ceilings. Domed glass doors led to a small balcony beyond the kitchen, cordoned off by an intricate Spanish wrought-iron railing. From there, they surveyed colorful tile rooftops dotting the hills below.

"This is a spectacular apartment," Zoey told her as they stood side by side on the balcony. "It has such charm."

Annie sighed. "I think so too."

"But why are you in such a rush to leave Carmel? You have an ideal situation there with Dot."

"I know, but this place just landed in my lap."

They debated the pros and cons of the move for several minutes, and Zoey kept bringing the conversation back to Carmel.

"You're walking distance from the village, and you have that great attic bedroom if you want privacy. And don't forget a built-in babysitter for Sherman when you need one."

"Gram? Or Evan?"

"Well, both," Zoey replied, chuckling.

"This is so much closer to the office."

"Yes. But far less space than you had in your old place. And the rent has to be a lot more for this location. How much is it?"

"Three hundred more a month," Annie admitted with an inward cringe.

"Three hundred! Annie, come on. You took a new job that pays less, and you want to move into a smaller apartment that costs more?"

"I can afford it," she insisted.

This is not going the way I'd planned.

"It's not about affording it. It's about being wise. I'm not going to tell you what to do, but it just doesn't seem wise to me. Leaving your gram to live closer to your folks? Is that really going to make you happy?"

"It's such a great apartment, Zo."

"It is. But you're in a gorgeous place now."

"I can't stay there forever."

"Well, that's debatable. But will you please just think it through before you turn in that application?"

Annie agreed, and they made their way in silence out the door and down the stairs.

"Listen, Annie," Zoey said with noticeable caution as they reached their cars. "I can see that you're going through something lately. Looking to change your life and all. But you don't have to change everything at once just for the sake of creating forward movement. Maybe get used to your new job and see if it's going to work out the way you hoped. In a few months, you can revisit this idea. But don't just dive off a cliff before you really know what's down there. Do you know what I mean?"

"Yes."

"Are you upset?"

"Yes."

"With me?"

"No."

"Okay," Zoey said with a sigh. "Call me later?"

"Yeah."

"Love to Sherman," she called back just before zipping out of the spot behind Taurie.

Annie's head began to ache on the drive home to Carmel. Probably from all the ricochets she'd been fielding lately.

After taking Sherman for a quick walk, Annie grabbed another Diet Coke from the fridge and headed upstairs toward her big, comfy bed and favorite pajamas. It took Sherman two tries to make it up on the bed beside her, but he snuggled close to her thigh and let out a groan as they settled in together.

"Zoey is right about one thing," Annie told him softly. "I need guidance." But Sherman was already halfway to sleep.

Propping her pillows behind her and forming a nest with her

folded legs, Annie grabbed the Bible Dot had placed on her night-stand when Annie moved in. She opened it at random, and her eye fell upon a single word on the page. Just as it always had, ever since the eleventh grade when she wrote an English composition about the similarity between humans and sheep, that one word captured her: *Sheep.*

"But He made His own people go forth like sheep, and guided them in the wilderness like a flock; and He led them on safely, so that they did not fear." She read the passage from Psalms over again and was reminded of her plan for change. She wondered if Zoey might be right. Perhaps all the change in her life didn't have to happen in one fell swoop; maybe God would lead her toward her future one bump in the road at a time.

A few minutes later, figuring it wasn't like she was making a decision or anything since she'd already bought it, Annie bounced into the bathroom and finally read the directions for her new teeth-whitening system. And two hours after that, she made a silly—kind of frightening, really—face in the mirror to admire her pearly *whiter-now* whites.

* * * * *

Annie hated dressing-room mirrors, especially on that particular day. She understood that they were designed to show how others would see a person, from every possible angle and all, and a certain degree of usefulness pulsed within that idea. But sometimes it was okay to just feel good about oneself from one angle, wasn't it?

"Try this dress!" Merideth cried as she rounded the corner and dropped a bunched-up pile of mauve silk into Annie's arms. She took a stack of other dresses with her into the dressing room next door, looking like a mound of walking fabrics—shiny, downright glittery, floral, and striped.

"If it works for you," she called to Annie from the other side of the wall, "you can get those beaded shoes we saw when we first came in."

Annie didn't know how to break it to her, so she just came out with it. "I'm sort of leaning toward this one."

The door flew open again on Merideth's side, and her head popped out like a jack-in-the-box. "I didn't see you trying that one on, over my mountain of dresses," she cackled. "All I saw was your head!" Then with a gasp, she added, "Oh, Annie. That looks really good on you."

Annie examined all four reflections: front, back, side, and other side. It did look pretty good—a champagne-colored silk bodice and floor-length skirt with long, sheer sleeves and yoke.

"You could still wear those beaded shoes we saw," Merideth added before disappearing on the other side of the door.

"And Gram's necklace."

She'd given it to Annie on her eighteenth birthday, mostly because Annie had been thinking of excuses to try it on every time she came to visit since she was nine. It was a lovely shiny, crystal choker, with two more tiers of crystals draping from the first. They weren't diamonds or anything—just an expensive piece of costume jewelry, really—but her grandmother had worn it on her wedding day.

"Okay, what do you think of this?"

Merideth emerged from the dressing room and all but stopped time. Such a gorgeous woman, with a certain style all her own but wearing this simple black dress with clusters of rhinestones scattered on the layers of her knee-length skirt, Merideth embodied elegance.

"Oh, Mer."

"Yes?"

"Definitely yes."

Merideth gazed at herself in the mirror for one long moment, then nodded and smiled.

"Okay, then. On to shoes and bags."

Shopping with Merideth, Annie decided, was a little like landing the role of understudy in a play. One knew what she was doing on her own but would never realize until that moment how much was still left to learn.

"I'm so excited you're going to be Colby's date, Annie. I knew as soon as I met him that the two of you would be a good match."

Annie held up a pair of earrings to one ear, inspecting them in the mirror. Merideth's face suddenly appeared behind hers in the reflection, her nose crinkled up and her head bobbing from side to side. "Mmm, no."

Annie replaced the earrings on the display. "What do you know about Colby?"

"Girl, I know it all," she replied, fishing through the handbags. "He's thirty-four, never been married. He's traveled all over the world—even lived in Germany and France when he was a boy."

Annie suddenly squealed, gathering the plastic bag to reveal the fabric of her dress to compare it to the beaded handbag on the display table. "Look at this!"

"It's a perfect match," Merideth told her. "Grab it, and we'll go find some shoes."

By the time they set out in search of Merideth's car, Annie had purchased a new dress, the beaded shoes and bag, Champagne Frost lipstick, a pair of panty hose, and a new cosmetic brush to replace the broken one in her favorite blusher.

"I haven't spent this much on myself in a whole year of shopping!"

"Wait until you see the menu for the gala," Merideth crooned as she turned over the engine. "Crab and shrimp, lobster, and prime rib. It's really going to be amazing."

Merideth chattered on as they wove through traffic, back toward Annie's office to pick up her car. Her friend had been working on the fund-raiser for three months straight, and Annie listened politely as she reviewed the evening's schedule, from a tour of three art galleries to an unstaged reading of a new playwright's work to an outdoor buffet in the courtyard between the galleries. But Annie's thoughts flipped the page a few times, leaving Merideth behind.

She could hardly wait for her second date with Colby Barnes. In fact, she drummed up images of herself in her new dress, on the arm of her handsome date…and those visions sustained her long after she'd said good-bye to Merideth and all the way back to Carmel.

Just before she reached the ivy-covered lattice gate of Gram's beautiful home, Annie stopped and took a hard look at the place. The two-story, sunny-yellow cottage evoked a sort of joy in her as it beckoned. The oversized front door, flanked on both sides by multipaned French windows, seemed to welcome her, and the upstairs windows to her bedroom sat open while the sheer white curtains wafted inward. Annie chuckled as Sherman's head popped up into the window at the mere hint of her return, and he seemed to grin at her happily.

Lugging her purchases inside, the familiar scrape of paws on wood floors announced his approach, and Sherman thudded into her leg by way of a greeting.

"Hi, Shermie. How was your day? Just give me one minute, and then we'll go."

By the time she hauled her packages upstairs and returned, Sherman waited for her, leash in mouth and his tail wagging a hundred miles an hour.

"Your turn now," she told him, clipping the leash to his bright blue collar and leading him through the kitchen and straight to the back door.

Stunned to find Evan standing on the other side when she yanked it open, his fist raised, just about to knock, Annie burst out with a surprised spurt of laughter.

"You scared me half silly."

"Sorry."

"I'm just walking Sherman. Want to come along?"

"Sure."

Evan didn't say much as they followed the concrete path around the back of the house, through the garden, then toward the street, with Sherman making stops every few feet along the way.

"So how are you doing?" she asked. "What's going on?"

"Not too much. How about you?"

"I'm going to that art gallery deal Merideth has been planning, so she and I went shopping for our dresses today after work."

"Oh. Find anything?"

"I did. Very elegant, way too expensive. But I love it. Wasn't it Ben Franklin who said that if you love the dress, it's worth the extra dinero?"

He smiled but didn't comment, and they walked on for several minutes more in complete silence.

"Hey, Ev, are you all right?" she asked as they rounded the corner and headed back toward the house.

"Yeah. Why?"

"You just seem a little subdued, that's all. Very un-Evanlike." She unleashed Sherman and let him toddle into the house.

"Well," he replied, "there is something I'm working up to, Annie. Something I've really got to do."

"What's that?"

Before she knew what hit her, Evan wound his arms tightly around her and his lips pressed down firmly against hers. They were nearly half a minute into the kiss before realization dawned.

Evan is…kissing me.

After too many years on the roller coaster, he'd never really kissed her before—not in this way, at least. Not just a quick peck to say hello or a warm smack good night, but an honest-to-goodness boy-meets-girl cinematic kiss.

And what do you know? I'm kissing him back.

It was a good one too.

The next thing you know, I'll be swooning or something!

He seemed to pull away reluctantly, and she wondered for a moment if he might just momentarily come up for air before heading back in.

"What was…that?" she asked him.

"A kiss, Annie. And I should have done it a long time ago."

She regarded him cautiously for a moment before it hit her.

"Yes, you should have," she replied. "You have no idea how long I've waited for you to kiss me like that."

"Really?" He looked hopeful, but Annie didn't actually mean to extend that branch.

"Yes. Really," she told him. "For three or four years, every time I thought we were getting closer to something meaningful, you pulled away. The reluctance of committing to something meaningful with me has been an unspoken wedge between us for a very long time, Evan."

"I want to change that."

"Why?"

"What do you mean?"

"I mean, why now? Why tonight?" Annie really wanted to know.

"I just figured…if I keep waiting to show you how I feel, I may not get the chance."

Time just kind of sat there, dormant—Annie didn't know for how long. And then she felt it winding up again as sorrow crested and flooded over her like a shower at the foot of a waterfall. She'd known this about Evan for such a long while, but it had never been so clear to her as in that moment: *He doesn't want to lose his ace in the hole. He doesn't necessarily want me…but he sure doesn't want anyone else to have me either.*

The truth ached inside of her.

"Good night, Evan."

"Annie, can we—"

"No, really. Good night."

Chapter Nine

....

"All right, Mr. DeMille.
I'm ready for my close-up."
Gloria Swanson, *Sunset Boulevard*, 1950

Change is a funny thing. It's a lot like a mink coat hanging in a closet. You know you want to approach it because it looks so glamorous and inviting, but where would you actually wear it without someone either dousing it in red paint or whispering about you behind your back for your audacity? And then there's the grief you'll take from your friends and family for even wondering what it might be like to try it on.

"I'm not nagging you. I'm just wondering what you decided, that's all."

"Well, Mom, I actually decided to stay put for a while," Annie said, and she adjusted her headset while rolling up to a red light. "As much as I love the idea of getting back to Monterey already, the truth is...something's telling me that being with Gram for a while in Carmel isn't such a bad idea."

"I suppose you don't need to uproot again so soon."

At first, she marveled at her mother's verbiage. *Uprooting.* It was just a change of location, after all. But that's what her five-point plan was all about, right? Uprooting her life, pruning it a little, shaping it, and helping it to thrive and grow into a whole other direction?

The only hitch being that every point on her list, aside from the new job, had been thwarted in some way. Annie couldn't seem to force change into her life with a whip and a chair!

"Listen, Mom, I have to go. I'm just pulling up at the office, and I'm running a little late."

"You're late this soon in starting a new job?"

"I won't be if I hang up right now."

"All right, honey. Come and see us soon."

"I will."

Annie tossed her cell phone into her bag then swooped the bag up along with her purse, jacket, and Diet Coke before sprinting across the parking lot and through the door. Deke stood in the doorway to his office as if waiting on her.

"What? Am I late?"

The front door swung open again and Nick Benchley blew through.

"A new low," he told Deke. "Now she's slamming the door right in my face."

"Oh, Nick, I'm sorry," she said, unloading her belongings on the top of the desk. "I didn't even know you were there."

"I went out to the car to get my phone," he stated. "And I ate a little bit of your dust, following you up the path."

"You got the number?" Deke asked him.

"Yeah, here it is."

Just after the two of them disappeared into the next office, Deke poked his head around the corner and grinned. "Morning, Annie."

"Morning, Deke."

"Wanna step in here when you're settled?"

"Sure."

Annie took a moment to catch her breath, stole a long draw from her soda, then checked herself in the mirror of the compact she kept tucked in the center drawer. Grabbing a notepad and a pen, she quickly went into Deke's office.

"Glad you could join us, Annie Gray."

"Thank you, Nick. How are you today?"

"Stellar. You?"

"The same."

Deke pulled a face that told them he wasn't fooled in the least by their pleasantries. But something else in his expression said he was in no mood for it, either.

"It would appear," Deke began, leaning back in his chair and clasping both hands behind his neck, "that I have a bit of a heart problem."

Annie waited for the one-liner to follow, but it didn't come. "Beg your pardon?"

"My doctor has suggested to me that surgery may be in order," he clarified.

"You're not joking, then."

"No."

"What's wrong, Deke?"

Annie eyes misted with tears, and she made every effort to angle herself away from Nick so he couldn't see them.

"It's nothing to worry about. A little blockage. They're going to check me into Community and clear it out, and I'll be good as new."

Annie gave a quick sideways glance in Nick's direction. His legs were crossed, his hands folded in his lap, as he stared down at the floor like something important might be going on down there. Annie almost wanted to take a look for herself.

"So what does this mean as far as...me? I mean, do you want

me to keep the office open? Should I...do something?" she queried Deke instead.

In the fraction of a second it took him to reply, Annie had already summoned visions of the unemployment line or, worse yet, returning to a call-center job and the umbilical-cord headset she had learned to despise. Her five-point plan began swirling, swirling, swirling down the—

"For you, this just means that you'll be deprived of my daily company for about eight weeks," Deke told her. "Bench has taken a leave of absence from the force, and he'll be keeping things going for me while I'm indisposed."

Bench...leave of absence...keeping things going...

It took a moment, but the reality of this news settled on Annie with a hollow thud.

Nick Benchley is going to be...my boss?

"Interesting turn of events, eh, Annie Gray?"

She turned toward Nick to find him grinning at her from one annoying dimple to the other.

Oh, this is so not *funny.*

* * * * *

On the drive back to the station, Nick found himself empathizing with Annie. Granted, he'd been given the news of Deke's condition a full twenty-four hours prior, but he would guess that his face had melted into a similar kicked-in-the-gut expression when he'd first heard.

She really cares about Deke, he thought. And it just made her more attractive to him, as if he needed that to happen.

Nick wished he could have wound his arms around her before

he jammed out of the office, to let her know that he shared her concern. Or just wrapped her in his arms for any good reason, come to think of it.

He wondered how long his friend had been suffering and whether the staunch and unflappable Deacon Heffley fought any anxiety over the notion of his chest being sliced open.

"Where ya been?" Greg Thorton asked as Nick passed his desk and headed toward his own.

"Alvarado Street," he replied as he flopped down into his familiar, lumpy chair. "Hey, your father-in-law had heart surgery last year, didn't he?"

"Triple bypass," Thorton replied. He gulped back the last of the coffee in his 49ers mug. "Hundred percent blocked in one and eighty in the others."

"Long recovery?"

"Endless." Thorton chuckled before he added, "But then, he came to stay at my house while he recovered. Might have just *seemed* endless."

* * * * *

Not the best Friday afternoon to ask Deke to let her go early, being his last day in the office before Monday's surgery, but he was amiable anyway, and Annie made it to Jake's in plenty of time for her manicure appointment. Concern for her employer and newfound friend formed a cloak around her.

"It sounds like a very glam evening you have planned," Jake said, standing behind Michelle and overseeing Annie's French manicure. "What do we have planned for the hair?"

"Something beautiful," she said. "Something, I don't know, over-the-edge-of-the-world gorgeous. You can do that, right?"

"It will be brilliant," he told her with a smile. "Just come on over to the chair when Shell finishes your nails."

Truth told, Annie's stomach resembled a swarm of butterflies, and she didn't have one clue about how she wanted her hair fixed for the gala and her date with Colby. She'd tried on her champagne-colored gown at least a half dozen times since she'd bought it, with three different bras, two types of slips, and with and without the beautiful beaded shoes. She'd held her hair up off her shoulders, let it cascade over them, and even tried clipping it up on one side.

She'd brought along a zippered bag holding a variety of rhinestone clips and shiny little hairpins, but she had no clear idea what Jake might do with them. All she knew for certain was that she wanted to look more amazing than any other woman at the gala. How she got there, well, that would be up to Jake.

He draped her in the familiar plastic neon cape and spread out the variety of clips and pins on the counter in front of the mirror. He looked like a painter considering his palette of colors before allowing one stroke to hit the canvas.

"Your dress is off the shoulder?" he asked her reflection.

"Only slightly," she replied, drawing the whole scope of the neckline with her index finger. "Like this."

"Okay," he said slowly, focusing a burning hole right into her. "O–kay."

Annie laughed off a comical memory of a cartoon she'd seen where the details of a makeover looked like someone diving into a blender and, once the power was cut and the craziness had subsided, a totally different person resulted. Hoping Jake didn't drag her into a blender, Annie closed her eyes and took a deep breath.

When she opened her eyes again a few minutes later, her new 'do was what Merideth liked to call "red-carpet ready." Jake had swept her hair upward and clipped it so the curls cascaded down her back, and then to decorate the style, he used a handful of her sparkly hairpins with the clusters of pastel rhinestones on the ends. With a small hot iron, he had randomly added more definition to the natural spirals of her hair and then sprayed it all into place.

"Oh, Jake."

"I know, honey."

"It's—"

"Perfect."

Always the first one in a room to hate her own hair no matter what the style, Annie surprised herself by loving what Jake had managed to do. She felt downright princess-like.

"Yes," she replied. "It's perfect."

"Now when you get to the makeup," he said, still fussing with the curls with the pointed end of a comb, "go easy. Soft and elegant. Muted colors. Nothing shocking or dramatic."

"Thank you so much, Jake."

When she got up from the chair, Jake gave her an unexpected hug. "Go and be the Annabelle of the ball."

And with that, Annie took her fantastic hair and new French manicure and headed home to get dressed.

When Colby arrived at her door two hours later, Annie had just clasped Gram's necklace and slipped into her beaded shoes. She glanced into the mirror before opening the door to make sure her fancy hair still looked fancy, and it did. She held her breath until Colby's reaction told her he was pleased; then she released it in a soft sputter.

"You're magnificent," he told her, and he took her hand and planted a kiss right on top of it. "Just beautiful."

Annie thanked him, refraining from commenting on the way he looked in a tuxedo—almost prettier than her but, thanks to Jake's efforts, not quite.

"Ready to go?"

"Absolutely."

The interior of Jake's cocoa brown Jaguar smelled spicy, like him, and the leather was softer than one of Sherman's ears. Elevator jazz clinked from the backseat speakers, and the drive to Carmel Plaza seemed much too short.

Colby offered his arm, and Annie's heels made the perfect little *click-click-click* on the stone walk toward the main gallery. When she saw their reflection in the double glass doors, she couldn't help but admire the way they looked—like something out of a movie or atop a very tall cake. The handsome prince with the perfectly chiseled jaw and the dainty princess at his side, glimmering and glistening with pure joy. She wanted to freeze the moment, just hold on to it somehow so that she could call it up again in the future after she'd been scrubbing the toilet or arguing with Evan or visiting her mother. It would be a beacon of remembrance that, for one flash in time, she looked and felt glamorous and had a strikingly handsome man at her side—a time when everything had been absolutely perfect, even if only for that one millimoment.

Once inside, however, she realized that the entire gala teemed with princes and princesses, probably all of them feeling a lot like she did in their new dresses and fancy shoes and sprayed-up hair. One of the most beautiful of them all turned out to be Merideth.

"Killer dress," she said to Annie, as if seeing it for the first time.

"Yours too." Just to prove she could play.

A small orchestra in the courtyard played old standards like "It Had to Be You" and "Moonlight in Vermont" while people milled between three small galleries framing the outer edges of the space, each of them hosting tables of silent auction items. Bistro tables for four dotted the courtyard, each of them adorned with a single white candle floating in a crystal bowl of water alongside a perfect white magnolia. Nets of crisscrossing white lights loomed overhead and captured the perfume of both the flowers and the women.

Annie and Colby followed Merideth and her husband, Frank, toward tables upon tables beckoning delicious offerings, and uniformed attendants stood waiting to serve at each chafing dish.

"I like to make it a point at events like this one," Colby half whispered as he handed Annie a chilled plate, "to have all the things I wouldn't normally have. For instance, how many times do you steam up a bunch of crab legs for yourself at home?"

"Not often," and she giggled as he loaded a half dozen of them on her plate.

By the time they joined Frank and Merideth at a table, Annie was working to balance the array of food.

"It's a buffet, sweetie," Merideth teased. "You can go back for more later. Pace yourself."

"He's a bad influence," Annie announced, nodding over her shoulder toward Colby.

"I can see that."

The instant Annie and Colby sat down, Frank popped up and hurried away from the table without a word.

"Something we said?" Annie asked.

"Oh, he's hung up on the possibility of being outbid on the sword-fishing expedition. He'll be right back. In fact, I'd better go keep an eye on him to make sure he doesn't bid the house for it."

Annie watched Merideth float across the room. "She looks radiant," she commented, and Colby nodded in agreement.

"This is my first time meeting Frank," he told her. "He's not the guy I would have pictured with Mer."

"No?" she asked curiously, watching the two of them across the room, holding hands, as Frank chatted with a fellow behind one of the auction tables. "Why not?"

"He's so…I don't know."

"Straitlaced?"

"Yes."

"I know what you mean. I always thought Merideth would end up with a jet-setter who could keep up with her—if that person even exists. But there's something quiet and peaceful in Frank that responds to the craziness in Mer. Whatever it is, it works."

"So it appears."

Annie glanced at Colby as he watched Merideth and Frank.

"I hope someone looks at me that way one day," he said, and he flashed her an awkward smile.

Keep watching. Maybe I'll be the one looking at you like that one day soon.

"Mmm, taste this," he said suddenly, popping a large chilled shrimp into her mouth. "The cocktail sauce is phenomenal."

Annie struggled not to choke on the thing as Merideth and

Frank reappeared at the table with another tuxedo-wearing man in tow. Colby greeted them, standing and shaking the man's hand.

"Dwayne, you know Colby already," Merideth stated. "But I want you to meet my friend Annie. She's a private investigator."

Annie nearly sprayed bits of shrimp all over them as she looked up into the narrowed eyes of Dr. Dwayne Biddle.

"Annie, Dr. Biddle is one of tonight's sponsors. Without him, our job would be worlds more difficult."

Biddle pressed a hole through her, his eyes thinning, turning ominous and dark.

"A private investigator," he commented. "That must be interesting work. I don't think I recall seeing that on the forms you filled out, Miss Gray."

"I'm little more than a secretary, really," she told him, trying to appear casual over the thunder of her own heartbeat. "I answer phones, type up reports, that sort of thing."

"You two know one another?" Colby inquired.

"I saw Dr. Biddle last week for my back problems."

Please, God. Please, God. Please, God.

"What back problems?"

Oh, Merideth!

"Miss Gray was in a car accident a few months ago, and she has had some problems ever since."

"No, she wasn't. Annie, you didn't tell me you were in a car accident!" Merideth cried. "When? Were you driving Taurie?"

Annie nearly fell to her knees with gratitude as someone tapped the microphone onstage and called for the attention of the room.

"Good to see you again, Miss Gray."

"You too, Dr. Biddle." *Not.* "Enjoy the evening."

Acid churned in her stomach, bubbling up into the back of her throat. How could just a few simple words out of Merideth's giant mouth completely ruin a budding new career?

* * * * *

Colby and Merideth seemed to see the benefit as a wonderful success, and Annie perceived her date with Colby in the same light.

On the drive home, Colby reached through the darkness and took her hand. She noticed the perfect fit as she looked down at them, clasped and resting casually on the console between them.

He walked her to the door, and they stood in the yellow glow of the light from the parlor window. Her insides flopped with butterflies in flight, her mouth went dry, and Annie felt like a high schooler again. The prom had gone even better than she'd hoped.

"Are you going to invite me in?" he asked as she turned the key in the door, and she felt his hand on her arm as he guided her around to face him.

Annie found it difficult to look away. He moved in slowly, wrapping her in his arms, and she dropped her keys to the porch floor as his lips touched hers in the kiss she'd been wondering about since the night they met.

After several moments, the perfect kiss evolved into something else. Something...*imperfect*. His lips pressed down hard, and his hands traveled the express train toward Alarmville.

"Colby," she whispered, firmly pushing both palms against his chest.

"Come on," he replied, undeterred.

"Colby, no."

"You don't have to play that game, Annie."

"I'm not playing."

"What, you're some sort of thirty-year-old virgin?" he asked, taking a full step backward and staring at her as if evaluating the level of her disease.

Twenty-six! she corrected, if only in her own thoughts.

"What are you protecting, Annie? It's been a perfect night."

"Yes. It has."

"No reason for it to end now, is there?"

"Well, yes, actually, there is. I know how cliché this will sound to you, but really...I'm not that girl."

"Are you kidding? You've been giving off signals all night."

"Signals?"

Annie backed up. She could hear Sherman's sniffing through the gap in the door. A different kind of dog might have inspired her to push open the door, letting him barrel out to protect her virtue. Being Sherman, however, he would probably barrel right on by in hopes of a little midnight roll in the grass.

"What kind of signals, Colby?"

"You know what I mean," he replied, taking a step forward.

"Those were not the kind of signals you're thinking they were," she assured him. "Those were romantic I-think-we're-starting-something-here signals. Not let's-go-home-and-well-you-know signals!"

"Come on, Annie. Let's go inside and get comfortable. We can talk about this."

"I'm serious, Colby. That isn't the kind of person I am. If that's what you're looking for, you'd better just continue on with your search. But do it somewhere else."

With that, Annie swept her keys from the ground, turned, stepped inside the house, and bolted the door behind her.

Annie's adrenaline surged, along with a short burst of pride at making such a graceful exit. In the past, she'd wanted to kick herself later over stumbles into walls, words that didn't come out, and fumbling with purses, keys, and what-have-yous. This time, however, it went smoothly and without incident, as if she'd practiced it. Which, of course, she'd never have thought to do.

Annie held her breath and then jumped when Colby pounded on the door with his fist, just once. Once she heard his footsteps take him away from the house, she peered out the window from behind the curtain. Sherman hopped into the bay window beside her and watched to see what was so interesting on the other side of the porch. As Colby climbed into his flashy car, Annie's hands started to tremble.

"How was your date?" Gram asked, meandering out of the kitchen with her favorite china cup in hand.

Annie reeled toward her, her mouth open but no words at the ready.

"Oh, Annabelle. How lovely you look! That dress fits you like a glove."

She sighed. "Thanks, Gram."

"Would you like some tea? The water's still hot."

"I don't think so. I just want to go upstairs to bed."

"Didn't you have a good time tonight?"

"It was fine." She kissed her grandmother's cheek before starting up the stairs, her heart still racing. "Goodnight, Gram."

"Sweet dreams."

Annie wondered if there were any sweet dreams to be had for

her just then. It wasn't so horrible with Colby; it hadn't gone too far. But his demeanor had transported Annie back to a time in college when she almost didn't get the door closed between herself and a date. That night so long ago was much different, but she couldn't help noticing the similarities.

The tall clock at the top of the stairs struck midnight as she passed.

Apparently my guardian angel's watch needs new batteries. The pumpkin returned a few minutes early tonight.

Chapter Ten

. . . .

"Mr. Allen, this may come as a shock to you,
but there are some men who don't
end every sentence with a proposition."
Doris Day, *Pillow Talk,* 1959

Saturday dawned as an unseasonably warm day, and Annie couldn't think of a better way to spend the afternoon than floating around in Zoey's pool. After a couple of hours in the water, Zoey made Diet Coke floats with vanilla ice cream, and the two of them lounged in the shade under the striped cabana.

"What a life you have," Annie told her, before taking a long draw from the plastic straw.

"What do you mean?"

"Seriously, Zoey, this is the life I dream about. A great husband, a fabulous house with a pool, Diet Coke floats whenever I feel like it…"

"Oh, yeah, that's my life in a nutshell," she replied. "I just sit around sipping floats all day, every day."

Annie slipped her sunglasses down her nose and looked at Zoey over them, trying to decide if the flush on her skin came from the sun or the conversation.

"I didn't mean to imply—"

"I know. Just forget it."

"Zo?" Annie broached. "Is everything all right?"

"Peachy," she replied, and she thumped her head back on the lounge chair and closed her eyes.

"What's going on? Something's wrong."

Her eyes still closed, Zoey sighed. "Wrong, here in Emerald City? Don't be absurd. What could be wrong?"

"Come on." Pulling her legs over the side of the chair, Annie faced her friend. "Talk to me."

"I can't right now."

She almost missed it, but Annie did a double take just as one lone tear cascaded down Zoey's cheek. Even with her eyes closed, it managed to escape, and Annie realized there was likely a whole waterfall in there that hadn't.

"I'm here when you're ready, Zo."

"I know."

Annie couldn't quite shake Zoey's cloud as the day progressed; she worried, burdened by her friend's obvious pain. Zoey had always been one of those people who didn't just *seem* to live the good life. She embodied it, even gave off the vibe that she was born for it. Zoey consisted of laughter, good sense, and refinement. The intermittent sadness Annie had sensed lately just didn't suit her.

Zoey and Annie could always talk about anything, even if they didn't agree. Or maybe especially when they didn't. Annie couldn't help wondering when that had changed.

Aunt Henri had always said, "Show me your friends, and I'll show you who you are." Annie used to take great comfort in those words when she looked at Zoey.

Annie arrived home to an empty house. Sherman didn't show signs of needing to take a walk, so she climbed the stairs and crawled across the bed, flopping down on her stomach and stuffing a pillow under her chin as she gazed out the window. It took Sherman an extra try at the bed before he joined her, and they lay there in silence. Annie's thoughts turned to the gala, and Sherman seemed to be considering something grand like a bowl of lettuce leaves or a ride in the car.

Annie rolled over to her side and snuggled up next to him, and Sherman sighed. She rubbed her cheek against the velvety softness of his long ear and whispered into it. "Love you, Shermie."

He knew. She could feel it.

The next morning, she awoke to the champagne-colored gown hanging on the back of the door. For a few minutes before sleep had found her, she'd considered returning it for a refund, but now it looked so stunning there on her door that she made the final decision to keep it in spite of the way her date turned out.

Colby's words came back to her so clearly, they were almost audible. *What, you're some sort of thirty-year-old virgin?*

So few people on the face of the earth knew the truth about Annie, and her stomach began to burn with shame at the reminder. Annie knew there was nothing much virginal about her, but those days were far behind her now. She'd made a choice at the age of twenty-two that she would not be that adventuresome, boy-crazy Annabelle Louisa-Kaye Gray again, that she would trust God to drop Prince Charming into her lap in His own timing. And since that time, her new leaf had influenced her decisions about everything: intimacy, her investment in the relationships she pursued, everything. It hadn't always been easy, of course.

Annie realized at that moment how fortunate she had been to have three years of...whatever that was...with Evan. He'd respected her choices from the very first. Never once had he pushed her like

Colby had the night prior. Never once did he ridicule her or mock her for wanting to wait and be sure about doing things that she couldn't take back.

Annie's heart sank, heavy. Heavy at the loss of Evan; heavy for Zoey and the burden she carried around, the one she couldn't share with her best friend; and heavy with disappointment as she gazed at the dress hanging on the back of the door.

The gala tripped over her mind in quick flashes, and it screeched to a stop with the memory of—

Dr. Biddle!

Without another moment's thought, Annie hopped to her feet and headed directly to the shower.

After a quick change of clothes, she bounded to the office with Sherman in tow. She could find Nick Benchley's phone number there.

* * * * *

Nick had just come in from a run and dropped to the sofa when the phone rang.

"Benchley." He answered it abruptly, and silence hummed on the other end. "What?"

"Oh, sorry. Um, Nick, it's—"

"Annie Gray. What can I do for you?"

"Well, I was wondering if you had some time?"

"Changed your mind, have you?"

"Nick, it's serious," she stated. "I need to talk to you in person."

And just like that, her voice trembling and concern coloring her demeanor across the phone lines, Nick dropped the attitude with a thud. "Where are you?"

"The office."

"I'll be there in twenty minutes."

"Thank you, Nick."

After a quick shower, he changed into green khaki shorts and a black polo shirt, tucking his slightly shaggy hair into a black police department baseball cap. His Birkenstocks snapped against his heels as he made his way up the path and into the office, and he sat in the chair across from Annie's desk.

Propping an ankle atop his knee, he asked, "What's up, angel?"

"Something happened, Nick. I don't know how to tell Deke. I'm just so—"

He glanced around the room. "Well, you didn't burn the place down. So what is it?"

"I went to a gala at Carmel Plaza the other night."

"I read about that. Black tie, silent auctions. So who was your date?"

"Please, Nick. Focus."

"Ah, I know. That Colby character, right?"

"Anyway—"

"Just tell me. Am I right?"

"Yes. I went with Colby."

He almost wished he hadn't pressed for an answer. "I'll bet he cleans up just dandy for a black-tie event. Did he wear a tux?"

Their eyes locked as they crossed paths, and what he saw stopped Nick in his tracks. Sadness, fear, and a little trace of panic drowned in a swirling greenish fire.

"I'm sorry. Tell me."

"Nick, Dr. Biddle was there."

"Who?"

"The doctor we've been investigating for Northern California Life and Casualty."

"And?"

"And it turns out that my friend Merideth knows him. And she introduced me to him and told him I'm a *private investigator.*"

"Eww." Nick removed the baseball cap and ran his hands through his damp hair a couple of times before replacing it. "That stings. What did the good doctor have to say? Anything?"

"Just that he didn't remember seeing that on the forms I filled out. I tried to tell him I'm just a secretary, but then he mentioned my supposed car accident and Merideth went off about how could I be in an accident and not tell her."

Nick let out a guffaw before leaning back in the chair. "You sure know how to work a case there, Annie Gray."

"What should I do? Deke will flip if I tell him."

"We're not going to tell Deke," he said decisively. "He's getting set for heart surgery. He doesn't need to worry about what's going on here."

"So—"

"Let me think a minute." He glanced over at Sherman in the corner and smiled. "Hey, buddy, I didn't see you over there. You're awfully quiet."

Taking that as an invitation, Sherman shoved himself to his feet and padded on over for a rub on the head.

"Good to see you again," Nick told him. Sherman wagged his tail in gratitude for the acknowledgment.

"My stomach hurts." Annie leaned down onto folded arms on the desktop.

"Come on, now. It's not that big of a disaster. We'll handle it. It's not like you got caught doing espionage or something, Annie."

She looked up at him curiously. Those hazel green eyes of hers killed him every time.

"You just…called me Annie."

"Is that not your name?"

"Yes. But you normally call me *Annie-Gray*, like it's one word or something."

Nick's mouth slanted upward on one side into what he felt certain took the shape of a smug, lopsided grin. "Thanks for noticing, Annie Gray."

"Nick, what are we going to do?"

"We're going to roll up our sleeves and put the reports together for NorCal. Then I'm going to go over to their offices first thing in the morning, tell them what happened, and encourage them to pursue the case as quickly as possible before Biddle has any more time to cover his tracks."

"I hope I haven't ruined everything."

"You couldn't ruin anything," he told her. "Now let's pull those files and get to work."

* * * * *

It took them four hours and three rounds of coffee, but Nick and Annie somehow managed to work as a team to pull the most pertinent information from Deke's files into an organized mass of evidence proving insurance fraud. While Nick ran down to the station to use the police computer to add to the background checks on the key players, Sherman and Annie remained behind.

After stopping to lap up the last of the water in his bowl, Sherman let out a little doggie belch and fell over on his side for a nap.

Annie paused to watch him for a moment before tugging open the credenza drawer and producing a three-hole punch. For some very odd reason, the serene inactivity of her dog never failed to fascinate her.

She closed the brackets on the final section of a six-sectioned file folder when Annie heard a car door slam outside.

Perfect timing.

Spinning triumphantly in her chair as the door opened, ready to allow Nick the opportunity to congratulate her on finishing the files, Annie didn't have more than an instant to consider the fact that the door didn't fly open with hurricane force in typical Nick Benchley fashion. She looked up to find Colby Barnes standing there instead, with what looked to be a whole shrub of scarlet roses overflowing in his arms.

"Colby."

"Your grandmother told me where I might find you. Annie, can you forgive me?" he asked. "I was an idiot."

"Yes. You were." It came out before she could censor it—not that she would have.

Urging her to accept the flowers, he flashed a grin that looked so well-rehearsed that her stomach turned slightly sour.

"I don't want your flowers, Colby. I appreciate the gesture, but I'm not interested."

"I'm apologizing to you, Annie," he said, slightly appalled at her unenthusiastic reaction.

"And I accept your apology. But you can keep your roses."

"What about forgiveness?" he asked just before Nick blew through the front door.

"Those for me?" he cracked. "For next time, I prefer tulips."

Me too.

"I'm trying to make up to this girl, but she doesn't appear to be having any of it," Colby told him, darting a quick glance at Annie.

"Good for you, Annie Gray. What'd he do?"

"Never mind," she said before she turned back toward Colby. "Like I said, I accept your apology, but you can keep your flowers. Now, Nick and I have to get back to work."

Out of nowhere, Sherman lifted his head and let a grumpy bark rip, as if to reiterate that they had had enough and Mr. Roses could be on his way.

"I'd say both Grays have spoken," Nick said with a grin. Holding the door open for Colby, Nick shot him a "be on your way" stare.

"Can I call you?" Colby asked Annie.

"I don't think so."

"Annie, really."

"Take care of yourself, Colby."

Annie had the feeling Colby Barnes didn't have much experience with rejection.

"Do you need some help with carrying those outside?" Nick asked him, and after a long moment, Colby looked down at the bouquet and shook his head.

"No, I'm good."

Colby slammed the door behind him and stalked down the sidewalk toward his car. Annie watched him through the window for a moment before turning back toward Nick, with what she imagined to be a blush stain heating her cheeks.

"So what'd he do?"

"He has high expectations," she told him finally. "I wasn't able to meet them."

Nick seemed to think it over before raising an eyebrow. "You want me to run him in? A few hours in a holding cell might—"

"Nick. Really, that's sweet but…thanks anyway."

Nick grinned at her, and those dimples of his curved into crescent moons. Leaning across her desk, he put his hand atop hers and turned serious. "Did he hurt you?"

"No."

"You're sure?"

"Yes. I'm sure."

"You're too good for him anyway, Annie Gray."

"You really think so, Nick?" she asked him with a smile.

"Yep. Besides," he added, snapping his fingers several times for effect, "it was only a matter of time before he was knocked out of the ball game. I mean, really. How could he compete with this?"

Okay. The moment was fleeting, but it was a moment.

Chapter Eleven

....

"You know how to whistle,
don't you, Steve?"
Lauren Bacall, *To Have and Have Not,* 1944

Deke's surgery went well but he took on a low-grade fever later in the day, so the hospital personnel began watching him closely and guarding against infection.

Annie placed the paper mask provided at the nurse's station over her face and fastened it behind her head before walking into his room. He looked ten years older than he had just a few days prior.

"Thanks for the flowers," he said, nodding in the general direction of the array of bouquets lined up on the windowsill, the evidence of a man well-loved.

"Is there anything I can get you? Do you need anything?"

"Update," he managed. But before he could expound, the door to his hospital room popped open with a sudden burst, slamming against the wall behind it.

"Deacon, my man, I'm hurt. You can't trust me not to run your place into the ground in a few short days?" Nick sauntered up behind Annie and rubbed her shoulder as he leaned down and shook Deke's hand gingerly, holding his paper mask in place with his chin pressed against his shoulder. "You know I'll need at least three months to make a real mess of things. Give me some time."

"Biddle?" Deke asked, turning his eyes to Annie.

"It's all being handled," she assured him. "Stop worrying about the office and concentrate on getting well."

Deke sighed. He didn't appear to have the strength for a dispute.

Annie reached up and tied Nick's mask at the back of his head, and he shot her a quick nod before patting the top of Deke's hand.

"Listen to her, Deacon. All is well."

Beeps and buzzes and flashing lights resonated from the mass of machinery behind Deke, reminding Annie of how serious the situation actually was. Connected to the equipment by tubes leading to his nose, his left arm and leg bent slightly beneath the cotton blanket, Deke caught her following the path and gave her a weary smile.

"It's not as bad as it looks."

Embarrassed, Annie chuckled.

"How about it, Annie Gray," Nick suddenly exclaimed. "Are you a praying kind of girl? Because I think a little prayer is called for right now."

She nodded, only slightly reluctant. "Count me in."

Nick turned his palm outward and Annie slipped her hand inside of his, reaching down and touching Deke's blanket-covered foot with the other. Nick massaged Deke's neck for a moment then rested a hand on the older man's shoulder.

After a quick prayer Annie opened her eyes and wondered how long she should wait before letting go of Nick's hand. Finally he squeezed hers one more time and did the letting go for her. Though somewhat humiliating to admit, Annie realized that her shoulder still tingled from Nick's touch throughout several minutes of inconsequential conversation following.

"Hang on a minute and I'll walk you down," Nick suggested

once Annie said good-bye to Deke. She felt strangely large and conspicuous as she stood in the doorway waiting for him. The feeling didn't subside as they rode the elevator down toward the lobby.

"He looks good," Nick commented when the door slid open. Pressing his hand against the small of Annie's back, her heart leaping at his touch, he added, "Are you on your way back to the office?"

"After a quick stop for supplies."

"Why don't I pick up some lunch and meet you there? Then we'll have a bit of a status meeting over the open cases."

"Sounds good," she told him. "Do you need anything?"

"Well, that's a leading question, Annie Gray," he replied, and the way he narrowed his eyes at her made her heart start racing again. "What are you suggesting?"

"Pens?" she replied. "Perhaps a few pads of paper? Brackets, brads, paper clips?"

Nick tossed his head back and laughed, and it struck Annie like a beautiful song, strong and resounding and sincere. He ran both hands through his thick dark hair and grinned. "Surprise me."

Annie watched him jog across the parking lot toward his black Jeep, and he waved his arm out the window as he rounded the curve and slipped into traffic.

She missed the paper aisle twice at Staples before she shook thoughts of Nick Benchley from the clouds surrounding her brain. She found herself smiling, and she waggled her head at the realization of how much he had changed in her view in such a short time. And then when he prayed for Deke…well, it got to her.

God-fearing men, being rather hard to come by in today's single universe, inspired reasonably intelligent, God-fearing women to be bowled over at a few reverent words. Standing in the checkout line,

Annie vowed not to be swayed toward romantic hearts and flowers over Nick Benchley.

Taurie made a soft squeal she hadn't heard before as she eased into the parking space in front of the office, but she forgot all about it when her cell phone rang.

"Hey, are we okay?"

Annie gathered her satchel and purse and Staples bags, propping the phone limply on her shoulder. "Hey, Evan. We're good."

"I'm so glad because… What are you doing tonight?"

"I'm not sure. I think I'm working late."

"Guess what's playing tonight, right down the street from your office," he prodded. He answered before she could form a reply. "*Casablanca!*"

"You're joking."

"I'm not."

"Ohh," she groaned. "I'm pretty sure I'm going to be stuck. But can I call you?"

"Sure. If you can get away before eight thirty, I'll meet you at the theater."

"Deal."

Evan sighed, and Annie waited for him to break the silence.

"You're sure we're good, Annie?"

Annie smiled. All of the ups and downs and bumps in the road aside, Evan still felt like a friend. Even an ill-timed kiss couldn't change that.

"We're good."

"Okay. See you at the theater if you can make it."

Annie folded up the phone and dropped it into her bag as she hurried into the office.

"Vanilla or chocolate."

Annie couldn't process the question as she struggled with the door, her packages and leather bag now flung forward, blocking her entrance.

Nick eased the load one package at a time, clunking them down to the desk before taking her bag and purse as well.

"Vanilla or chocolate?" he repeated.

"That depends. In what form?"

"Milk shake."

"Oh! Vanilla."

"Good."

She followed Nick around the corner into Deke's office, one side of the desk impenetrable beneath organized stacks of files. On the other side, two unfolded napkins served as placemats beneath neatly placed, loaded cheeseburgers and milk shakes with curved straws.

"Impressive," she commented with a smile, dragging a chair toward the desk.

"Yeah, I get that a lot."

* * * * *

Annie checked the clock on the wall behind Nick. Already 7:00 p.m.

Nick smiled at her and winked. "As far as we're concerned, my curly-headed friend, we can now officially close the case on NorCal Life and Casualty."

"Have you heard anything back from them about their next step? Have they contacted the authorities?"

"By the end of the week, they'll have nabbed three doctors and two attorneys," he told her. "I'm guessing this was quite a network of fraudulent behavior."

"Awesome."

"Awesome, indeed. We done good."

Nick stretched his arms out above his head and eased his neck from side to side until it cracked.

"I have a status meeting at NorCal first thing in the morning, and I'll meet you here at the office when I'm through."

"Sounds like a plan," she replied. "Don't forget we've got a new client meeting tomorrow afternoon."

He nodded and stretched again. "So what are your big plans for this evening, Annie Gray?"

"Well," she said, as she tidied up the top of the desk, "I was thinking about meeting Evan to see *Casablanca*."

"Oh, that's right. I saw the sign."

"But all I really want to do right now is go home to a hot bath, an early night, and my waiting dog."

"You've earned it. Go ahead. I'll finish up here and be right behind you out the door."

Annie tossed a used napkin into the trash and, at the doorway, turned back to share a comfortable smile.

"You know, I was a little worried about working with you."

"And now?"

"Well, you're still sort of a pain in the fanny."

"Goes without saying," he acknowledged with a straight face. "But aside from that?"

"Well, you don't ruin *every* day. That's saying something."

"You're not so excruciating yourself. Now get outta here."

Two slices of peanut butter toast and a glass of milk later, Annie felt ready for bed. Sherman crossed the finish line first, but she made it under the covers with her head buried in the pillow before the stroke of nine.

"Long day," Annie said on a yawn.

Sherman groaned in agreement as she turned off the light.

* * * * *

Lunch with Merideth had been planned around catching up. Instead, it became a walking public-relations seminar on behalf of Colby Barnes.

"I'm sure he didn't mean it in those terms," she assured Annie. "He was carried away by the moment. And he probably thought you were too."

"The moments that were carrying us were very different moments, Mer. Seriously, I'm not interested in anything else he has to say."

"So you're just going to toss away a perfectly good man and—"

"Your idea of a good man and mine are apparently polar opposites. Would you let this topic die, please?"

Merideth waved her hand and turned up her nose in dismissal. Knowing her friend the way she did, Annie realized the matter of Colby Barnes was by no means dead, but she decided to settle for a short coma if it meant the chance to enjoy her Cobb salad.

"I'd like to express my compliments to the chef," Annie told Abby, the waitress. "Would you ask him to step out here for a moment?"

Abby grinned. "Sure thing, Annie."

A few minutes later, Evan appeared through the swinging door of the kitchen, his white chef's smock as clean and bright as if he'd just put it on.

"I didn't know you two were here," he declared with a broad smile. "Hi, Merideth. How are you?"

"Good, Evan. The primavera was perfect again today."

"Glad to hear it. What did you have, Annie?"

"Cobb salad. Wonderful. Your record stands."

"Abby," he said softly as the waitress passed with a pot of coffee, "their lunches are on me."

She nodded without pausing.

"Evan, you don't have to cover our meals every time we come for lunch," Annie exclaimed. "We come here because we enjoy your food!"

"And we're willing to pay for it," Merideth added.

He grimaced, turning the topic on a dime. "So what are you two talking about today?"

"The usual. Clothes, shoes, gossip."

"I'm trying to bring Annie to her senses," Merideth interjected. Annie shot her a disapproving glance. "What? I'll bet Evan would agree with me."

"About what?"

"One bad moment during an otherwise perfect evening. Do you throw the date out with the bathwater, or do you give him a second chance?"

"Oh." Evan nodded knowingly. "Nick Benchley?"

"No, not Nick!" Annie cried, then reeled in her reaction and let out a modulating sigh. "Why would you assume it was Nick?"

"Well, I saw him last night at The Monterey. His date was an absolute knockout."

This one-two punch nearly knocked *Annie* out.

"What do you mean? Nick went to see *Casablanca*?"

"I forgot that was showing," Merideth commented. "I love that movie."

Ignoring her, Annie pressed Evan for further information. "Are you sure it was Nick?"

"Oh yeah. I was in line for popcorn, and I was watching the door in case you were able to make it after all. And in walks your buddy with this auburn-haired *beauty*."

"Really."

"She seemed a little, I don't know, *sweet*? to be dating Nick Benchley, I have to say. But they were pretty chummy, so I'd guess they've been going out for a while."

Her conversation with Nick before leaving the office for home brushed across Annie's memory.

I'm the one who gave him the brilliant idea for his perfect little date with his auburn beauty.

Acid roared through her stomach, and Annie sipped her iced tea in an attempt to dilute it. Questioning why the mere thought of Nick and Auburn together played such havoc with her equilibrium, she decided she didn't have the time to wait for the answer.

"I'm sorry," Evan said sincerely, and Annie could see that he wished he hadn't delivered the news so casually. "I didn't mean to—"

Using Merideth's trick of waving her hand to assimilate the ability to deal, Annie shook her head. "No, it's fine. Nick is free to do whatever he wants. There's nothing going on between the two of us."

Neither of them appeared to believe her, but their failure to call her on it evoked deep relief inside of her.

"Well, it's good to see you both," Evan said, breaking the awkward silence. "If you're up for dessert, I've got a berry tart with your names all over it."

"I couldn't eat another bite," Merideth groaned, patting her flat little stomach.

Evan looked to Annie, and she shook her head, forcing a smile that felt more like an open wound.

"I'll see you later," he said. The quick squeeze to Annie's shoulder repeated his apology.

"See?" Merideth said in a whisper as soon as Evan returned to the kitchen. "There aren't many good men out there, Annie. Give Colby another shot, would you?"

Annie actually stopped to weigh the idea then sniffed out a firm "No" when a three-second instant replay reminded her of the Colby Barnes who walked her to her door the night of the gala. "Not happening, Mer."

"Your loss."

Annie dug into her purse for Abby's tip when the front door jingled. She instinctively glanced up at the two women making their way inside, and she watched with increased intensity as the hostess greeted them and led them to the nearby table. Her heart thumped. Her vision became tunnellike, and she kicked Merideth under the table before mouthing her message.

"Dor–is Da–ay."

"Huh?"

"Doris Day," she whispered.

"What?"

Annie groaned just as her eyes suddenly met those of her idol.

"Hello." She smiled sweetly.

Unsure of how she managed it, Annie lumbered to her feet and took three or four cautious steps to bridge the gap between them.

"Miss Day. It's such a pleasure to meet you," she stammered. "I'm Annie Gray. My grandmother is Dorothy Gray."

"Ohh, Annie. What a pleasure to meet you. How is Dori?"

"She's great."

"Please give her my best."

"I will. Thank you. I'm such a big fan of yours."

"It's true," Merideth added, startling Annie. "She's seen every one of your movies until she can say the lines right along with you."

"Did you both enjoy your lunch?" Miss Day asked them.

"Y–yes," Annie answered. "My friend Evan is the chef here, and he's just one of my favorite chefs in all the world. So I come and eat here as often as I can. I had the Cobb salad today and Merideth— that's Merideth—she had the pasta primavera."

It was rather like roller skates racing downhill. She knew she should somehow apply the brakes, but the rush of adrenaline kept her from it. When she finally shut up, Doris Day's polite smile broke into a wide, pearly-white grin.

"The Cobb salad sounds good to me," she told her companion. "I think I'll try that too."

"Miss Day, I just admire you so much."

"Thank you, Annie. I appreciate that."

"I just loved the movies you did with Rock Hudson." She clamped her hand over her heart. "Those were just…beautiful films."

"Annie, thank you so much."

"Would you mind?" Merideth asked her, producing her cell phone. "Could I get a picture of the two of you together?"

"Oh…Mer…"

"Certainly." Doris Day stood up and slipped her arm around Annie's shoulder, smiling as Merideth snapped a digital image.

"Can I get you something to drink?" Abby asked—and Annie felt the yank of reality.

"I'm sorry. Go ahead and enjoy your lunch. It was really a pleasure to meet you."

"Thank you. Please remember to send my regards to Dori."

Annie nodded, feeling like a bull in a china shop as she gathered her things and made her way to the door.

"Have a great day," Merideth said from behind her. "It was a real kick to meet you in person. The highlight of Annie's whole year, I can tell you that for sure."

Squeezing her eyes shut, Annie pushed the door open and escaped into the warm Carmel sunshine.

"Good grief," she said on a groan.

Once safely in the car with the doors shut, Annie turned sideways in her seat and bore down on Merideth with a glare that could cut glass.

"Well, that was exciting, huh?" Merideth looked at her curiously for a moment and then added, "What?"

"I've seen her movies so many times that I can *say the lines along with her*?"

"What? She was flattered."

"And I was humiliated."

Merideth considered that for an instant before letting out one solid chuckle.

"You're laughing?"

"Oh, come on, Annie. She thought it was adorable. You probably made her whole day."

"And yet she made my whole *month*! Isn't that what you said? A month?"

Annie looked out the window for a moment before glancing again at Merideth, who looked like a total innocent and inspired Annie to laugh right out loud.

"It's such a pleasure to meet you, Miss Day," she mocked herself. "Oh, Miss Day, you're just my complete and total idol. Me? Oh, I'm just a dewy-eyed, Cobb salad–eating, running-off-at-the-mouth, *idiot* granddaughter of Dorothy Gray."

"It wasn't that bad," Merideth promised. She held up her cell phone to display the photo of Doris Day, timeless and beautiful, and Annie, who looked very much like she might toss her entire lunch to the floor.

Annie shook her head and buried her face in her hands as they both got a good, hearty laugh out of it all. A passerby leaned over to look in at them as he made his way down the street, causing them to laugh all the harder.

They needed to post a sign, Annie decided. BEWARE OF CAR. LUNATICS ONBOARD.

* * * * *

Rather than heading straight back to the office, Annie popped in on Zoey first, confident that her close encounter with Doris Day would bring at least a giggle or two. When she arrived at the house, she saw Zoey through the slatted window of her office, on the telephone and massaging her forehead.

Walking around to the front door, Annie tried the knob. Surprised when it slipped open, she let herself in.

"Yes," she heard Zoey state as Annie made her way down the hallway. "I'm well aware of that, Bobby, and we'll have it to you before the end of the week. Okay. Yes, okay."

Zoey hung up the phone and leaned back hard into the chair with her eyes tightly closed.

"Zo?"

She jumped to her feet, startled. "Annie! Don't scare me like that."

"I'm sorry. I saw that you were tied up, so I let myself in."

"Oh." Zoey slumped down into the chair again with a sigh. "I don't have time for lunch today."

"I'm not here for lunch. I just stopped by to chat."

The phone rang, and Zoey pursed her lips at Annie and shrugged as she picked it up. "Canyon Restaurant Supply."

She pulled up a screen on the computer and began verifying a list of numbers with the caller as Annie folded into one of the chairs around the conference table in the corner. The maple table-top could scarcely be seen beneath the pile of invoices, file folders, and unopened mail.

"Okay," Zoey said. "I'll run them again and get back to you in an hour."

She hung up the phone, releasing a long sigh as she did. Turning toward Annie, Zoey opened her mouth to speak, but the phone rang again and sliced her words at the tip.

"Sorry," she groaned. "Canyon Restaurant Supply. Yes, Angela, how are you?"

As Zoey answered a barrage of questions that made no real sense to Annie, Annie floated back to thoughts of Nick Benchley's Auburn Beauty once again.

Then came the familiar acid chaser.

She'd told him she might join Evan at the theater that night but had decided instead to make it an early night. When he'd rushed her out the door so she could do just that, Annie had believed it was motivated by uncharacteristic sweetness.

I should have known better.

The truth was, she'd given him a great idea about how to spend his evening with another woman. And all the while, she'd been warming up to Nick in the time that they'd been working together for Deke, thinking she saw something special in him—something compelling and rather magnetic that drew her to him.

"I'm sorry, Annie," Zoey said, interrupting her stream of thought. "I just don't have time for a chat today. Can I call you later?"

"Sure."

Annie tried to maintain the smile until she reached the front door then let it lapse as she made her way toward Taurie. Looking back through the window, she spotted Zoey tapping at the computer frantically, the phone to her ear once again.

She tried to remember if she ever knew what Zoey's days were like, running the administrative end of her husband's business, and she decided that she couldn't have known. No wonder she seemed more on edge each time Annie had seen her lately.

What kind of best friend hasn't figured this out until now?

Annie felt around in her bag as she drove until she produced her cell phone. Unfolding it, she pressed number eight on the speed dial, and Nick answered promptly.

"Benchley."

"Nick, it's Annie. I'm headed in to the office from lunch. I wanted to see how the meeting went with NorCal."

"Great. I'm just pulling in myself. I'll fill you in when you get here. What time is the new client meeting? Is it three thirty?"

"Yep. I should be there in ten."

"See you in ten."

A very civilized conversation, considering.

As she pulled into the parking lot alongside his Jeep, Annie wondered how to bring up Nick's date night at the movies. Once inside, she found him sprawled in Deke's big chair, a broad grin on his face as if he had nothing more important to do than wait on her arrival.

"Afternoon, Annie Gray."

Annie decided then and there, in that single instant, that Nick's date was none of her concern.

If he wants me to know, he'll tell me.

That grin he flashed, however—that unbelievable, dimpled smile, right there and right then—that was just for Annie. And no Auburn Beauty could take that away from her.

"Afternoon, Nick." She slid a chair up to the edge of the desk. "Tell me how it went."

Chapter Twelve

....

"As Miss Golightly was saying
before she was so rudely interrupted…"
Audrey Hepburn, *Breakfast at Tiffany's*, 1961

Nick had sat across the desk from Annie for several hours that day and spent most of them wishing he could invite her to join him that night. One of the guys at the station had hit him up to buy a couple of tickets to the charity thing at the Cherry, and he couldn't shake the thought that it might be something Annie would enjoy.

For the umpteenth time, however, he reminded himself that he'd already invited Jenny to join him. And if he'd learned any one thing about women over the years, he was certain that a guy didn't go around breaking a date at the last minute, especially with the shallow notion of taking someone else. Besides, with Jenny staying at the house for the next few weeks, he couldn't get away with such a thing even if he could find the justification.

Or could he?

No, not cool, he decided as he picked up the remote to set the DVR.

As if things weren't bad enough already, now he had to miss the Lakers game and watch a recorded version later.

* * * * *

"I'll bet the Staples Center is packed to the rafters tonight," Annie muttered to Zoey.

"Will you forget the Lakers game? You can watch it tomorrow. This is why God made TiVo."

"It's not the same."

Annie sighed and pushed up a smile as she rounded the car and offered her arm to her grandmother.

"I'm so excited," Dot beamed as they headed into the Carl Cherry Center for the Arts. "I've been looking forward to this for weeks. I'm happy you could come with us, Zoey. I think you're going to really enjoy the show."

Annie had been a patron-by-default of the center for years, accompanying her grandmother to art exhibits, lectures, and small stage productions. The artistic hideaway, an established entity in Carmel's eclectic cultural scene, revolved around a commitment to providing accessible interaction between the arts and the local community. It was only natural that Dorothy Gray would become a regular patron soon after moving to the village. For all her elegance and dignified grace, Gram also possessed a certain bohemian quality that fit right in with the Cherry.

Annie perused the program for the musical revue dedicated to the Golden Age of Movies, taking her seat between Gram and Zoey once inside the intimate theater.

"Look, Dot," Zoey said, waving the program. "They included a song from *Devonshire Pass*. Weren't you in that movie?"

Gram chuckled and squeezed Annie's arm. "I was 'Girl on Train.' I had three lines."

"Three *pivotal* lines," Annie told Zoey. "Gram set up the whole plot."

"That's why Annie's my favorite granddaughter. She sees the significance of being 'Girl on Train.' "

"You sound just like Aunt Henri."

"Well, I raised her."

Turning to Zoey, Annie reminded her, "I was Henri's favorite niece because I like to wear hats."

The theater filled up quickly, and several of the patrons stopped to greet Dot. Just before the lights dimmed, Zoey leaned over toward Annie and poked her in the side with her elbow.

"Hey. Isn't that Nick Benchley?"

His name brought her surroundings to a screeching halt. Annie followed Zoey's nod down to the end of the second row.

She groaned. "Yep, that's Nick."

"Who's that girl with him?"

"His Auburn Beauty, no doubt."

The small village of Carmel-by-the-Sea just keeps shrinking by the day, Annie lamented. And Nick Benchley appeared to be everywhere!

"What are you talking about? What Auburn Beauty?"

"Evan said he saw them at the movies the other night. He didn't know anything about her but that she was an auburn-haired knockout."

As the production opened, Auburn beamed at Nick, applauding and grinning.

"She looks too young for him. What is she, about twelve? And she doesn't look like such a knockout," Zoey said with confidence. "She doesn't hold a candle to you."

"You're a good friend," Annie whispered. Then, "Evan was certainly taken by her."

Trying to focus on anything except Nick and his young date, Annie peeled her eyes away and focused on the revue. After a few minutes, she actually did forget about Nick and began to enjoy the show. Even more fortuitous, the happy couple left as soon as the show concluded, while her own departure moseyed along, dictated by Dot's social interaction.

Zoey had left her car at the house, and she decided to stop in for a few minutes when they returned. Sherman, excited to see her, slipped on the kitchen linoleum and fell prostrate at her feet.

"Oh, honey, be careful," Zoey cooed at him, and she lifted his front paws while Annie lifted from the rear to get him to his feet again. He forgot the embarrassment almost instantly, and he hopped from Zoey to Annie and back again.

Gram headed straight to bed while Annie took Sherman for a quick walk and Zoey filled two tall glasses with ice and Diet Coke. Decaffeinated. A new thing Annie had decided to try.

"Are you feeling sad over seeing Nick with a date?" Zoey asked when they finally sat down at the kitchen table.

"A little. But what about you?"

"It doesn't really bother me if Nick sees someone else," she replied, her eyes narrowed. "Unless it bothers you."

"No, I mean, are you sad about something?"

"Oh. No. I'm fine."

"Please don't lie to me. We've known each other far too long for that."

"I'm fine, Annie."

"Zo. It's me. Talk to me."

And that's all it took.

Zoey melted like candle wax, and before Annie knew it, she'd folded her arms and crumpled into them atop the table and begun to sob. She saw a weariness in Zoey that she'd never seen before, and Annie scuffed her chair up next to hers and enclosed her friend in an embrace.

"Whatever it is," she whispered, "it's going to be okay."

Annie continued to tell her that, believing it for her, knowing full well that Zoey didn't have the strength to believe it for herself. Annie had floundered in similar emotional waters a time or two; she knew the signs.

For just a moment, she began to wonder if the unthinkable had happened. Had Mateo cheated on her? No, she decided. Not possible.

Is the business going under? Is someone sick?

"Please, Zoey. Tell me what's wrong."

"I'm just so tired," she told the table through her folded arms. "I can't keep going like this."

"Like what?" Annie asked, nudging her to look up. "What's going on?"

When she lifted her head, Zoey almost looked to Annie like a watercolor painting left out in the rain. She handed her a clump of napkins, and Zoey used them to blow her nose and wipe off her face.

"I'm sorry," she said, the pile of rumpled napkins on the table in front of her. "I didn't mean to do this."

"You had to," Annie corrected. "You can't just walk around like this. I'm your best friend. Would you talk to me, please? Has something happened? Is Mateo all right?"

"Define 'all right.' "

"Healthy?" she articulated. "Faithful. Safe."

She tried to smile through the tears, and she took Annie's hand and squeezed it.

"Then yes. He's all right."

"Are you?"

"I don't know," she admitted. "I thought I was. I thought helping Mateo run his business was what I should do, so I left my job and picked up the slack. But it seems like it's just one big sand trap, and now, instead of just him being swallowed up in it, we both are."

Annie gave her a nod. "Keep going."

"Don't get me wrong, I'm thankful for everything we have. The business is the right move for Mateo. It's just that it's become this huge elephant in the middle of our lives that we can't walk around."

"Can you hire some help?"

"We do. We hire drivers and administrative help, and they work out for a couple of weeks but then they leave without notice or they show up to work intoxicated or they steal from the warehouse. Annie, we just can't catch a break. And there's no end in sight. I can't even remember the last time we went out for dinner together or took a weekend trip or did anything at all that was just the two of us that didn't involve paperwork or deliveries."

She paused to nurse her drink for a moment, and Zoey looked up at Annie with more tears standing in her eyes.

"He's always out on the road or at the warehouse. And I'm at home handling the rest of it. This just isn't the way I pictured our lives, you know? Seriously, sometimes I find myself daydreaming about just packing a bag one day, getting in the car, and disappearing."

"Oh, Zoey."

"I know how awful it sounds. Believe me, I do. But I just can't take this much longer. And I don't know what to do about it."

An hour later, Annie's best friend left Gram's house looking wrung out but at peace for the moment.

"Thanks for listening," she said, and she planted a kiss on Annie's cheek. "I really needed to let it out."

The smile she managed left Annie with a sense of well-being all her own. She hadn't realized how long it had been since she'd seen that smile from Zoey, and a bitter taste of guilt rose in the back of her throat for not noticing much sooner.

* * * * *

An arrangement of tulips and roses swallowed up Annie's desk. A card bearing nothing more than a huge question mark and signed *Colby* sat on her calendar.

Nick had been behind closed doors for the last twenty minutes after she'd passed a phone call to him from someone named Jenny. An auburn-haired child, no doubt, and each minute that ticked by with him still tied up on that phone call irritated her a little more.

To divert her own attention, Annie looked up Colby's number and dialed it.

"Colby Barnes."

"Colby. It's Annie."

He greeted her with a short, silent pause, followed by a sigh to punctuate it. "Annie. I'm so glad you called."

"Well, I'm calling to ask you not to send any more flowers, Colby."

"I tossed in some tulips for your friend," he said on a chuckle. "I hope he appreciates it." After an awkward moment, he added, "Please, please forgive me, Annie. Let me make it up to you by taking you to dinner?"

"I don't want to have dinner with you, Colby. Please understand, and stop contacting me."

"Listen, I know I pushed too hard. I have no excuse except—Let me take you to dinner. I'll wear a muzzle and oven mitts. I promise you'll be perfectly safe."

"I'm sorry, Colby. But no."

"Just some linguini? Seven thirty at Casanova?"

"Good-bye, Colby."

The door to Deke's office flew open just as she hung up, and Nick stepped into the doorway.

"I'm headed out early today. I have something to do. Will I see you in the morning?"

"Bright and early."

As Nick's Jeep zipped out of the parking lot, Annie bit her lip and shook her head.

This is ridiculous. I'm hating a Jenny I've never even met.

* * * * *

Deke's eyes were bright and sharp again when Annie went to visit him the next day, and she felt a surge of relief to see him sitting upright and ready for visitors.

"Come in here and tell me about my business," he said by way of a greeting. "How far into the ground has Bench run it anyway?"

"Just far enough," she replied, and Deke let out a resonant laugh that did her heart good. "Any idea when they'll let you go home?"

"Another few days, I'd guess. Then another few weeks at home before I come back to work. Think you can stand him that long?"

"Well, he is pretty hard to take," she said with a grin. "But I think we can manage for your sake."

"Once I'm out of here, I expect to start getting weekly updates.

No more of this 'keeping me in the dark for the sake of my health' bit that Bench has you both playing."

"Sir, yes sir," she replied with a mock salute.

"I mean it."

"He means what? What does he mean, Annie Gray?"

For the first time since she'd known him, Nick Benchley walked into a room without making a thunderous entrance.

"I was just telling Annie that, once I get out of here, I'm going to start expecting updates on what you're doing. We'll start with weekly meetings, then daily ones, before I come back to work."

"What makes you think there will be a business to come back to after that long, Deacon? You know I'm working hard at running it into the ground."

"Oh-ho-ho-ho," Deke chortled, and he clutched his heart gently.

As different as the two men were, Annie realized as she watched them together that they were a perfectly matched pair. At the root of their sarcasm and digs and humor, a true affection and brotherly spirit always emerged.

A male version of Zoey and me.

"So how is Jenny getting settled?" Deke asked, and Annie's heart plopped down into her stomach.

"Good. She's with me, actually. But she made a stop in the gift shop. I told her you didn't need anymore flowers in this place, but you know Jen."

Jen. Deke knows Jenny?

Annie wondered how long she and Nick had been dating. The sudden realization that she wasn't just a casual date brought her pulse to thudding.

"There she is!"

As suspected, Auburn Beauty entered the room.

"How are you feeling, Deacon?" she asked sweetly. Then she smiled at Nick knowingly. "We've all been so worried."

"Not all of us," Nick added. "I haven't been worried in the least."

"Oh, hush," she countered playfully, and their rapport caused an ache so deep inside Annie that she couldn't even pinpoint its exact locale.

"You must be Annie," she said, extending her hand.

Annie forced a smile and nodded. "And you're Jenny."

"Nick has told me so much about you. Honestly, I don't even know how you put up with him."

"Well, it isn't easy," she returned.

Jenny presented a charming bunch of daisies wrapped in blue paper to Deke and sat down next to him on the bed before smacking his cheek with a kiss. "It's so good to see you again."

"How are you surviving living with this slob?"

The words echoed through Annie as if she were a gaping cavern, and she didn't even process Jenny's reply.

Living with—

Living with—

Living with??

"You're living with Nick?" Before Annie could stop them, the words dove out of her mouth and into the room.

"Temporarily. Until I find a place of my own."

"Uh… Oh. I see."

"If you know about any apartments for rent, let me know? I'm desperate."

Jenny and Nick exchanged a laugh, but Annie couldn't even fish out a polite one.

He's living with her?

"I—I—" She forced her mouth shut, but all eyes rested on her. "I have to go."

"Already?" Deke exclaimed. "You just got here."

"You have a nice visit with Nick and Jenny," she told him. "And I'll be by to see you again in a day or two. Jenny, nice to meet you. Nick—" Annie couldn't think of one thing to say to him. "Bye."

"I'll walk you to the elevator," he offered.

"No! I mean, no need. That's okay. I can walk on my own."

"Bye, Annie," said perfect, auburn-haired Jenny.

"Good-bye."

Annie wished times like these didn't inspire such bad behavior. Not a woman without her faults, passing Red's Donuts on her way home proved just too compelling to resist.

"Two glazed and two chocolate-filled. And an extra-large Diet Coke."

"Anything else?"

"Probably not."

Four donuts and twenty-two ounces of caffeine. Yep. That should do me quite nicely.

While she waited for her order, Annie marveled that she didn't weigh three hundred pounds. Then, after pausing to thank God for her good genes, she dipped into the bag to indulge in her spoils.

Chapter Thirteen

....

"Insanity runs in my family.
It practically gallops."
Cary Grant, *Arsenic and Old Lace,* 1944

Nick powered up the computer and flipped on the webcam, twenty minutes late.

"I'm sorry, I'm sorry. Have you been waiting long?"

"Oh, you're finally here," his aunt Tess cried as she came into full view on the screen. "I thought I was doing something wrong with this gadget."

She'd been using it every week for two months, ever since he made the trip out to Illinois and set it up for her. He'd taught her how to use it so they could communicate face-to-face, but Tess called the webcam a *gadget* and wondered if she might have broken it each and every time he'd spoken to her since.

Her silver hair looked like spun silk pulled back into a loose bun, and her tawny brown eyes sparkled as she moved in closer.

"You look good, Nicky. Can you see me?"

"You look beautiful, Tess."

"I tried something new on the market. It's a face-lift in a bottle," she told him, using both hands to stretch the skin at the sides of her face. "Do I look any younger?"

"You look perfect," he told her with a grin.

"I thought about getting one for real."

"Getting what?"

"A face-lift."

"Don't you dare."

"Well," she croaked, "I gave up on that idea once I saw Lois Brighton at bingo on Thursday. She had hers three weeks back, and I walked by her twice without realizing who she was. Nicky, she looks like a flat, waxy mannequin. Like one of those dummies on the Old Navy commercials."

It amused Nick to hear Tess talk like that. And it particularly surprised him that she knew about Old Navy commercials.

"What else have you been up to this week, Tess? Aside from bingo."

"Oh, don't discount the bingo, sonny. I won a face-lift in a jar and two free bingo cards."

"Score!" he replied on a laugh.

"It was like Christmas."

"I bet."

"Ooh, and the big news around here is that Joe Deemis found a mouse in his shoe. He nearly wet himself!"

Nick chuckled. "A mouse?"

"His place is on the second floor. He opened his closet door and poked his foot into his loafer, and a little gray mouse popped out."

Nick frowned, wondering if he needed to have a talk with the administrator about maintenance.

"Oh, don't pucker up like that, Nicky. There's no rodent problem here at *the home*. It turned out to belong to Nellie's grandson. He brought it to show her and it got out of his coat."

He leaned back in his chair and laughed, gazing at her image on his computer screen. He'd lived with his mother's sister for several years while he floundered around after high school, trying to figure out where he was headed. If not for Tess, there was no telling what he might have become, but she'd gently led him toward the idea of law enforcement and following in the footsteps of his uncle. He'd been badgering Tess to leave the assisted living facility in Des Plaines and give northern California a try, but Tess was well-planted and stubborn about it. She had no intention of leaving her friends at *the home* behind.

"And let me tell you what happened to Karen Jarvis, Nicky. You won't believe this!"

"It's never a dull moment with you, Tess."

"Oh, none of it happens to me, honey. But happening to my neighbors is the next best thing to being there."

"Do you need anything?" he asked her. "I'm packing up a box this week. If there's anything you need me to include—"

"I'd love some more of those chewy chocolates you sent last time. Now that my dentures are locked down, I could really enjoy them."

"You got it. Anything else?"

"Well… Is there another visit from you in my future?"

"Next month, Tess. Like clockwork."

"Oooh, good. I can't wait to show you my artwork. We're into pastels now, and Cloris thought mine was so good that she hung it on the rec room wall. I call it *Spring Flowers*. I feel like a real *artiste* every time I walk by it. Maybe you'll bring Jenny with you, Nicky?"

"I don't know. She's started a new teaching job, and I'm not sure she can get away until the summer."

"Oh. Well, you'll give her my love, then?"

"She sends hers as well."

* * * * *

As she pulled into the driveway, Annie wondered if she could actually smell whatever her mom had cooking on the stove or whether she just had a very keen sense of memory, like Pavlov's dogs when they heard the bell. Perhaps whenever she approached her mother's house, a bell went off inside her head and she automatically smelled stew. Or stuffed peppers. Or baking bread.

Approaching the front door, she realized to her horror that the treat of the day appeared to be cinnamon rolls. The four Red's Donuts from the night before saluted in respect as her stomach flopped over.

"Annie! Nathan, it's Annie. Are you hungry, honey?"

"No, I've had din—"

"I made a ham for supper. There's plenty left. I'll make you a plate."

"No, Mom. Really."

"Nonsense. I'll make you a plate."

Her mother stood before her, examining Annie's hair like a questionable painting hanging on the wall of a museum, before reaching out and smoothing it with both hands.

"Go in and say hello to your father. And Linda's here. We're making cinnamon buns."

"I didn't see her car."

"Teddy dropped her off, and he's picking her up after his meeting. Go on in, honey. Say hello."

Her father lounged in his favorite chair, and his heavy breathing told Annie he didn't care much about watching the news playing on the television before him. Linda, curled quietly into the corner of the sofa, raised one finger to her lips to shush her as she walked in.

She scooted to the edge of the sofa and stood up, the small bulge in her belly catching Annie's eye, first thing. When Linda noticed, she molded her blouse around it and turned sideways with a broad, toothy grin.

"Mom and Dad told you?" she whispered as they stepped into the kitchen.

"Yes, and I'm sorry I haven't called."

"I hear you have a new job," Linda replied. "You're probably all tied up with that. How's Evan?"

"Oh, he's fine. I don't see as much of him as I did before. Both of us are just—"

"Linda, there's just two more minutes on the timer and our cinnamon buns will be ready to come out!"

Annie pulsed with gratitude for the interruption. She just hated being there on the verge of having to explain once again that *Annie* plus *Evan* did not equal *Couple*.

"Tell me when you're due."

Ask an actor for his resume or a pregnant woman about her pregnancy and you're guaranteed a lovely one-sided conversation for at least a half hour. The cinnamon rolls dripped with icing, three of them half eaten and coffee having been served, in the time it took for Linda to recount the day she found out, what the doctor said, how adorable Ted's reaction had been, and the progress of the future nursery.

"I'm really happy for you, Linda." *Okay. I know. But it's not a total lie. Just a fraction of one.* "You're going to make such a great

179

mom." *And that's the truth, isn't it? You've had years of practice on my brother.*

"I think Ted is hoping for a boy, of course. But can I tell you a secret? I'm really counting on a little girl."

"Don't let her fool you, Annie. That is no secret. My wife is completely transparent."

They looked up to find Ted standing in the doorway, and the way he looked at Linda just about melted the icing on what was left of Annie's roll.

"Oh, honey, good. You're back. I'll pour you some coffee."

Annie watched her mother move around the kitchen, always at her absolute best when hungry people surrounded her. Or people she perceived to be hungry, anyway.

"If you won't eat this now, I've packaged up a little ham and some scalloped potatoes and a few string beans in here," she said, placing a large green plastic container in front of Annie. "You can take it for lunch tomorrow or save it for dinner after work."

"Thanks, Mom."

No use declining. Annie figured her mother would just hide it in her bag before she left or chase her car down the street until she stopped to take it.

Annie made more polite conversation about the baby and the possibility of Linda quitting her job so that she could really enjoy the planning stages.

Linda, being one of those people just courteous enough to know when to ask the obligatory question or two about someone else when the whole world had been revolving around her for long enough, said, "So tell me about your new job, Annie."

"I love it, actually. It's something different every day, and with my boss in the hospital, I have a lot more responsibility sooner than we'd expected."

"Your boss is in the hospital?" Annie's mom always honed in quickly on subjects involving health. After food and the ever-discouraging state of Annie's hair, it ranked high among her very favorite topics.

"He had to have heart surgery. But he's doing very well. Now it's just a matter of keeping him out of the office and at home long enough for a full recovery."

"It's a shame I didn't know," she replied in earnest. "I could have sent him some flowers—or a cake."

"The man is in for heart surgery," Ted exclaimed with a chuckle. "Don't send him butter cream cake."

"All right. Flowers, then."

"You know, Mom, Deke has so many flower arrangements in that room that we can hardly find him in there. Flowers aren't necessary, but I'll send him your good thoughts."

"Yes, do that, honey. Tell him your father and I wish him well."

Out of nowhere, Annie found herself thinking about the flawless bunch of daisies wrapped in blue paper. With all the roses and gladiolas and carnations on every tabletop and filling every inch of windowsill, those daisies really stood out.

A sour taste at the back of her throat, having nothing to do with her mother's cinnamon rolls or hazelnut coffee, choked her until she derailed the train of thought completely on purpose.

"You know, I have a really early day tomorrow, so I'd better get going."

"How's Gram doing?" Ted asked as she started to gather her things.

"Fantastic," Annie replied with a smile. "She's got more energy than anyone I know. You two should come visit her and let her pat your new belly."

"We should, Ted," Linda piped up.

"Give Dad a kiss for me when he wakes up," Annie continued. "He needs his beauty sleep."

"Well, don't forget your care package."

The ham dinner, now adorned with a cinnamon bun wrapped in plastic and a small thermos of creamed hazelnut coffee, ended up in a large brown paper bag with the edges neatly folded down.

"We love you, honey."

"Love you too, Mom. And congratulations, you guys."

Annie tried to hum along with the radio on the drive back to Carmel, but her heart wasn't completely in it. So many issues buzzed around in her head, making it hard to pinpoint which one had brought about the strange heaviness on her heart.

Linda had the makings of a great mother, and Ted looked happier than Annie ever remembered. Her little brother just always seemed to excel in every situation, leaving Annie behind in his dust. He finished law school and became an attorney while she meandered around at Equity Now; he got married before her; and now he would give their parents the grandchild they'd longed for, all before Annie even had a dateable prospect.

There was Evan, of course. But he'd been a moot point for much longer than Annie would admit. And Colby, but the bloom fell off that rose the night of the gala, and no amount of replacement roses seemed likely to change that.

And then…Nick.

Ah. Now I know what's weighing down my insides.

The mere thought of him drew tears to her eyes, and with one blink, they cascaded down her cheeks like huge raindrops down a windowpane. At a stoplight Annie closed her eyes, but all she saw was Jenny. With her perfect little daisies and her sparkling, radiant smile.

What kind of woman wanted to kick a perfectly sweet Auburn Beauty simply because she was first to wrangle the Perfect Man?

Nick Benchley? The Perfect Man? Have I been drinking?

What otherworldly planet had she drifted toward, where the Nick Benchleys of the universe became *perfect*?

But what kind of person didn't call her own brother upon hearing the news that he would soon be a father and made his miraculous news all about her?

What is wrong with me?

With that question hanging loudly unanswered, Annie made a U-turn and headed back in the direction of Monterey before fishing out her cell phone and dialing Zoey's number.

"Can I come over?"

"I'll frost up a soda glass."

"See you in fifteen."

* * * * *

The last time they'd poured Diet Cokes, it had been Zoey slumped over Gram's kitchen table, weeping about the troubles plaguing her life. And now, Annie's turn. Collapsed onto the counter, a half glass of cola standing near her limp hand, she wiped her tears with a wad of tissues.

"I don't know what's wrong with me. Why can't I be happy for

Ted and Linda? And for Nick and Jenny, for that matter! *Echh*, you should see them together. They're perfectly suited to one another, Zo. It's like they came out of the very same mold."

"I did see them together. And she's too young for him."

Annie loved that about Zoey. Complete and loyal support available at any time, day or night.

"She is. She really is too young for him," she sniffed in agreement. "But he doesn't seem to care. When he looks at her, all he sees is someone he adores."

"You don't know that, Annie. You don't know what he sees when he looks at her."

"He sees what the rest of the world sees, Zo. Silken auburn hair… big, round doe eyes…and…and…" She spat out the final word like the pulp of a lemon. "Daisies."

"And what about Evan?" Zoey asked, rubbing a comforting circle on Annie's back. "Are we over him?"

"Yeah. Evan's not The One."

"Yes, I know." Annie looked up at her, and Zoey grinned. "I'm just glad to know you know it, too."

"I do."

"And Colby Barnes?"

"Colby's beautiful. And successful. And he drives a great car."

"But?"

"Yeah. But he's not The One either. I just can't get past that picture of him at my door that night. Having a little tantrum, like a teenaged boy who didn't get what he wanted."

"Me either." Their eyes met for a moment, and Zoey smiled lovingly. "He was out of line."

"I know."

"What about Nick? Are you thinking he might be The One?"

"I don't know."

"Or maybe he's just The One You Can't Have?"

Annie wanted to object, but she didn't have the energy. "Who knows."

"You know," Zoey began, pausing as she bit her lip, "Mateo hired a new guy to help with the administrative things over at the warehouse."

"Zoey, that's great!"

"His name is Randall Burgi. He goes by Rand."

Annie lifted her head slowly, narrowing her eyes, wondering if Zoey might be headed in the direction that she seemed to be—

"He's very cute. And you know, he's coming over for dinner tomorrow night. Why don't you come too? Mateo is making salmon on the grill."

"Are you kidding me with this?"

"He's just a nice guy, Annie. And it's just dinner."

"Dinner."

"And options. Options are always nice, right?"

Annie dropped her head into her arms again, but this time she started to laugh. And the laughter built until it felt almost maniacal somehow.

"Forget it, Zo."

"Annie."

"For–get—it. No more boys. No more *options*, or my brain will explode."

* * * * *

Annie signed online to check e-mail, and a news headline waited there, just for her:

Too Much Diet Soda Can Be a Buzzkill for Weight Management.

Okay, take my donuts and pizza and all the tacos on the planet. Even my mom's cinnamon rolls. But leave my Diet Coke alone.

Sherman bounced into the room as if he had news too, then plopped down to the floor beside her and rolled over to one side.

"Somewhat anticlimactic, boy."

He looked up at her momentarily and stretched.

Merideth had attached the picture of Annie and Doris Day to one e-mail and then sent a second one telling Annie about a two-for-one on a package deal at a local spa. The third came from Evan, a bit unusual for him since he didn't normally appreciate the more technical sides of life. Things like e-mail and faxes and digital cameras—all were somewhat of an abomination to Evan despite the fact that he fancied himself a bit of a Renaissance man.

"I'll bet you're surprised to get an e-mail from me, huh?" he said.

He read my mind.

"You've been a little hard to catch up with these days, and I thought this might be a better idea than just dropping by or leaving another voice mail."

Fluent in EvanSpeak, Annie recognized the underlying message: Evan felt neglected.

"Next week's retrospective is on Cary Grant," he wrote. "And I know you'll want to be there for that. They're playing *Charade* and *To Catch a Thief*, the latter being one of your favorites and a great one to see on the big screen. Can we set aside a night to go? It's on me. I'll even get the popcorn and soda."

Annie determined there and then to make the date with Evan. He may not have turned out to be the right man for her, but the friendship had so many aspects worth salvaging. Hitting the REPLY button, she tapped out her response.

"You've got a date. How about Wednesday night?"

DELETE, DELETE, DELETE to the spam junking up her mailbox, then she opened the last one, an e-mail from Linda and Ted.

"Can't tell yet whether it's a niece or a nephew, but Baby's first photo is attached."

She downloaded the file and watched as a surprisingly clear sonogram picture slowly revealed itself. The baby, turned on its side, looked like a little peanut of a fetus, and her heart swelled as she viewed it. Tracing it on the screen with her finger, realization set in.

This is Ted's son or daughter. My baby brother...is having a baby of his own.

Annie felt so selfish, and before another minute ticked by, she snatched up the phone from its cradle and pressed number four on the speed dial.

"Linda? It's Annie. I just got the photo."

They chatted for nearly twenty minutes before Linda put Ted on the line at Annie's request. Not much of a telephone conversationalist, Annie's brother. But something needed to be said.

"I want you to know how happy I am for you and Linda, Ted. I really mean that."

"Thanks, Annie. That means a lot."

"It was a little daunting," she confessed. "You got married before I did, and now you're having babies before me."

"But you've always been slow, sis. We all understand."

They both broke into laughter at that, and it did Annie's heart good to share a moment like this with her brother when there had been so much unnecessary distance between them over the years.

"I love you, Annie," he told her. "I know you don't think I do, but I do."

Too stunned to reply at first, Annie sighed.

"Linda loves you too."

"And I love you both right back," she told him in earnest. "And your little peanut too."

"It does look like a peanut, doesn't it?" he cried. "Linda swatted at me when I said that, but it's a perfectly shaped peanut shell!"

Linda objected in the background, and their laughter harmonized into music.

Chapter Fourteen

....

"Lions, tigers, and bears? Oh my!"
Judy Garland, *The Wizard of Oz*, 1939

Annie changed into a tie-dyed T-shirt and denim shorts. Her head bobbed from one shoulder to the other, keeping time with the music wafting through her head as she tore lettuce, chopped tomatoes and cucumbers, and tossed whole green olives haphazardly into a large porcelain bowl. She squeezed a little ranch dressing into the mix then vaulted up to the counter, her legs swinging as she mixed the salad with an ornate fork.

Sherman eyed her torturously, deprived of his favorite snack. He cocked his head to the side, one ear tilted back and the other pushed forward, and he let out one solid yelp.

The lyrics of the song she sang broke up with guffaws as Annie watched him, so intent as he was on the lettuce clinging to her fork that she could easily make him dizzy just by conducting with it above his head. When he began to whine mournfully, Annie gave in and tossed him one large lettuce leaf. Received like a prime-rib dinner, Sherman lapped it up.

"You are a very strange dog."

Sherman didn't break eye contact for even a moment. He didn't blink, didn't even flinch, as he waited for another delectable bite of lettuce.

"Seriously, Sherman. You're psycho."

He panted for a moment, and it looked like doggie laughter.

Annie sighed then moved to the refrigerator and foraged through the items on all four glass shelves. Finally! At the back of the bottom shelf, she found the treasure for which she searched: one lone can of caffeine-powered soda.

The good stuff.

She snatched her prize and headed into the parlor, flipping on the television. She helped Sherman up next to her as Ty Pennington began yelling to another needy family through a megaphone.

"It's on, Gram. Are you coming?"

* * * * *

Annie stopped at the hospital for a leisurely visit with Deke before work, and she learned that he would be released before the week's end. She arrived at the office afterward a few minutes earlier than her usual start time, her arms loaded with her purse, satchel, and a bakery bag. She dropped everything to the desk, opened the blinds on the window behind her desk, and sauntered over to the mini-fridge to grab a Diet Coke.

Frozen in silence, she could only just stand there, gawking into the gaping refrigerator. She wanted to scream, but it pushed up and out of her as a simple, horrified grunt.

Not a single aluminum can in sight. Not one. Instead, neat stacks of water bottles, juices, and yogurt filled the fridge to capacity.

"Is this some kind of joke?" she finally managed. When she turned around, she noticed Nick in the doorway to Deke's office with a lopsided smile on his irritating face.

Sweeping her arm toward the refrigerator like Vanna White showing off a few vowels, she asked, "Uh, what is this?"

He stalked toward it and peered inside curiously.

"What is this?" she repeated.

"I believe it is a miniature refrigerator. They make them for offices and wet bars and the like."

"What's *in it*?" she clarified, staring at him in incredulous disbelief.

Nick leaned in again for a moment, taking stock. Standing back, he folded his arms. "I do believe it's water and juice."

"Right." Annie nodded at him. "That's *right*."

"Okay, then. Now that we've established—"

"No. You're not hearing me. Who is going to drink that water and juice?"

"Anyone who wants to," he replied, maddeningly calm. "Help yourself."

Nick started back toward the office, but the pitch of Annie's voice seemed to stop him in his tracks, kind of like Sherman responding to a dog whistle.

"*Where is my Diet Coke?*"

"I thought I'd restock the thing with something a little more beneficial."

"More... A little more *what*?"

"You drink a half dozen of those things in the morning, Annie," he announced. "It's just not healthy to ingest that much caffeine and artificial sweetener. Now when you're here at the office, you can stick to water and fruit juice. If you're hungry, there's yogurt or string cheese or seedless grapes instead of"—he lifted the bakery bag from her desk and showed it to her as if she'd never seen one then dropped it again before finishing—"this harden-your-arteries junk you normally eat. It will be much better for you, and you'll thank me for it one day."

"I will not thank you for it," she told him confidently, sitting down at her desk and opening the bakery bag, producing a large cinnamon-crunch muffin. Retaining eye contact with Nick, she took a huge bite of it and crooned, "Mmmm."

"Fine," he said with a shrug. "That's fine. But will you at least try a little raspberry juice with that? Or a bottle of ice-cold water? I'm telling you, you'll learn to prefer it after a while."

"Whenever someone tells me I'll get used to something, I know that's a sign it's no good."

Annie wished she'd had the foreknowledge to stop and buy a soda on her way into the office. Without a word, she accepted the water Nick extended in her direction and smacked it to the desktop, refusing to give him the satisfaction of opening it until he disappeared into the office.

Nick smirked, grabbed a juice and a package of string cheese out of the refrigerator, nudged the door shut, and departed without ceremony.

Annie lifted the water and stared at it for a moment before unscrewing the cap and taking a few gulps. Not so horrible. But largely unsatisfying by comparison.

"Hate you," she called after him.

"No, you don't," he sang back to her.

The phones rang off the hook all day, and Annie hardly had time to complete the data entry and filing she had planned. The last call before sending the phones to the answering service at day's end came from a reporter from *The San Francisco Chronicle* looking for a quote on Heffley Investigations' role in the NorCal insurance fraud case being examined by the district attorney.

"Can you hold for a moment, please?"

When she told Nick the purpose of the call, he instructed her to tell them they had no comment except that the facts of the case would come out when and if it went to trial. Anything else, he explained, might jeopardize effective prosecution.

The cop in him showed, and Annie liked it.

"I'm out of here early tonight," he told her as he slipped into his jacket. "Can you lock up?"

"I think I can manage," she said, urgently trying to curb the resentment creeping up out of nowhere. "Hot date?"

"Not at all. I have plans with my sister."

Leaving poor Jenny behind at home?

Annie resisted the sarcasm making every attempt to crest out of her, and she simply nodded. "Well, have fun."

"You have a good one too, Annie Gray."

She watched him through the window, leaning back into her chair after he faded from sight. She gulped down the last swig of water from the bottle on her desk and tossed it into the trash, vowing to get a large Diet Coke and popcorn with extra butter at the movies that night. Just to spite him.

She picked up the phone receiver and dialed her grandmother's number. "Hi, Gram."

"Hi, sweetheart. Are you still at work?"

"I am," Annie replied, tracing the buttons on the phone with her index finger. "I was thinking of meeting Evan at the Monterey for a Cary Grant retrospective."

"Oooh, that sounds like heaven."

"Do you want to come along?"

"No, not tonight," Gram answered. "It's yoga night. There's a downward dog with my name all over it."

Annie chuckled. "Would you mind walking Sherman before you go? That way I don't have to drive all the way home and back again."

"Sherman and I just returned from a walk in the village. He's sacked out on the kitchen floor."

Annie laughed. "That's my boy."

"You have a good time tonight. And give my best to Mr. Grant."

"Will do."

At the theater, Evan greeted Annie with a hand to her shoulder and a soft kiss to her cheek. Familiar...and comforting somehow.

"I bought the tickets. Let's get some popcorn."

"Extra butter," she added.

"Oh, feeling wild tonight, huh?"

They both laughed at that, chatting in line about inconsequential things like the unusual flood of business at the office and the new salad dressing Evan had concocted that day.

"Uh-oh."

Evan stared at the entrance, wide-eyed.

"What is it?"

She followed his line of vision. Walking in the door, as chummy as two sardines in a can: Nick and Jenny.

He lied.

The words stuck to the back of her throat like peanut butter.

He said he was meeting his sister. Clearly, he lied.

Nick Benchley was a lot of things—tough as nails, somewhat crass, and even surprisingly tenderhearted at those infrequent moments when a person might least expect it. But one thing Annie never expected him to be: *a liar.*

"Annie!"

Jenny spotted her first, and Annie plastered on a smile so false that it seared her cheek.

"Jenny. Hi."

"Are you a Cary Grant fan too?"

"He's Annie's all-time favorite," Evan chimed in, handing Annie a large Diet Coke while Nick eyed her like a traitor.

"This is my off time," she warned him. "I can eat or drink anything I please."

"Indeed you can."

Jenny looked from Nick to Annie and back again. Turning toward Evan, she asked, "Do you know what this is about?"

Evan shrugged. "Nope."

"I've been trying to introduce Annie to the fine art of nutrition," Nick clued them in. "Unfortunately, she's a reluctant student."

"Oh, Nick, not really," Jenny chuckled. "He doesn't look like the health nut that he is, does he?"

"No!" Annie piped up. "In fact, I clearly remember sharing a burger and a shake with him on at least one occasion."

"I didn't say you should never have something you want, Annie Gray. I just think you could be a little more concerned with what you put into your body on a consistent basis. But if Diet Coke and gargantuan cinnamon muffins are what float your boat, by all means, chow down."

"Evan Shaw."

Annie turned to find Jenny and Evan shaking hands. "Oh, I'm sorry," she cried. "Evan, this is Jenny. And you remember Nick."

Evan merely nodded at Nick momentarily, turning back toward Jenny afterward. "I'm looking forward to seeing *Charade* again. It's such a classic."

"Right, but *To Catch a Thief* is really the most beautiful film ever made. All of that gorgeous landscape and the wide, sweeping shots. Can you imagine it up on a big screen?"

"That's what I was saying to Annie!"

Nick moved around them and stepped into line at the concession stand. Annie followed him casually.

"So what happened to getting together with your sister?"

He looked at her as if she spoke another language. "Pardon?"

"When you left the office, you said you had plans with your sister. But here you are with Jenny."

"*Jenny* is my sister."

Their eyes locked for an instant, and Annie broke the grasp, staring at the air over Nick's shoulder.

"Wait a minute. You thought—?"

And suddenly Nick burst into a fit of laughter, drawing Evan and Jenny toward them.

"All this time," Nick told Jenny, placing his arm around her shoulder, "Annie Gray thought you and I were an item."

"You did?" she asked. "Where would you get an idea like that?"

Annie looked at Evan, and her glance pushed him to shrink back a step. He had been the one to put that thought in her head. But then, nothing had ever occurred at the theater or in Deke's hospital room to make her think they were anything other than a couple.

One by one, each episode rolled across her mind neatly, like stacked playing cards dropping cleanly through a shuffler. Relief began to summit, and she held back a rush of emotion that truly wanted to evolve into tears.

"Annie, I'm so disappointed," Jenny said. Then she peeled back a broad grin, adding, "You thought I would date someone like *Nick*?"

"Well, I wondered," she managed as a comeback. "But then when you said you wanted to move out to your own place as soon as possible, my opinion of you brightened considerably."

Chapter Fifteen

....

"Years from now when you talk about this…
and you will…be kind."
Deborah Kerr, *Tea and Sympathy*, 1956

The four of them walked outside after the second movie, Evan bending Jenny's ear about anything and everything film-related. Nick wondered if the guy always talked so incessantly.

"Yes, and you know that curvy road where they drove together that one afternoon?" Jenny exclaimed. "That was the very same road where Grace Kelly died in a car crash twenty-some years later."

"I think I read that somewhere."

Come to think of it, Jenny's contributing her share of the chatter. Maybe the two were made for each other.

Nick moved in beside Annie and placed an arm loosely around her shoulder.

"Great California night, isn't it?"

"Beautiful," she replied.

"Up for a café au lait?"

"Caffeine? You?"

"They do make them caffeine-free, Annie."

She smiled up at him, and his gut took a sudden and unexpected flip when their eyes met.

"Did you hear that?" she asked him.

He gazed at her for a moment, wondering if the thumping of his pulse could possibly be audible outside his own body.

"Hear...what?"

"Evan, that's a wonderful idea! Let's do all go for a coffee. Do you want to, Nick?"

Annie raised her palm toward Jenny and Evan, and she grinned. "Kismet. They're talking about getting coffee too."

They walked over to the café on the corner and pulled two small tables together near the window. The waitress delivered cappuccinos for Jenny and Evan, a café au lait for Nick, and a hot chocolate with extra whipped cream for Annie. As Evan and Jenny chattered on, exchanging all the Grace Kelly and Cary Grant trivia either of them had stored up, Nick and Annie gravitated toward one another.

"I saw Deke this morning," she told him. "He looks good."

"Yeah, I stopped by the hospital last night just before visiting hours were over. He was eating orange gelatin and talking baseball with one of the nurses."

Annie popped with laughter.

"You should have seen him when that nurse dared to infer there was another ball club in the league that might make it to the next World Series outside of his precious Chicago Cubs. His face was all bunched up. I thought he might have another heart attack."

"But of course it's a given," she interjected, "that the chances of the Cubs going to the Series—"

"Yes, but we won't tell that to Deacon. We want him healthy again as soon as possible."

Annie released a rolling chuckle before she took a drink from her hot chocolate. Nick loved the way her nose wrinkled each time she took a sip from the cup.

She's a real beauty, this one. He wondered how a woman could be so exquisite and so childlike at the same time.

When Annie set the cup down again, she immediately noticed Nick gazing at her, and she smiled at him. He felt the poke of that perfect smile in a deep spot just beneath his ribs.

"What?"

"Nothing," he said with a slight shake of the head. "I just can't believe you thought I was dating Jenny. She's barely out of college!"

"Well, how was I to know you're not a dirty old man? How old are you anyway? Fifty? Sixty?"

He narrowed his eyes at her, an intentional threat dancing within them. Annie started to giggle, and Nick melted into a grin. "Thirty-plus."

After a moment, he fell quiet again, lowering his head. "I guess I thought you realized I was interested in someone else."

"Someone other than Jenny?"

"Yes," he replied, looking her squarely in the eye. "I thought you and I might be building toward something."

His heartbeat doubled, pounding hard against his chest. Before Annie, it had been something like five years since he'd declared any real interest in a woman. But here he was again with Annie, putting it all out there.

Nick's palms turned to ice in an instant when it seemed as if Annie's breath caught in her throat.

"Am I wrong?"

She opened her mouth, but nothing came out besides a tiny fraction of a noise. She tried again, with the same result.

"Okay. Maybe I'm wrong, then."

"N–no," she managed. "You're not...*entirely* wrong. I'm just—"

"So happy to learn that I'm not involved with Jenny?"

"Well. Yes."

"And so relieved to discover that I'm still interested in you, after all these weeks of being a good boy."

She released one hard chuckle, and Nick breathed again.

"And you can't find the words to retract your former position on the issue of me kissing you."

"Pardon?"

"I told you I'd never kiss you again unless you asked me. Go ahead, Annie Gray. Ask me."

Annie glanced over at Evan, and Nick followed her gaze. Evan nattered on, completely oblivious to the presence of anyone at all besides Jenny.

"I'll have to give that some further consideration," she said. "I'm not entirely sure you're kiss-worthy."

"Ahhh," he groaned, holding his chest in wounded amusement. "Me? Not kiss-worthy? Annie Gray, you are so sadly mistaken."

"I think that remains to be seen," she told him with confidence. "I'll get back to you."

* * * * *

The afternoon mail brought a few checks, some junk mail, and a beautiful Italian postcard.

> *Thank you so much for everything you did to get us here.*
> *We're having the time of our lives. God bless you both.*
> *—Marion and Davis Armbrewster*

Annie flipped it over and admired the mesmerizing Tuscan valley pictured there.

Peeling a tab of tape from the dispenser on her desk, she displayed the card from the top of her IN box where she could look at it every day. Not just because of the spectacular scene, but also because the card served as a wonderful reminder of her very first case with Heffley Investigations. It seemed more like three years ago than three months since she'd made the leap, but Annie had enjoyed every minute.

Her concentration on Italian wine country broke as the front door opened. She squinted against the light, and a familiar and expansive smile drew one of her own.

"Tyra!"

Annie leaped around her desk and tossed her arms around her friend, and the two of them squealed in a sort of dancing embrace. Nick appeared in the doorway in response to their high-pitched sounds. When he found Annie safe and sound, he waved a hand and disappeared back into the office.

"Come on in and sit down. Tell me all the dirt about Equity Now."

"Oh, it's the same old place, girl." Her face dropped, and she looked at Annie so seriously that it scared her a little. "That's not why I'm here."

"Uh-oh. That sounds ominous."

"I need your help."

It took Tyra more than a half hour to unfold the entire family drama centering around her widowed mother of sixty-two and the thirty-eight-year-old Casanova romancing her.

"I'm so worried about her, Annie. I know there's something sinister going on there. He's just not right."

"What's his name?" Annie asked, picking up a pen and turning to a clean page on her pad of paper.

"Marques DeLeon."

"And what do you know about him? Anything at all? Where is he from? Where did he go to school? How did they meet?"

"Mama took a seniors' cruise with her girlfriends from her garden club," Tyra began, pausing to glance down at the floor. She shook her head and looked at Annie, her dark eyes brimming with tears. "He was one of the tour guides that showed them around at the ports."

"So he works for the cruise line?"

"Yes."

Annie made a whole page of notes before their conversation concluded.

"How much is this going to cost me?" Tyra asked. "I don't have a lot of money."

"This one's on the house, sweetie," Annie told her, squeezing her hand. "It's just a background check, and we do those all the time. I don't think Nick will mind."

"Nick's the guy in there?"

"Right."

"Are you sure?"

"I'm sure. Just hang in there, and I'll get back to you in a day or so. Okay?"

"Okay."

Tyra accepted the tissue Annie handed her from the box on her desk, and she dabbed it at her nose before telling Annie, "He's kinda hot."

"DeLeon?"

"No," she whispered, nodding toward Deke's office with a quick grin. "Your boss."

"Oh, Nick? Yeah. I guess."

Tyra sniffed. "Thanks, Annie. I didn't know where else to go."

"You came to the right place. I'll find something out, and I'll call you."

The second Annie rose up from her chair, Tyra rounded the desk and wrapped her in her arms again, burying her damp face in her neck and thanking her over and over again.

"I don't want you to worry, Ty. Trust me, okay?"

"Okay."

"Now tell me about the job," Annie urged, hoping to introduce another subject that wouldn't be so emotional.

"Oh, *giiiirl*," she cried in her own inimitable style. "The calls are backed up in the queue from the first thing in the morning until the last thing at night. You know? And the big deal this week is how nobody's keeping to their break and lunch schedules, so now we're going to be docked if we deviate, even the least little bit. And girl, I'm too old to be asking for permission every time I have to use the little girl's room."

Before long, they were giggling and gabbing like teenagers at a slumber party, and Tyra's spirit appeared to be a few hundred feet higher than when she arrived.

"I've got to finish up these reports on my desk today," Annie told her as Tyra prepared to leave. "But first thing in the morning, I'll run a complete background history on our friend DeLeon. It usually takes twenty-four to forty-eight hours to get the findings, but I'll call you as soon as I have something."

"Thank you so much, Annie."

"If this is what it takes to get you to come and see me, then so be it," she teased.

"I know. I'm sorry. I really have missed you."

They hugged again, and Annie watched her departure through the window behind her desk. Leaving Equity Now was a blessing, of course. But leaving Tyra behind had been one of the few things that hindered the celebration.

"Friend of yours, I take it."

Nick collapsed into the chair Tyra had occupied, and Annie turned toward him and relaxed into her own.

"Very good friend."

"And her mom's a mark?"

"You heard? Yeah, it looks that way."

"Charging her the deep discount rate?"

Their eyes met, and Annie cringed. "It's just for the initial background check. If we need to go further, I can—"

"Settle down, Annie Gray. I get it."

She narrowed her eyes, regarding him with curiosity.

"She's a friend. She came to you for help. I get it."

He gave her one of those Nick Benchley lopsided grins, dimples flying like a flag, and her heart started to thump again. "Thanks, Nick."

"Don't thank me," he cracked as he stood up. "You're the one who will be doing all the work."

* * * * *

"I heard you met up with an old friend of mine."

Annie glanced up at her gram and smiled. "Did she tell you what a dork I was?"

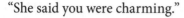
"She said you were charming."

"Charming like a stalker."

Dot chuckled as she dunked a tea bag into her cup. She sat down at the kitchen table across from Annie and rubbed the top of her hand.

"Want to know a secret, Annie?"

Annie nodded.

"I'm a little awestruck by Doris Day myself."

Annie grinned. "All those great movies, so elegant and beautiful."

"She still is."

"She sure is."

"There's only two of the greats," Gram told her, pausing to take a sip of tea, "who always seemed to have that radiance about them, almost like they had their own backlighting wherever they went: Doris Day and Grace Kelly."

"That's the truth," she agreed. "I really envy you, Gram, being part of that whole thing. Hollywood was so glamorous then."

"Certainly not like today."

"No. It was pre-paparazzi."

"Oh, they weren't called the paparazzi, but we had them back then. The only difference was that they pretty much printed what agents, publicists, and studio executives told them to print. We had our Lindsay Lohans and Mel Gibsons. We just didn't wear them like a community-wide badge of honor."

"Does life seem awfully boring to you now?" Annie asked her.

"Boring?" she replied with a chuckle. "Oh my, no. I'm living the life I always dreamed about."

"You had all that, and *this* is what you were dreaming about?"

"Don't get me wrong, it was fun. But this life here in Carmel, with my garden and my cottage and the Pacific Ocean rising up to greet me every morning, and especially now, with you and Sherman here—this is real life, Annie. This is the sweet and gentle whisper I kept hearing but couldn't quite reach."

Annie threaded her fingers into her hair and leaned on her elbow.

"Do you know that scripture?" her gram asked.

"I don't think so."

"Elijah went running for his life, and he hid out in a cave in the mountains. When God found him, He told him to stand outside and wait because the presence of the Lord was going to pass by."

"Oh, right," Annie said. "And the wind came."

"But God wasn't in the wind. Nor was He in the earthquake or the fire, as you might expect. When the Lord's presence arrived at Elijah's door, it was a sweet, gentle whisper that greeted him. All the other stuff was just Hollywood drama."

Annie giggled. "That's a beautiful verse."

"I love that passage because it tells us that our destiny doesn't always have to be in the big, showy things, Annie," Gram explained. "Sometimes it's going to be in the softer, sweeter things of life, the ones that bring that safe feeling, like the comfort of home. Wasn't that what you said you were looking for the night that you made your list at this table?"

Annie tilted her head and sighed. "Are you trying to tell me something, Gram?"

Dot just smiled, and Annie reached across the table and stole a sip from her grandmother's teacup. "Mmm. That's good. What is it?"

"Darjeeling."

She took one more sip before placing the delicate cup on the saucer again. When she began to pull her hand back, Dot caught it and gave it a squeeze.

"Do you know how much I love you?" she asked.

"I think so," Annie replied.

"I'm very proud of you for setting out on this search for what will make you happy. It's a little like a spiritual sojourn."

"A happiness safari," Annie added.

"As long as you keep things in perspective along the way, I think this pursuit will be an adventure you'll never forget."

Annie smiled thoughtfully. "Thanks, Gram. Can I make a cup of that tea for myself?"

"Certainly."

As she filled the kettle and put the water on to boil, Annie wondered what might be ahead of her. Adventures in *Casablanca*? Romance and *An Affair to Remember*? Perhaps some intrigue and a *Maltese Falcon* or two.

The Scripture verse fluttered across her memory, and she said a silent prayer that any whispers that crossed her path might be heard above the din of heavy winds and roaring earthquakes.

Chapter Sixteen

....

"Bond. James Bond."

Sean Connery, *From Russia with Love,* 1963

Marques DeLeon had a relatively clean record aside from a couple of parking tickets and a citation for lapsed insurance. Prior to gainful employment with Elegance CruiseLines, he'd been a waiter, a bartender, a dance instructor, and a messenger. He married in 2006, divorced a year later; no children resulted.

"Anything interesting?" Nick asked when he emerged from Deke's office for the first time all afternoon.

"Nothing at all. Marques DeLeon seems pretty much like a regular Joe."

"*Mar-kez Day-lee-own,*" Nick enunciated with dramatic flair, and he clicked his heels in punctuation.

He looked silly, and it drew a chuckle out of Annie.

"Plans for dinner?" he asked.

"Nope. You?"

"I was thinking about checking out a new place near the village. Want to join me?"

"Sure."

"I have to warn you, the cuisine might be a little cleaner than you're used to."

"Oh, please. Don't start with me on that. Just let me tidy up my desk."

Ten minutes later, Annie followed Nick's Jeep toward Carmel and through the village. Not until he whipped into one of the driveways at the end of a cul-de-sac did it occur to her that the "new place" nearby might actually be Nick's home.

He lives in Carmel? Annie wondered why she didn't know that.

A stone arch shielded the front door from the street, creating a lovely Mediterranean courtyard entrance; simple and non-ornamental, kind of like Nick. Casement windows framed by slate blue wooden grills matched the heavy tile roof. Annie parked in the driveway behind him and smiled as he sauntered toward her.

"Nice place. What's it called?" she asked through her open car window.

"Casa de *Me*."

"Does this mean you're cooking for me?"

"If you think you can handle it."

Never one to back down from a challenge, Annie rolled up the window and got out of the car. Nick gave her a satisfied nod and led the way up the brick walk.

Beyond the arch, a beautiful fountain built from blue-and-yellow porcelain tiles and graced by cascading green plants ushered them toward the house. The simple front door, made of weathered planks of wood, displayed an iron knob and ornate brackets.

"How long have you lived here?" she asked him as they stepped inside. "It's really beautiful."

"About two years now," he told her. "It's a work in progress."

He tossed his keys to a Moroccan mosaic console table in the foyer leading into a warm living room with light cinnamon walls. A dark hunter green leather sofa and chairs with copper studs provided inviting contrast. The broken ceramic tiles across the top of the coffee table seemed a perfect match to the flawless, shiny ones bordering the fireplace. Framed photographs congregated in natural groupings along the mantel and on tabletops.

"Nick, this is really nice. Did you do it yourself?"

"Everything from the fireplace to the windows to the hardwood floors," he stated matter-of-factly, leaning against the doorjamb leading to the dining room. "It went from a weekend hobby to my life's work in no time at all."

"The efforts have paid off."

"Come on into the kitchen. I'll pour you a drink and you can keep me company while I cook."

He paused in the dining room to flick a switch on the massive stereo system, and soft strains of Spanish guitar seemed to whisper from every corner. Three chairs arranged in a neat row cordoned off a section of broken wall and a large plastic curtain.

"Like I said," he told her with a wave of his hand in the direction of the curtain, "a work in progress."

Nick produced a glass pitcher from the refrigerator and poured a fruity-looking concoction into large glasses.

"Nonalcoholic sangria," he told her as he sliced an orange and tossed the pieces into the glasses. "You'll love it."

Annie took a sip and acknowledged with a nod that he was right.

"Too sweet?"

"No. Perfect."

"And caffeine-free."

Annie poked her tongue out at him playfully.

The front door opened and voices carried through the house, one of them oddly familiar, striking a chord in Annie.

"Hey, Annie!"

Looking up, only mildly aware that she must have looked like she'd just seen something resurrected, she said, "Evan. What are you doing here?"

"He's with me," Jenny said as she stepped up to the island and took a drink from Nick's glass. "Are you cooking tonight, big brother?"

"I thought I might. Want to join us?"

Jenny turned toward Evan, and he shrugged in agreement. "If it's all right with Annie."

"Of course," she managed, just coming to the realization that the shocked expression on her faced needed to be tamed.

"I'm gonna show Evan how the pool is coming along," Jenny declared, and the two of them left the kitchen, hand in hand.

"I take it from the deer-in-headlights look on your face," Nick remarked, "that you had no idea your boyfriend was dating my sister?"

"Uh, no. No idea at all." Annie chewed on her bottom lip for a moment. "I mean, Evan's not my boyfriend. He—he can date whomever he chooses. I was just a little...*surprised*...to see them together. That's all. I didn't know they...I mean, I'm just a little taken back because...well, how long has this been going on?"

"They've been pretty much inseparable since that night we all met up at the movies last week," he told her, using tongs to flip the steaks now sizzling atop the gas grill top in the center of the island.

She watched mindlessly as he placed long, thin slices of yellow squash, zucchini, red peppers, and onions into tight foil packets and placed them around the outer edge.

"Do you like corn on the cob?"

"Hmm? Yes."

The rest of the preparation process became a blur as Annie

went over that night at the movies in arduous detail inside her mind. She recalled the way Evan had looked at Jenny, especially once it was revealed that she was not in fact Nick's date at all, but his sister. And then the way she had sized him up in response.

The twosome had discussed movies and music, books and art. They'd even touched lightly on politics, as Annie recalled. And while Nick drank his coffee and she had her hot chocolate, Evan and Jenny had shared identical cups of cappuccino lightly dusted with cinnamon—and two refills.

The oddest feeling pinched her ribs as the memories bounced around in her aching head.

This feels a little like— Am I...jealous?

Jealous over Evan? She couldn't be.

Am I?

Evan and Annie had been over for a very long time. Oh sure, there had been a season long, long ago when she'd entertained visions of a future for them. But so much raging river had passed beneath the bridge since then—so many disappointments and stumbles and obstacles—that the water had gone all the way out to the bay, emptied deep into the ocean, and been obliterated from sight.

So why is my stomach churning at the thought of Evan with another woman?

And what about that throbbing in her temple? The sweat on her palms? She felt like—

Oh good grief. A woman scorned.

Annie knew she shouldn't be feeling like she'd just caught her boyfriend in the act of cheating. In fact, "Evan" and "boyfriend" had no place in the same sentence! The time he spent with Jenny had absolutely nothing to do with Annie.

And yet—

Annie squeezed her eyes shut and rubbed her temples. When she realized Nick had been speaking to her for she didn't know how long, she opened her eyes and squinted them again.

"How do you like your steak? Medium rare okay?"

"Fine."

Nick and Annie sat side by side at the table with Evan and Jenny facing them, Annie flinching inwardly as the new couple recounted their versions of Adventures in Dating. Watching the two of them together made Annie want to brush her teeth, and she wondered if sweet little Jenny could honestly be *this sweet*. Or if anyone could, really.

"Evan packed us a lunch and we went over to Monastery Beach for a picnic. You know that spot where the shore curves and that bluff of rocks juts out into the water?" Nick nodded before she continued. "We watched the children playing and walked barefoot in the sand, and he put flowers in my hair. We just had the best time!"

Oh. Come. On. Flowers in her hair? Really, Evan?

Annie didn't like the version of herself that arose just then, the bitter and mean version, jealous of something making one of her best friends deliriously happy, possibly for the first time in his life. How could she actually be thinking, *Evan never put flowers in my hair* while his eyes blazed with adoration for the auburn beauty seated next to him?

Annie plunked a bite of steak into her mouth and set the fork down on her plate. As Jenny and Evan's eyes met one more time, they reminded her of a pair of carefully folded cashmere gloves, completely bound up in one another. And despite her best reasoning against it, her ridiculous heart felt as if it might just break right in two.

* * * * *

Annie couldn't sleep that night.

Sherman, however, did not have that problem, and his snoring irritated her. She pulled on a pair of socks, padded downstairs to the kitchen, and flipped on the light over the sink. She knew that caffeine would be a huge mistake at this juncture, and she congratulated herself for thinking clearly enough to realize it.

She poured herself a glass of cold water and hiked herself up onto the counter to drink it while she mulled over the dinner at Nick's. Absurdly, she found herself wishing she had one of those raspberry juices from the fridge at work.

Annie's mom had given her the clock that hung on her kitchen wall, a beagle puppy whose little paws swung as time ticked by. Her mother had said it reminded her of Sherman when, of course, the dog-clock looked nothing like him at all except for the coloring. But for some reason, Gram liked the friendly way the strange little beagle showed her the time. She'd suggested hanging him on the kitchen wall over the back door, just where he used to hang in Annie's Monterey apartment.

Dog-clock told her it was nearly 11:00 p.m., but she dialed the phone anyway.

"Hello?"

"Is it too late to call?"

"Annie, what's wrong?"

"I need to talk."

"But you're okay."

"Yes. I'm okay."

"Let me go out to the other room and call you back."

Mateo would be getting up in a few hours to go to the warehouse, and Zoey didn't want to wake him. Annie wished she'd thought of that.

"I'm sorry," she told her, after answering in the middle of the first ring.

"It's fine. He didn't even budge. Now tell me what's going on."

"I was hoping you could tell me."

"Okay."

Annie started at the beginning, how Evan had told her that Nick's date was so beautiful and that he was really taken with her, and then how they'd run into them at the theater and discovered she wasn't his date at all, just Nick's sister. She recounted the way they'd gravitated to one another, how they didn't seem to run short on things to talk about, how Evan had looked at Jenny in a way that Annie had never seen him look at anyone before, including her. She moved on, filling Zoey in on dinner, from picnics to flowers in the hair to the perfect fit they seemed to make, leaving nothing out.

"That is so great for Evan," Zoey said, when Annie wound down to silence.

"I know."

"And?"

"And what?"

"And why is it bothering you so much?"

"I was hoping you could help me get a handle on that very question."

"Ah."

"Evan deserves a little happiness, Zo. He's great, and so is Jenny. So why am I feeling like the angry, rejected girlfriend?"

"For the same reason you found it so difficult to be happy for

Linda and Ted, Annie. You feel challenged by it. Evan's always been your sure thing. If you needed a date, he was there. If you wanted to watch a movie, Evan was your guy. You each provided something very secure for the other, but now he's not going to be your beck-and-call boy any more. Someone else has his attention."

She mulled that over for nearly a minute, hating the realization that landed on her.

"I am a really terrible person."

Zoey chuckled. "You are not a terrible person. You are a human person."

"I'm not terrible?"

"No," she reassured her. "What would make you a terrible person is if you didn't come to terms with those feelings and see them for what they are so that you can overcome them."

"I don't know if I can."

"You can," Zoey replied with confidence.

"How do you know?"

"Because I know you. And I know that you are not the type of person to try to hang on to someone like Evan simply because you don't have someone of your own. And I also know that you are too kindhearted and too good of a friend not to encourage the joy that Evan and Jenny have found in each other. A joy, by the way, that has nothing whatsoever to do with you."

I hate when she does that.

"I do have one question, though," she added. "What was Nick doing while you were reacting to Evan's newfound relationship?"

"I don't know. Cooking, I guess. Why?"

"And you don't think it was the least bit rude to ignore him while indulging in your jealous side?"

"I…hadn't really given that much thought."

"Maybe you owe him an apology?"

Annie bit her lip. "Maybe I do."

* * * * *

Nick grew irritated. He couldn't rein in the focus necessary for the speed bag. Pulling the boxing glove from his right hand, he smoothed down the wrap before replacing the glove and moving on to the heavy bag behind him.

Jab—jab—cross.

This is more like it.

Nick lit into that bag with a vengeance. It wasn't Evan's face on the front of the bag; he couldn't exactly blame Evan for what he felt. And it wouldn't be right to place Annie's cute little wrinkled nose and sweet, fragile jaw in the path of an uppercut; he only entertained the notion for about a millisecond. But Nick needed a target for all his misplaced anger, and for the moment, the worn-out punching bag hanging in the station's workout room wore the bull's eye.

He threw the power of his entire body into several right crosses until the bag began to shimmy and Nick's knuckles ached, even beneath the padding protecting his hands.

"Yo, Bench," Thorton called out as he plunked down on the rowing machine across the room. "A little less rage, a little more focus, bud. Or are you *trying* to put yourself out of commission?"

Nick ignored him.

Linking his punches with combinations, he moved around the bag, throwing fast jabs and following with powerful crosses. One final thrust, accompanied by a booming groan, sent the heavy bag flying.

* * * * *

Nick had been out of the office all morning, and that afternoon he seemed unusually somber. It took over an hour for Annie to screw up her courage to do it, but she finally stepped into the doorway of Deke's office and waited for Nick to notice her there. It felt like another hour before he did.

"What's up?" he asked, before returning his attention to the computer screen before him.

"Can I talk to you?"

"Sure."

He busied himself at the keyboard as Annie sat down and began to fidget.

"So talk."

"Well," she managed, staring at the floor around her feet, "I feel like maybe we need to talk about what happened the other night."

"What happened? What night?"

"You're not going to make this easy for me, are you?"

"Not in the least." He only looked up at her for a second or two, but those seconds were heavy with meaning.

Well, he's honest anyway.

"I think I was a bit…rude when you invited me to your house for dinner."

"Do you?"

He didn't look up this time.

"Yes. I do."

Nick closed the laptop before him and leaned back into the leather chair, crossing his arms over his chest and regarding her with such intensity that she suddenly wished he'd go back to ignoring her.

"The thing is—I was a little stunned when Evan came in with Jenny. I had no idea they were seeing each other, and it just took me completely by surprise."

"And this inspired your behavior how again?"

"I'm not entirely sure, if you want to know the truth," she admitted with a weak smile. "Evan and I had a rocky time of it when we were dating, if what we were doing could even be called that. Anyway, we've struggled a little in moving forward, and our relationship just isn't quite…defined."

"Let's cut away the fat, Annie. You were jealous."

She paused, biting her lip. "I was jealous," she said with a nod. "Even though it makes no sense at all."

"You were holding out hope for something more to come of your friendship with Evan?"

"No. At least I didn't think I was."

"And now that you've had time to mull it over," he stated, "what do you think now?"

"I think Evan and I were never meant to be anything more than friends. I think I spent a long time hoping for something more because we seemed so well-suited to one another," she told him. Swallowing hard, she added, "And when he couldn't seem to take that leap forward with me, I blamed it on his inability to commit."

Nick's face seemed to soften slightly. Or at least Annie imagined that it did.

"The truth is," she added with reluctance, "he just wasn't able to commit *to me*."

Nick fumbled with a pen for a moment or two before he lifted his eyes toward her. "I don't think the two of you are really so well-suited to each other, Annie."

"No?"

"No. There's no spark. And whatever there is that's going to ultimately follow, doesn't it have to start with a spark?"

Annie thought that over for a moment as Nick got up and rounded the desk. Sitting on the edge of it right in front of her, he leaned forward and looked down into her eyes so deeply that she felt his gaze practically gouge her in the pit of her stomach.

"You and I, Annie Gray—now, we've got sparks."

Truer words were never uttered. *But do we have anything to reach for beyond that?*

When she looked up and met his gaze again, for just one moment, Annie thought how wonderful it would be to just lean into it, to just let Nick kiss her.

"You're entitled to your feelings, whatever they are, about Evan and my sister," Nick said, rising from the edge of the desk. "No apology is needed for reacting in whatever way your heart led you."

Nick returned to his chair and opened the laptop. "Was there anything else?" he asked her.

"N–no. That was it."

"Okay, then. Do you want to work on completing this week's updates so we can report to Deke? I spent an hour with him over at the house this morning, and I don't think we have much more time before he starts poking his nose in to see what we've been doing."

"Sure. I'll get my notes."

"Bring the Riley case file too, will you?"

"Sure."

Chapter Seventeen
....

"I'll get you, my pretty.
And your little dog, too."
Margaret Hamilton, *The Wizard of Oz*, 1939

After a solid hour of updating the week's activity file, Annie looked on as Nick popped to his feet and slipped into the jacket he'd left hanging on the back of the door.

"Hey, do you want to grab some dinner?" Annie asked, trying to sound as casual as she could manage.

"Nah, not tonight, Annie Gray. I'll see you in the morning."

Once Nick closed the front door behind him, the silence in that office began screaming relentlessly, bearing down on Annie. Sitting there beneath the weight of it became unbearable. For no reason in particular, her heart pounded so hard that she found it hard to breathe. At last she pushed up out of the chair and made her way into the reception office to gather her things and leave. She sank down into the chair at her desk, yanked open the drawer, and pulled her satchel out of it.

The rumble came first, the one that sounded like a semitruck barreling too fast down the road outside. And then came the shaking, followed by the shattering of glass somewhere nearby.

Earthquake!

Annie watched the supply shelf in the open closet fall and crash on top of the small refrigerator, and she dropped her bag as she and her chair rolled swiftly away from the desk and thumped hard against the window nearby. She slipped from the seat down to the floor and crawled beneath the desk, waiting there for what seemed like several minutes as the floor shifted underneath her and the desk lurched above.

More glass shattered, and thick wood splintered noisily overhead. A framed photograph of Sherman crashed to the floor beside her, sending her thoughts hastily home. Annie said a quick prayer for Sherman and Gram's safety.

This has got to be at least a six on the Richter scale.

When it finally ended, Annie didn't move an inch. She remained frozen beneath the desk, trying to find her breath and then struggling to regulate it.

In through the nose, out through the mouth. Then again.

Alarms sounded all over the area, and then came the sirens. She jumped at a loud *pop!* and realized that an electrical line close by had fallen.

"Annie?"

The door banged open. Nick appeared and squatted before her.

"Are you all right?"

She thought so but for some reason couldn't find her voice to tell him. She finally gave up and just nodded.

"Are you hurt?"

Pain throbbed softly in the back of her head, and she realized she must have hit it pretty hard when she rammed into the window. She raised her hand to where it stung, and her palm came back with blood on it.

"I'm hurt," she managed, showing him the proof on her hand as tears began to fall.

"Okay, hang on to me," Nick told her.

She crawled out from under the desk and grabbed her leather satchel from the floor then slipped her arms around his neck, burying her face in his shoulder, as Nick lifted her and carried her straight out the front door.

He eased her into the passenger seat of his Jeep then reached behind the seat for a black gym bag. "Everything will be okay," he seemed to promise, as he produced a towel from inside the bag.

He wrapped it around his hand and gently applied it to the back of her head.

"Just let me get a look here and see how bad it is. You're going to be fine. I don't want you to worry."

Annie appreciated the soothing quality about Nick just then, and she sighed.

"It doesn't look too bad. Do you know what hit you?"

"I was on my ch–chair, and it rolled me back into the wi– window," she stammered.

"Did you hit your head on the metal frame or the glass?"

"I don't know."

"Okay," he repeated, pressing the towel against the back of her head again. "You're going to be fine, angel. Just relax. You're going to be just fine. Can you tell me what day it is?"

The corner of Annie's mouth quivered. "The day of the earthquake?"

"Oh, fine," Nick replied, nodding. "I'm trying to help, and she gives me sass."

"I need to check on Sherman and Gram, Nick."

"Okay," he answered, and he handed her the towel, got in the vehicle, and tossed the Jeep into gear.

She struggled to produce her cell phone from her bag, finally dialing the house. No answer.

Annie made a couple more calls as Nick drove her toward home.

Zoey and Mateo had sustained no damage at all, and her mother seemed more shaken than anything else. Some glass fixtures had broken at the bistro, but the earthquake left Evan and his prized kitchen intact.

She left a quick voice mail for Merideth and Frank; then Nick used her phone to check on Jenny, despite Evan's report that she had weathered her first earthquake with nothing more serious than a case of nerves. All seemed well between Monterey and Carmel, aside from the massive, throbbing gash at the back of Annie's head.

Nick parked diagonally across the small driveway. "Woozy" and "ladylike" presented cross-purposes as she climbed out of the Jeep with gratitude coloring the memory of the skirt she'd been considering that morning. She was happy that she'd opted for jeans instead.

"Can you walk?" Nick asked her. Annie nodded.

Before they reached the front porch, Sherman's head popped up in the bay window. He barked out a message when he spotted her, one Annie translated with no trouble at all: *Something unusual has happened, and it scared me. Get in here. I want to tell you all about it.*

He practically knocked her down as she opened the door, rushing her with a childlike eagerness that spoke volumes about their relationship. Still scratching Sherman's head, Annie sighed with relief as Gram whooshed down the stairs, talking a mile a minute.

"Oh, Annie, that poor little dog of yours was scared out of his wits, and he's been whining and barking ever since the quake. We've already had two aftershocks, you know. They were small and the newsman on the television said we probably didn't feel them, but I'll tell you I sure did. Goodness me! Hello, Nick. Annie, your head is bleeding."

Nick held the towel, blotchy with her blood, and he wrapped it around his hand and pressed it to the back of her head again.

"Is everything all right here?" he asked.

"I think I fared quite well."

"I'm going to take care of a little first aid, then," Nick told her with a smile and a nod toward Annie.

"I'll get the kit and put on the water for tea."

"Come on, Sherman," Nick announced, guiding Annie into the kitchen. "Let's tend to your mom, huh?"

Sherman bounded ahead of them, making a couple of wide circles before standing guard over the kitchen table until they reached it. His ears pinned stiffly forward, he looked curious and alert.

"It's okay," Annie assured him. "Just a little bump on the head."

Nick guided her to a chair, and Sherman lifted his head and shot her a panting grin over his shoulder.

An aftershock kicked in just as Gram sat down at the table and opened the kit. Nick pulled both of them close, an arm around each of their shoulders, as it rolled and shook for several noisy seconds. Sherman pressed against Nick's leg until it passed.

"That was a good one," Nick commented as he resumed triage duty without missing another beat. "I'm guessing a 5.2. Maybe 5.3."

Annie's scalp stung, and Nick instinctively leaned toward her and blew on the wound. "This is going to hurt when you wash your hair. Be careful to rinse it clean—and I'd suggest no conditioner or product until it has a chance to heal."

She didn't use gel or mousse and the like, so that wouldn't propose a problem. But no conditioner? Sudden visions of a small, pale Annie with twice-her-size Diana Ross hair shot across her mind.

"Listen, I need to run over and check on things at my place," he told her. "Will you two be all right here for a few minutes?"

"Certainly," Gram commented, just as Annie cried, "No!"

The objection had hurled from somewhere deep inside of her, right out there in the air between them before she knew it.

She sighed, modulating herself a few octaves softer this time. "Can't you stay with us until the aftershocks settle down?"

"It could be days before they stop entirely, Annie Gray."

"Couldn't we come with you, then?"

"Nonsense," Gram said. "We'll be just fine here. Well, you and Sherman could go ahead with him while I head down the street to check on Myrtle. I phoned her and she said she was fine, but that woman is a shrinking violet, afraid of her own shadow. I just want to see her with my own eyes."

Annie watched Nick as he deliberated. Finally, to her great relief, he asked, "Where's Sherman's leash?"

She pointed to the hook by the back door. The instant Nick's hand touched it, Sherman rushed toward him, his little paws scampering noisily across the checkerboard floor.

Sherman had never ridden in an open vehicle before. The closest he'd come, in fact, might have been Zoey's old Volvo with the sunroof. But any doubts Annie might have had about his safety were quickly alleviated as Nick adeptly converted the leash into a sort of harness and hooked the dog into the seat belt. As they flew along Ocean Avenue, Sherman sat upright on the driver's side of the backseat, his eyes nearly closed as he leaned forward into the breeze. His long, floppy ears pelted him mercilessly, but he barely seemed to notice.

Annie twisted her hair into a knot and leaned back against the headrest to hold it in place. Even after a lifetime in California, Annie had never gotten used to earthquakes or how they just appeared out of nowhere, unpredictable and menacing.

"There's some sort of something everywhere," her aunt Henri used to say. "Quakes at your house; tornadoes at mine. When I get to heaven, I think I'll have a chat with Him about that."

Annie wondered if Aunt Henri had gotten a definitive answer yet.

From the front, Nick's house looked perfect. Not a flower or a pot out of place. But they walked through the door to find Jenny on her hands and knees in front of the fireplace, sweeping shattered glass into a dustpan and emptying it into the small trash can beside her. The many photos Annie remembered seeing on the mantel were now gone, and glassless frames sat nestled into safe piles on the hearth.

The moment she saw them, Jenny's eyes darted to Nick and she burst into tears. He chuckled and invited her into an embrace that she hurried toward. Sherman and Annie just stood there for a minute, feeling conspicuously out of their loop until Nick's arm twirled back toward her. Stepping forward, Annie joined the circle.

"My two favorite girls," Nick muttered. "Everything's going to be all right."

Annie thought it funny how they both seemed to believe him.

Evan stepped through the open front door, and when Jenny saw him, she raced toward him, hopping into his embrace. Seeing the two of them there like that, Evan holding her like a treasured parcel he'd long-awaited, made Annie's heart beat double time. At that moment, she realized: *Evan is really and truly in love.*

He'd been waiting for Jenny his whole entire life, without ever really knowing it. And now there she was, in his arms, looking for all the world as if she'd just settled into her own proper place. Annie had thought her heart might break over Evan finding with Jenny what he could never seem to find with her, but then she realized that she'd witnessed something amazing, firsthand. Destiny had found its place within unsuspecting lives, right before her eyes.

Jenny is the right fit for Evan. I never was.

Whining drew her attention, and Annie scanned the floor for Sherman. He sat regally at Evan's feet, with not a peep out of him.

"What is that?" Nick asked.

"I thought it was Sherman," Evan chimed in.

"Where is it coming from?" Jenny inquired.

Nick made his way toward the kitchen, and they all followed like a funny little parade with Sherman trailing at the end. When he reached it, Nick pulled back the plastic sheeting that curtained the wall he'd already torn down. On the other side, the beautiful wood flooring had collapsed in one spot in front of the window.

"Oh, Nicky!" Jenny exclaimed. "You were almost finished with securing that floor!"

" 'Almost' only counts in horseshoes, I'm afraid," he countered, hands on hips and feet planted firmly as he surveyed the damage.

The whining started again, quickly evolving into full-fledged cries, and Nick motioned them back from danger as he crossed the remnant of the open deck and hopped to an exposed beam beneath it.

Evan held Sherman by the collar as he squirmed, wanting to follow Nick toward the animal trapped beneath him.

"What in the world are you doing under there?" Nick commented, reaching into the gaping hole in the middle of the collapsed flooring.

"Nick, what is it?" Annie asked him.

It took him several tries to get a firm grasp on the animal, but then he lifted something from the opening. Grinning, he held up a wiggling little beagle puppy and suggested, "Sherman's little brother?"

He held the dog close to him, stepping from the beam to the flooring and through the plastic curtain. All the while, the beagle squirmed in his arms, yipping as if he'd been mortally injured.

Sherman whined as Nick set the dog on the floor of the kitchen. "He must have been out there under the deck when the quake knocked that part of the floor down, and then he was trapped."

Though barely half his size, Sherman welcomed the newcomer, and they exchanged a low-pitched growling version of the adventures of their day.

"He's so cute," Jenny said. "Can we keep him?"

"Ah, I'm sure he belongs to someone," Nick objected. "A neighbor kid or something."

"But we can keep him until we find out, right?"

"Oh, you have to," Evan added, scooping up the dog from the floor for a quick rub.

"He can't be more than a year or two old," Annie said as Evan set him loose again. Sherman led the way as the beagles romped out of the kitchen, down the hall, and into the living room. "He shouldn't be outside by himself."

"Maybe he wasn't," Nick suggested. "Maybe there was damage at his house too, and he got out through a broken window or a fallen door."

"What should we do?" Jenny asked.

"Evan, why don't we take a walk around the neighborhood and see if anyone is missing their dog?" Nick said. "Jen, I want you to get

Annie off her feet. She has a nasty gash on the back of her head and a bump to go with it."

Evan looked at Annie, worried. "What happened?"

"Earthquake," she told him. "Tossed me around like a rag doll for a minute, but I'll be fine. Nick took care of it."

"You can collapse on the sofa," Jenny told her. "I'll make tea."

Ah, tea. The whole world's answer to any trouble that plagues a person. A nice cup of tea and everything is set right.

"Do you have any Diet Coke?"

"Are you joking?" Jenny replied with a chuckle. "Artificial sweetener? In my brother's house?"

Nick placed both hands on Annie's shoulders, a serious edge to his gaze. "Sit. Rest. Drink orange spice tea." Looking to Jenny, he added, "She won't make it easy on you, but give it your best shot."

Nick picked up the newcomer and Evan snapped Sherman's leash into place at the back of his collar. Watching the four of them walk out the door together amused her somehow, and Annie giggled.

Jenny brought a tray into the living room a few minutes later, and she placed it on the ottoman and poured two cups from a small ceramic teapot.

"The kitchen seems okay," she said. "A few broken glasses." Dropping a perfect cube of sugar into one of the steaming cups, she said, "I'm glad we get this chance to be alone, Annie." Annie looked up to find Jenny's sparkling eyes pressing in on her. "I want to thank you."

"Thank me? For what?"

"For introducing me to Evan," she replied, and she placed her hand against the center of her chest. "He is the most wonderful man I've ever known."

Annie took it all in, mindlessly dissolving the sugar in her tea with a very small spoon.

"I really think he could be *The One*."

Annie remembered thinking that about Evan once upon a time too.

"I can just see it so clearly," Jenny continued, and Annie couldn't help the surge of envy. The girl seemed to radiate with light as she told her, "I didn't think I would ever meet someone who would make me feel like this, Annie."

"Well, I can certainly see that the two of you are smitten."

"I know. I would never have thought I could fall in love so quickly."

Fall in love.

Annie's pulse kicked it up a notch and began to race, and the bump on the back of her head expanded and contracted with every heartbeat.

"You're in love with Evan?"

"Yes," she replied. "I'm sure of it. I know I haven't been in California long enough to call it home, but the really funny thing is that, when I'm with Evan, I just know that's where I'm supposed to be."

Annie considered asking if the emotion was reciprocal, but she realized she didn't need to ask. She'd just seen Evan's face while he held Jenny in his arms. He undoubtedly loved her too.

She thought about all the times she'd wished for that feeling that Jenny described, that contented feeling of home she'd found in Evan, and she remembered Zoey telling her once that the concept of home had nothing much to do with where you lived.

"Mateo is my home," Zoey had declared.

Annie wondered if she would ever find that person, place, or thing to fill the gaping home-shaped hole inside of her.

The pint-sized dog's thunderous, bouncing return preceded Nick, Evan, and Sherman, and he skidded to a stop at the end of the sofa.

"Murphy, come back here," Evan called from the front door.

"Murphy?" Jenny repeated, and she shot Annie a wide grin. "He has a name already."

"Murphy?" Annie tested, and the little dog cocked his head to one side. He pushed his ears forward until they appeared to be about three sizes too large for his head and caused his brow to furrow comically.

"How do you know his name is Murphy?" she asked when Nick and Evan entered the living room. "Did you find the owner?"

"No, but we found this," Nick said, holding up the remnants of a bright red dog collar. It had just the last two digits of a phone number and the letters M-U-R-P embroidered into it. "What else could it be?"

"Murp," Annie suggested, and everyone laughed.

In just that speck of an instant, Murphy disappeared. Nick walked around the corner and into the bedroom and let out a resounding laugh. Annie followed and found the pup poking his head out from beneath the bed, one sock hanging diagonally over his head and covering an ear—and another one protruding from both sides of his mouth.

"You know, I think he really could be Sherman's little brother!" she exclaimed. "I wonder if he likes lettuce."

The mere mention of the word and Sherman waddled quickly into the room, stood hopefully before them, and waited.

"Oh, sorry, bud. I didn't mean to tease you."

He seemed to think it over for a few seconds and then he circled around to face Murphy. After a moment of watching him, Sherman dove forward and snatched one end of the sock in Murphy's mouth; the two of them began growling and yanking with all their might. Finally Sherman walked away with it, Murphy still attached to the other end and dragging alongside him.

Nick watched them pass, and he smiled thoughtfully. "I think I'll place an ad in the paper," he said. "Found, lost dog named Murphy. Reward offered. Come quickly."

Chapter Eighteen

....

"I want to be alone."
Greta Garbo, *Grand Hotel,* 1932

Things had been heating up a little with Nick Benchley. Not entirely sure where it might be headed or if it had anywhere to go at all, Annie still found herself thinking about him an awful lot. Like the day before, at the grocery store, for instance. Standing in line, casually waiting her turn, Annie had no idea how much time had elapsed, only that the woman behind the register called out to her. She'd completely lost her place in real life, stuck there in Fantasyland, thinking about what it would be like to kiss Nick Benchley again.

Snap out of it!

She'd spent an entire week trying to style her bohemian, free-spirited hair without conditioner, and she'd just about reached the end of her hair follicle. In the shower, she carefully applied a blob of conditioner to her palm and distributed it freely to the ends of her hair, allowing it to inch upward slightly but nowhere near the wound at the back of her head. She had a sudden mental image of nappy little locks extending down into silky tresses, like before and after pictures, all in one shot. In the end, it didn't turn out to be quite that horrifying, but she certainly wasn't rocking her normal hair by any means.

Annie and Nick climbed into the back seat of Evan's Camry that afternoon, and Jenny sat up front with him as they all headed to the youth center fund-raiser together.

"So what's the latest on Murphy?" Annie asked.

"He's just the cutest little thing," Jenny piped up. "And he adores Nick."

"I've had an ad in the paper all week," Nick added, "but we haven't received a single call."

"I think that dog is just destined to be yours, bro."

"Yes, Jen. I'm sure it's part of the overall plan for my life."

"You never know," she sang hopefully, and Nick shook his head.

"The dog is a menace," he told Annie. "He's into everything. He's not destructive, like chewing or anything. But his nose is into every drawer, every closet—everything! And not one day has passed where he hasn't lined up all of my shoes in front of the fireplace. It's like a daily mission or something."

Annie laughed at that. She remembered when Sherman used to situate her unmentionables in front of his food bowl in the kitchen. She finally had to get a laundry hamper with a locking lid.

"He was probably out running loose because his family couldn't stand it anymore," Nick stated before grinning at Annie.

"You should see the two of them together," Jenny told them. "Nick will sack out on the couch to watch television and Murphy jumps right up next to him and falls asleep with his chin on Nick's arm. It's adorable."

"Yeah, that's me. Adorable."

"Not you. Murphy."

"So, Jenny," Annie interrupted. "How is the apartment hunting going?"

"Just awful!" she exclaimed. "I can't find a nice place anywhere near the school where I'm teaching."

"She drives thirty minutes every day," Evan said.

"I'd really like to settle in Monterey, if I can find something."

The small Spanish apartment she'd considered just after starting to work for Deke crossed Annie's mind.

"I know the area. I looked at a darling place over there, but that was months ago. I'm sure it's rented by now."

"Do you still have the owner's number?" Evan suggested. "Maybe Jenny could call him and see if he has any other buildings in the area."

"You know, I think I kept his information. I'll check for you and e-mail it this week."

"Thanks, Annie."

She could easily see Jenny living in that beautiful old place. She struck Annie to be just as charming as the building itself.

As they arrived at the community center, Nick helped Annie from the car, shielding the back of her head from the frame of the door, and offered his arm as they walked up the cracked concrete sidewalk together.

An old building sorely in need of attention, the center teemed with people, most of them African-American or Latino, some dressed in jeans and T-shirts, others in faded garments that had truly seen better days.

"There's Deke!" Jenny exclaimed, taking Evan by the hand.

Nick and Annie arrived just as Deke stood and embraced Jenny warmly.

"Hey, old man," Nick said. "Good to see you out and about."

"I thought I'd take a stab," he replied, as he moved toward

Annie for an unexpected hug. "What are you doing in this part of town, Annie?"

"I thought I'd take a stab," she said, repeating his words.

"Well, we're happy to have you. Make yourself at home."

Deke patted Evan on the back as he passed, and the five of them sat down in the third row as hundreds of others took their own seats. Nick seemed to know about every third person who came into the building, from young to old, black to white, male to female. He called them by name and knew all their stories.

The center director, an African-American man, took the podium. He told the audience about the day's festivities, including music performances and handmade crafts for sale. While a children's choir performed, Annie happened to glance down the row and noticed Evan holding Jenny's hand between both of his. She felt a bit like an interloper when she glimpsed the smiles they exchanged.

The moment the director released the crowd to enjoy the fun set up outside, Annie excused herself past Deke and Jenny, and she slipped an arm around Evan's neck to pull him close.

"What's this for?" he asked.

"Just because."

When she pulled away enough to look into his eyes, Evan smiled. "My life is changing, Annie."

"I can see that," she replied. "And I'm really happy for you."

"Honestly?"

"Honestly."

They embraced again, and he whispered into her ear. "I love her, Annie."

"I know you do. And she feels the same."

As they headed toward the door, Annie scanned the crowd for

Nick. When she located him, arm in arm with a Penélope Cruz–alike and their heads together as if sharing a very private moment, Annie's insides did a little dance before they splatted back into place. Disappointment scorched, poking her right in the heart as "Penélope" planted a tender kiss on Nick's cheek. Nick squeezed her hand affectionately.

"I'll call you tomorrow," she heard him say, as she approached.

"I'll look forward to it."

In much the same way as an obsessive-compulsive goes back again and again to make sure the stove is turned off or the door is locked, Annie's brain took to repeating certain key phrases after hearing them.

I'll call you tomorrow.... I'll look forward to it.

She heard their exchange a hundred times or more in the short ride back to Carmel that night, and after each repetition, she rationalized.

You're being ridiculous.... It's none of your business.... Things probably aren't how they looked.

None of it washed away the despair she felt when remembering the way the two of them had looked into each other's eyes.

Nick had squeezed her hand in such a familiar way. And this time the recipient *wasn't* his sister.

Nick is a very kind man, she reminded herself. And the freight train carrying that excuse derailed when it reached the one thought that had always been there but never acknowledged.

Perhaps he's just being nice to me too.

The four of them stopped for lunch, and over a spinach-and-mushroom omelet with Swiss cheese, Annie replayed encounters that had meant something to her. Each and every one was now consistently banished to the "He's just being nice" column.

In between rounds, Annie nodded politely and tossed a comment or two into the ongoing conversation, her cast-iron focus still fixed on the running tournament of "Figuring Out Nick."

Evan was due at the bistro, so they didn't linger over their good-byes when they dropped off Nick and Jenny.

"I'll see you at the office in the morning," Nick said, the break quick and clean from there.

Annie felt drained, and she couldn't even muster up polite conversation with Evan on the ride back to her gram's house. She hummed with the radio, her head pressed against the glass, occasionally thankful that Evan had been her friend long enough to know when to stay quiet.

* * * * *

"Believe me, Ty, I really dug deep on this one. And I can't, for the life of me, find anything dark and foreboding about Marques."

Tyra looked so disappointed. Annie wondered why her friend yearned for there to be some ulterior motive for a young man romancing her mother.

"I guess your mom is enough of a reason, Tyra."

She raised her dewy eyes and tried to smile at Annie, but it didn't quite reach her lips.

"She's fabulous. But…I don't know."

She'd asked for a background check on the guy, and that's what she'd been given. *Does she want me to make something up?*

"Tyra. He's clean."

This is definitely a girl from Kansas…or is it Missouri? Which one's the Show-Me State?

Tyra shrugged her shoulders and nodded. "Well, thanks for your help, Annie. I appreciate it. I really do."

As soon as the door closed, Annie Googled "show me state" and learned the answer: Missouri.

Nick left the office early that day for destinations unknown. The Penélope Cruz–alike crossed her thoughts unexpectedly, and she tried to shake her away. Thinking that Jenny might be a good source of information on the subject of Ms. Cruz, Annie would have paid her a friendly visit right then if not for the dinner she'd agreed to have with her parents.

Swayed from wisdom with the promise of marinated steaks and steamed clams.

Her mother called it *teriyaki*, but what she could do with a steak was something else entirely. Soy sauce and ginger and garlic… It made a steak melt right in a person's mouth with every single bite. Annie had tried making it herself once; it had been a bitter disaster. She'd taken to the belief since then that her mother purposely left things out of her shared recipes so that no one else could ever reproduce them. It was cruel, really. Like something she'd seen on television once, where a pusher had said he would innocently offer an addict some designer drug, knowing full well no one else could ever supply them again.

She could smell the soy sauce and ginger from outside the front door. When she opened it and stepped into the house, her taste buds started to sing and do a little happy dance.

"Nathan, it's Annabelle."

"Hi, Mom. Hi, Daddy."

"Come and kiss the cook," her dad called out to her from the patio, as he turned the steaks on the grill.

"Take a look at the silly apron your father is wearing," her mom said too loudly as Annie headed out back.

Her father stood there awaiting her comment with his hands on his hips, displaying the apron proudly. Black, with bright red letters: KISS THE COOK. He obviously thought he looked quite adorable, so much in fact that it made him right.

Annie planted an obedient kiss on his cheek and chuckled. Her father sliced off a corner of one of the steaks, stabbing it with a fork before offering it to her. Her taste buds exploded with the bite.

"Ooooh, that's so good."

"We're having steamed clams with your aunt Henri's tartar sauce," her mom tossed out the door. "Oh, and I found the most beautiful asparagus at the market today."

She really should have a cooking show. At least a once-a-week thing, à la Paula Deen.

"Come in and set the table, Annie. We're having five tonight."

Ted and Linda.

"Teddy and Linda are stopping by."

She wondered about whether to offer to host a baby shower when they arrived, and the voice in her head called her an idiot while her heart told her something else entirely.

She'd expended all that energy in mustering up forgiveness toward her little brother, and he blew it with one sentence almost immediately upon arrival.

"So, Annie. Tell me about your love life."

"Oh, yes, Annie," her mother chimed right in. "We haven't heard anything for such a long time."

"What's become of Evan?" Linda asked.

"Evan has met someone. She's the younger sister of a man I've been working with while my boss has been recovering from heart surgery."

"Nick Benchley."

It brought a chill up her spine that her mother knew his name so readily.

"Yes." She swallowed and attempted to breathe. "His sister Jenny is an elementary school teacher, and she and Evan seem to be a very good pair."

"Oh, I'm sorry, sweetheart," her mom said, doling out more asparagus. "I always kind of thought you and Evan would find your way to each other."

Get in line.

"There's no accounting for chemistry," Annie commented, as she cut her steak into tinier pieces than necessary. "And Evan and Jenny were just...meant to be."

Hearing herself say it out loud for the first time, Annie realized that she actually meant it. It left her feeling a little hollow in the spot where that old dream used to sit.

"And what about you, Annie?" Ted asked—and she couldn't discern whether he was only having a bit of fun at her expense. "Who were you meant to be with?" he continued.

"After the importance of chemistry," she replied, "is the issue of timing. I just haven't reached mine yet."

And with that, Annie wanted to go home without even pausing for banana cream pie in a perfect graham cracker crust.

* * * * *

With the date set for Deke's return to the office, Annie realized they had less than a week to go. Excited that his health had improved and everything had turned out so great for him, she also knew that with his return came Nick's departure.

She wiped up the coffee-cup stains and ran a dust rag over Deke's desk to remove the crumbs, then replaced his favorite coffee mug that she'd re-washed. When all of the pens stood straight in the pencil cup and the file folders in the metal rack fell into a neat line, Annie stood back and looked around the office in search of anything else she could do ahead of time for Deke that Nick wouldn't mess up too much before Monday.

The tidiness of Nick's home struck Annie as funny when she considered the slob he turned into at work. His jacket only made it to the hook on the back of the door about 50 percent of the time, and remnants of crumbs of several lunches gravitated to the closed laptop at any given time.

Just about the time she mused over the tornado he created every time he entered a room, the front door to the office erupted from the jamb and clunked into the wall behind it. Nick had arrived.

"What's up, Annie Gray?"

"I'm just cleaning up a little before Deke comes back to us on Monday." She folded the rag in her hand.

"Hey," Nick said offhandedly, "what ever happened with the background check for your friend?"

"Tyra? It went fine. Everything looked clean."

"Good. She must have been relieved."

"You'd think so, wouldn't you?" she replied with a shake of her head. "She seemed more hopeful that I'd find something, rather than clearing his name for her."

"Why, do you suppose?"

Annie glanced up at him as he leaned casually in the doorway, and she noticed that the light streaming in from the window behind him formed a sort of halo around him. It made her pause a bit.

"I'm sorry. What did you say?"

"I was just wondering why she was so hopeful about hearing the bad news instead of finding the good."

"I don't know."

Annie shrugged and headed into the reception office.

"How far did you go with the check?" he asked, following to her desk and leaning against the corner.

"The usual stuff. Criminal record, lawsuits, DMV."

"Did you try a similar name search?"

"What's that?"

"Come on into the office," he suggested, motioning as he headed back that way.

Annie paused to grab a bottle of water from the refrigerator first.

"What's his name?"

"Marques DeLeon. M-A-R-Q—"

"Okay," he interrupted. "Watch this."

Annie rounded the desk and stood behind him. He had some sort of national Web site on the screen, and he fed in a password for the right to access. Nick typed Marques's name into the search box, chose California from the drop-down selection, and clicked on a button marked Similar Name Search. Within seconds, several options appeared.

Marcus DeLeon

Marcus Leonard

Mark DeLeonardi

Mark Lyon

Nick began clicking on the highlighted links, one at a time, viewing the pictures associated with each name on the list.

"Have you met him?"

"No," she told him. "I just know he's African-American, about thirty-five, and works for a cruise line as a tour guide."

Nick clicked on the last entry and smiled, turning the screen toward her. "Could that be our boy?"

"Maybe."

Within the space of about five minutes, Nick generated pages of information on Mark Lyon, and his rap sheet read like a Who's Who of America's Most Wanted. He'd done three chunks of jail time for fraud, and he'd been investigated enough to warrant about twenty lines of information links.

"Do you know Tyra's e-mail address?"

Annie leaned over him and typed it into the blank e-mail box on the screen.

"Go call her. Tell her I'm sending over a photo. Have her take a look."

Spinning the phone around, Annie quickly dialed Tyra's number and then pressed the speaker button so Nick could be in on the conversation.

"Hey, girl," Tyra answered on the first ring. "What's going on?"

"Can you pick up e-mail while you're on the phone?"

"I can now. I just got broadband."

"Welcome to the universe, Ty. Check your e-mail, would you?"

"Sure. Why?"

"Nick was helping me do some final checks on your mom's admirer, and—"

"You found something! I knew it!"

"Well, we don't know. I want you to take a look at the photo and tell me if it's him."

A few seconds later, Tyra gasped. "That's him."

She mouthed the words to Nick as if he hadn't heard them. *That's him!*

"It looks like he's going under an alias, Ty. His real name is Mark Lyon. He's been in jail three times for fraud."

"What kind of fraud?"

Nick took it from there. "He's written a half dozen bad checks. Also stole someone else's checks and cleaned out their accounts for over ten grand. He's been investigated for embezzlement and racketeering. This is a very bad guy, I'm sorry to tell you."

Tyra remained silent for a very long moment before they heard the telltale *sniff-sniff-sob* that betrayed her.

"Tyra? Are you okay?"

"Yes. I knew it, Annie. I absolutely knew it. And no one would believe me. When you came up empty, I just figured—" After another moment, she continued. "Thank you so much."

"If you want something to show your mom when you talk to her," Nick said thoughtfully, "I can e-mail you something you can print out in the next few minutes."

"That would be great."

"He'll send it right away, Ty."

"Annie, you are the best."

"No, I'm not. But Nick is."

"Thank you, Nick."

"Welcome, Tyra."

Annie flicked the button on the phone and collapsed into the chair at the outside corner of the desk.

"What's wrong?" Nick asked after hitting SEND on the e-mail to Tyra.

"I feel sick to my stomach, Nick. There I was, telling my friend she had nothing to worry about and even getting a little irritated with her for not believing me. I could have really made things worse, if not for you."

"Well, Annie, I've been a cop for a lot of years."

"I know, but—"

"Don't beat yourself up, angel. You're doing a great job here. You have some things to learn, that's all. In time, you'll be cracking cases right and left."

"You really think so?"

"I do. I think you'll be a great investigator. And having Deke to show you the ropes, you're way ahead of the game. He's one of the savviest PIs around."

"You've known him a long time?"

"A few years. But more important than how long I've known him is that I know him really well. He has great intuition, which, of course, makes an exceptional investigator. You either have that or you don't. And you have it, Annie. Your instincts are good. You just need to polish them a little."

"That's a nice thing to say, Nick."

"Well, I can be nice when it's warranted."

"Apparently," she said with a grin. "Color me surprised."

"I'll color you sarcastic."

"That too. I'm a rainbow."

"You said it, angel."

This might be the warmest moment I've had with Nick.

It was a little annoying, the way the thought lit up her heart and set the butterflies to fluttering around in the pit of her stomach.

Chapter Nineteen

....

"There are four ways of doing things onboard my ship:
the right way, the wrong way, the navy way, and my way."
Humphrey Bogart, *The Caine Mutiny*, 1954

"Annie, sweetheart. It's so good to see you again."

Nick listened carefully as Annie greeted someone in the front office.

"Mrs. Armbrewster! And Mr. Armbrewster! How are you both?"

"Just dandy," came the reply.

"How was Italy?"

"Oh, it was downright beautiful," the woman replied. "I meant to bring the photographs along today, but we left the house in such a hurry that I completely forgot. I'll have to bring them by another time."

"Oh, please do," Annie told her. "What can I do for you today?"

"Is Mr. Heffley around?"

"He's been out for a while after heart surgery," she explained. "But Nick Benchley has been filling in for him, and he's here. Would you like me to see if he's available for a meeting?"

"Would you, dear?"

"Sit down and make yourselves comfortable," Annie told them. "I'll just go and see what Nick's schedule looks like today."

When she entered, Nick waved them all in.

"Mr. and Mrs. Armbrewster? Come on in and meet Nick Benchley."

When the pleasantries were exchanged and the parties seated, Mr. Armbrewster cleared his throat in a transparent announcement that said "Ready to get down to business." Nick stifled a chuckle at the remembrance that this man's wife had suspected him of infidelity.

"Your colleague, Mr. Heffley, and Miss Gray here did a wonderful job for my Marion when she came to them."

"I have no doubt," Nick returned with a smile.

"I especially liked the way Miss Gray kept my little secret. Do you know about that?"

"In fact, I do," Nick told him. "I read the case file."

"Because of that, Marion and I wanted to do something to thank them both."

You paid your bill in record time. That's all the thank-you they need!

"That's certainly not necessary," Nick said instead.

"I was going to make you some of my famous pecan tassies," Marion advised Annie. "But I think we've got something even better."

The two of them looked as if they might burst from the pressure of holding the secret. Then, almost as if they'd rehearsed it, they both started to spill the beans.

"Over at the—"

"Oh, I'm sorry," Marion said. "You tell them, dear."

"Well," he started with a smile, "we were having lunch over at the golf course where I was working when we ran into Franklin Usher."

"He's the gentleman who owns that course and about six or seven others throughout the country," Marion explained.

"Lovely man. Four grown children and eight grandchildren. He attends our church."

"He happened to mention that he's working on a special project right now, which led us to thinking about you and Mr. Heffley, Annie."

"Oh?"

"He's in the process of screening investigation agencies to find someone he can put on retainer to do background checks for his golf courses…and some of his other businesses besides."

This sounds promising.

Annie's gaze dragged toward Nick, who had a smug grin waiting.

"Every one of his courses is first-rate," he continued. "And they have restaurants and a pro shop and the like. So they have a lot of employees turning over. Every time they interview, they have to screen those applicants."

"And he has how many golf courses?" Annie asked, and Nick could see her effort to keep her enthusiasm down to a manageable, professional level.

"Eight, including the one here. And he has some other interests too. Do you think that would be something Mr. Heffley might be interested in entertaining?"

Nick let out a slight chuckle before replying. "Absolutely."

"We were hoping you would say that," Marion added.

"We told Mr. Usher all about you," her husband continued. "That you're a small agency, like what he was hoping for. You're local, which is a requirement because this is where he's headquartered."

"I appreciate your thinking of us, Mr. and Mrs. Armbrewster," Annie told them. "It's very generous of you."

"I told him I would touch base with you and just inquire about your interest." He reached into the breast pocket of his jacket and produced a linen business card, which he handed to Annie. She looked it over before passing it to Nick.

"If you could just call him at this number, he'd like to set up a meeting with you to discuss the details."

Nick eyed the business card before setting it down on the desk and reaching over it to offer his hand. "Thank you."

"You're quite welcome. We were happy to do it. You were all so kind to Marion and me."

"We'd love to have you both to tea sometime if you'd like to come," Marion offered hopefully.

"I'd love to come," Annie told her. "And I can see your Italy pictures then."

"You are such a dear," she told her, and Marion gave Annie a hug before she led the way out to the reception area.

Once they'd gone, Nick and Annie looked at one another in frozen silence for a long moment before Nick began to laugh.

"This is good, right?" she asked him.

"Yes," he stated firmly. "This is very, very good."

"Deke will be happy."

"If we can set this up, Deke will be downright ecstatic, Annie Gray. Franklin Usher is to golf courses what Donald Trump is to resorts. His courses are first class all the way. Putting this place on retainer with him will change everything for you and Deke."

Nick suddenly realized that, with Deke's return, he would be faced with the very unappealing idea of not seeing Annie every day, and that left him a little cold. When served alongside that reality, the good news, while still good, tasted a little sour.

* * * * *

Dinner with Merideth always played out like an event. Just the two of them getting together at her place for a meal equaled an elegant dinner party with five-star cuisine and decadent dessert. No casual, everyday dishes on this girl's table. Instead, Royal Albert bone china and Waterford crystal glasses graced two place settings while hand-embroidered Battenberg lace place mats and napkins adorned center-pieces of deep burgundy dripless candles atop fine silver candlesticks. Never a *get-together* when Merideth played hostess—a *happening*.

"I'm so glad you could come tonight. Frank is traveling, so it's a perfect time for a night with my girl."

Over spinach-and-mushroom salad with hot bacon dressing, they chatted about Frank's work and the background check Nick saved for Tyra. And over a gorgeous grilled-chicken entrée, the conversation took a natural swing toward the opening of a new restaurant her firm promoted. That's when Annie saw it coming before it ever left the ground.

"So Colby told me the split between you two is pretty firm."

"I don't know how a non-couple can really split up, but I'm not seeing him anymore, if that's what you mean."

"Annie, he's a wonderful guy."

"Have you dated him, Mer?" The words popped out on a tone far more hostile than she'd intended.

"No, but I work with him every day at the agency. He's just—"

"Not the man for me," she completed for her. "Maybe if you weren't married to Frank, he'd be the perfect man for you, Mer. But he's not the one for me. Can we talk about something else?"

"I just want to know why you're so unforgiving with him," she said, ignoring Annie's request. "That's not your usual way, and I want to understand."

Annie sighed and glanced at Merideth. Hair that stayed in just the right place, turquoise blue eyes that sparkled when she smiled, a tiny turned-up nose, and full lips that were always smartly outlined and stained in some wonderful shade. And cleavage. Whether she wanted it or not, Merideth rocked some girlish curves. But remarkable in every way, not just physically. Intelligent, assertive, and, at times, downright hilarious to be around.

This was not one of those times.

Annie set her fork on her plate and wiped the corner of her mouth with the beautiful cotton napkin before drawing in a slow, deliberate breath.

"He is a very forceful person, Merideth. And he doesn't show his best light when being refused something he wants."

"Well, how forceful was he?"

Their eyes met for a moment, both unwavering. Finally Merideth blinked and frowned. Could it be that she finally understood?

"Annie. He didn't hurt you, did he? Tell me the truth."

"He didn't hurt me, Mer. He scared me."

She thought it over for a moment. "Like when you were in college?" she asked. "That kind of scared?"

"Those memories were right at the surface in a heartbeat and a half," Annie told her.

"And you're sure it's about Colby and not about the past?"

"It's about both. He's not the man for me, Merideth. Can you trust me on that?"

She pondered that before shooting Annie a luminous grin. "I can do that."

"Thank you. Now let's not talk about Colby Barnes anymore, okay?"

"Okay. Who would you like to talk about now?"

"Marion Armbrewster," Annie stated firmly.

"Who?"

"I've never told you this story, but she was my first case when I started to work for Deke. Mer, she's adorable."

Annie unraveled it all for Merideth, from their first meeting to following the woman's husband, even about finding Sherman eye-deep in lettuce leaves inside a produce delivery truck at the course. And then she shared the exciting visit from the Armbrewsters the previous afternoon.

"It's really funny how things work, isn't it?" Annie commented. "I thought that lovely old couple was just nothing more than the first of many cases I would work on in my new career. And now they could be the catalyst to taking Deke's business up a notch."

"When will you know?"

"Nick is meeting with the guy tomorrow."

"I hope it's good news."

"From your lips to God's ears."

* * * * *

Waiting for Nick to return from his Friday afternoon meeting with Franklin Usher presented an exercise in patience that Annie simply didn't have. She wanted the deal so much for Deke that she could hardly stand just twiddling her thumbs in anticipation of the answer. When she finally saw the black Jeep pull into the parking lot, she couldn't even stay put until he came through the door.

Annie rushed out to the lot and leaned on the open window on the driver's side. She clutched Nick's arm. "Well?"

"Better than well."

"What! Tell me."

"He's willing to pay an obscene monthly retainer, with an additional fee per background check. There are a few stipulations, of course, but as long as Deke is agreeable to them, it's a done deal."

When he climbed from his Jeep, Nick bear-hugged Annie before closing the door behind him.

"Details," she said. "I need details."

"Well, the primary condition of getting the business is that Deke moves his office."

"Move? Why?"

"Not upscale enough, I guess," he told her, leading the way toward the office. "But the good news is, he's willing to foot the bill for the move and put the office in one of the buildings he owns."

"Do you think Deke will go for that?" Annie asked as they filed through the front door.

"I don't know. It's a leap of faith to take for a new client. But Deke will make the right decision. We're having dinner tonight at his place, and I thought I'd tell him then. Do you want to join us?"

"If I'm not intruding."

"You, Annie Gray? Intruding? Get outta here."

He grinned at her and tweaked her shoulder before disappearing into Deke's office.

Annie heard him push-dialing the phone and then heard, "Deacon, my man. I've invited Annie to dinner with us tonight so we'll have something better to look at than each other.... Yeah, I thought so too."

Deke met them on the front porch of his small brick house in worn blue jeans, tennis shoes, and a long, white gauze shirt. He looked healthy and well-rested, which was a relief to Annie.

"Welcome, welcome," he greeted them. "Perfect timing. Supper's just about finished."

They followed him through the clean and inviting house of minimal furnishings tastefully coordinated in deep blues and resonant browns. Following a path of large white stones, they made their way toward a lovely wooden pergola hanging over a small picnic table at the center of the backyard. Three enormous ham steaks sizzled on a grill off to one side.

"There's an ice chest over there with soda," he told Nick. Then he winked at Annie and added, "There's Diet Coke for you, Miss Annie."

"Bless your brand-new little heart."

"Speaking of your brand-new heart," Nick teased, "is all this meat going to be good for it? We want it to keep beating, after all."

"You worry about getting the drinks. The Lord and I will worry about whether my heart keeps beating."

"If I know you as well as I believe I do, I think it's about to start beating much faster," Nick said casually as he slid across the bench and stared off toward the horizon.

Deke looked to Annie and asked, "What has he done?"

She laughed as Nick told Deke, "You'd better sit down."

As Franklin Usher's offer unfolded, Deke remained steady, and Annie examined his face for some trace of a reaction.

"That sounds interesting," he stated once Nick had finished. "I'll set up a meeting with him first thing Monday morning."

"I took the liberty," Nick replied. "You're expected at his Pacific Grove office at eleven a.m."

Annie couldn't help but think about how strange men could be. If she'd delivered this sort of news to Zoey or Merideth, they'd be hugging, jumping up and down, and maybe even doing a silly victory dance. But Nick checked out the view while Deke tended to meat he probably shouldn't eat, and Annie decided they were missing out on a lot of fun.

Conversation flowed steadily over the delicious dinner, running from Deke's medical instructions for the immediate future to the damage at Nick's place from the earthquake to some special project Nick had been spearheading at the youth center.

"Are you going to make it on Sunday, do you think?" Nick asked, and Deke nodded.

"I'm signed up for the ring-toss booth from noon until four."

"I have someone standing by in case you're not feeling up to it."

"You kidding me? I'm looking forward to it."

"Are you holding a carnival or something?" Annie asked them.

"Festival," Nick explained. "We do it every year to raise money for the various inner-city charities associated with the center. There's even pie-eating contests and old-fashioned games."

"And some of the finest soul food you've ever tasted!" Deke added with a shake of his head. "Some of the ladies in the hood sure can cook."

"Again with the food," Nick teased. "Ham for dinner and fried chicken and greens on Sunday. Do you want to be back in for heart surgery before your meeting on Monday morning?"

"This boy sure can nag, Annie. How on earth have you been putting up with him?"

"Wait until you see the fridge at work!" she exclaimed. "My Diet Cokes have been replaced with bottled water and fruit juice."

"Oh-ho-ho-ho-ho," Deke marveled with a broad grin. "I'll bet she had your head over that one."

"At least she's listening. You could learn a thing or two."

"Oh, she's listening, huh?"

They both turned toward Annie as she guzzled down the last of the soda from the can. She shrugged and made a bank shot into the trash can at the end of the table.

Chapter Twenty
....

"We'll always have Paris."
Humphrey Bogart, *Casablanca*, 1942

The Ferris wheel and Tilt-a-Whirl could be seen from far away, the bright California sun glinting off them as they beckoned. Parking proposed a challenge, but Annie finally found a spot in the dirt lot adjacent to the center.

She fluffed her hair and straightened her camel Eugenia Kim fedora, tossed her bag over her shoulder, and took off toward the entry gate. She hadn't expected such a huge crowd, and she began to wonder if she'd be able to find Zoey and Mateo in its midst.

As she passed the carousel for the second time, she spotted Zoey beside the steel gate, waving her arms above her head.

"Hey! You made it."

"What a great festival," she said. "Are you having fun?"

"Just arrived. But it looks great."

"Mateo is over there playing the ring toss. Want to come?"

"Absolutely."

Just about the time they reached his side, Evan and Jenny were there too, and Jenny gave Annie a warm embrace. "Have you seen Nicky?"

"No. Do you know where he is?"

"He and Deke are running the pie-eating contest in about fifteen minutes."

"Pie eating! Can we go watch?" Zoey exclaimed—and suddenly the group of them was on the move.

Remembering that she'd meant to ask Jenny about Murphy, Annie turned back but stopped in her tracks at the way she and Evan walked along, lost in one another.

Zoey linked arms with Annie and patted her own heart. "Evan's in love."

"He sure is."

At the contest site, Deke greeted Annie with a hug, and she told him, "These are my friends, Zoey and Mateo."

"Enjoying yourselves?" he asked them, and their enthusiasm lit him up. "Excellent! That's just excellent."

"Nick around?" Annie asked.

"Right there." Deke pointed him out at the contest table; several custard pies were stacked in his arms.

When Nick saw Annie, he nodded and grinned then pretended to prepare to eat the pies himself. Once the contestants found their seats and Deke got things underway, Nick ambled to Annie's side and tugged on the brim of her hat.

"Good to see you. I'm glad you came."

"It's a spectacular festival," she told him. "I'm very impressed."

Nick faced Annie, holding both of her arms gently. "Listen, Annie, I wanted to talk to you about something, and I thought—"

"Nick!"

Interrupted by the Penélope Cruz–alike Annie had seen with Nick when she attended the fund-raiser at the center, Annie watched the woman dart toward them and toss her arms around his neck.

"How did it go?" he asked her.

"It was fun. You were right; I enjoyed it."

"Lisette, this is Annie."

"Oh, you're Annie?" she asked. "It's so great to meet you."

"You too."

"Nick is an angel, isn't he?" she asked.

Annie spontaneously expelled a burst of a chuckle. "An angel? Well, I don't know about that."

"Oh, take my word for it, he is. He's helped my kid brother more than I can tell you. In fact, this man has single-handedly turned Jose's life around."

"Jose has turned his own life around," Nick corrected. "I just helped to show him the way."

"Well, you're a very lucky girl to have someone like Nick interested in you," she said—and Annie's heart began to pound out a rhythm in double time. "I'll see you both later. I'm off to help at the Ferris wheel."

As she ran off, Nick raked his hair with both hands and looked at Annie.

"Am I?" she asked him.

"Are you what?"

"The girl you're interested in."

He puffed out a breath and shook his head. "You don't know that by now?"

I hoped.

"Look. I feel like it's time I throw my hat into the ring. Put my cards on the table."

"Fish or cut bait?" she teased.

"A stitch in time saves nine."

"Waste not, want not," she added, and they both started to laugh.

Nick placed his arms around Annie and pulled her toward him with a sigh. "You are a very special girl, Annie Gray."

He briefly glanced down at the ground between them and then raised his eyes provocatively.

"Annie, you've got to see this!" Zoey rushed toward the two of them and grabbed Annie by the wrist. "Hey, Nick. Annie, Mateo is going to eat pie. You have to come watch!"

Annie looked at Nick. He gave her a weak smile and nodded.

"Go ahead."

* * * * *

Dog-clock told Annie that midnight had just passed, and she asked herself why she sat on the kitchen counter, swinging her legs and watching Sherman sleep underneath the table at this time of night.

She never did find Nick again before she left the festival, never heard what more he had to say, and her imagination pulsated with possibilities. It had sounded like he might declare his intentions... issue an invitation. Maybe a date? Love? More?

The unquestionable chemistry between Annie and Nick could not be denied. But what else did they have? They both appreciated Lakers basketball and classic film. And they had their work.

But he'll be returning to the force now that Deke is coming back.

She wondered. Would the relationship grow, or even manage to be sustained, without the daily contact?

Annie racked her brain, reaching in every possible direction for something to add to the list of things that might hold them together.

"Is Nick Benchley *The One*?" she asked out loud, hoping someone might hear her and answer.

She listened intently. Aside from the thunderous pounding of her own heart—silence. And of course the ticking of Dog-clock on the wall as he swung his paws and smiled at her.

"Am I going to die alone, then?" she asked the thing.

Still nothing more than a creepy little dog smile.

After that, morning came much too quickly, and Annie's heart still raced a bit as she woke up feeling as if she hadn't yet slept at all. As she brushed her teeth, she remembered that Deke would be meeting with Franklin Usher, and she hoped Nick might utilize the free morning to finish the discussion he'd tried to initiate at the festival.

Instead, though, he'd left a voice mail message at the office saying that he wouldn't be in until noon. Disappointed, Annie filled the time by finishing up the overflow of filing from the previous week.

When the door popped open at 11:13 a.m., she expected to see Nick entering with his usual flair. However, when she looked up from the filing cabinet, she met a different scenario entirely.

"You Annie Gray?"

She nodded at the young African-American man standing before her, who looked a lot like a bull getting ready to snort at any moment.

"You the one who told Tyra's mom about me?"

Marques DeLeon.

"I did an investigation into your background, but—"

"That's an invasion of my privacy!" he exclaimed, and he picked up the stapler from her desk and held it over her head.

Annie's heart lurched, and her mouth went completely dry.

"You had no right!"

"Look, Mr. DeLeon, it's nothing personal. We're an investigation agency, and a client came to us requesting—"

"Requesting private information about me, and you gave it to them, didn't you?" He followed with an insulting expletive just before he drew back the stapler and—

"Wait—"

Wham!

He...hit...me? Annie decided that seeing stars wasn't just something "they say"—because she saw a million of them. Just before they stopped shimmering and faded to black.

* * * * *

"Annie?"

Her head throbbed, and she wondered why her right eye didn't open. Her left one began to focus, and she saw Nick standing over her, looking more worried than she might have thought he knew how to be. A gray box with green-and-white lights behind him blinked *Hospital* into the path of her thoughts, and she looked down at the IV taped to the top of her hand.

"Can you see me, angel?"

It came back to her in a rush. *Marques DeLeon. Mark Lyon.* "He hit me. With my stapler," she told him.

Nick grinned. "Yes, I know."

"Wh–why did he do that?"

"Because he was angry."

"Better call Tyra and make sure she's all right."

"She's just outside," Nick told her. "Lyon is in jail. And if you can believe the gall, he called Tyra's mother to come bail him out. Which, of course, she did not."

"They caught him already?"

"I pulled up outside and caught him trashing the office, with you on the floor behind your desk."

"You're the one who got him, Nick?"

"Yep. I got him."

Annie thought that over and let it process for a long moment. "Thank you."

"You're welcome."

"You're always saving me."

"Only when you really need it."

"What's wrong with my eye?"

"It's swollen shut, and you've got some kind of shiner there. But aside from a nasty headache for a day or two, you'll be fine."

"Why is it always my head?" she asked.

Nick squeezed her hand and smiled. "Better your hard head than something softer."

Tyra floated into the room, wafting on apologies that started before she even hit the door. The high pitch of her voice nearly reduced Annie to tears, and the instant she raised her hand to her temple, Nick stepped in as if he could read her mind.

"She's a little fragile right now, Tyra. Why don't we just let her get some rest?"

"Oh. All right," she surrendered. "But, girl, I am so sorry."

"Nobody blames you," Nick reassured her. "Let me walk you out."

"Annie? You call me, okay?"

"I will."

When Nick returned, he inched up next to Annie on the hospital bed and placed his arms around her. It felt so good to sink into him and just let him hold her. She closed her eyes and listened to his heartbeat thump against her ear.

"What about Deke's meeting with—"

Nick shushed her softly, caressing her hair and holding her close. "Shhh."

"Did they strike a deal?"

"Annie. They struck a deal. And you'll know all the details soon enough. Just relax and let the pain medication work, angel."

"What about Sherman?"

"What about him?"

"Gram left for Los Angeles this morning."

"I'll take him to my house."

"Did you call Zoey?"

"I left her a message with my cell number and asked her to call me back."

"And there's—"

"There's nothing else, Annie. There's just you and me, and peace and quiet. Just be quiet, angel, and give in to the sleep. It's good for you."

Annie took a deep breath, and as she released it, she felt her entire body begin to relax. Her ears tingled, and her skin felt as if it vibrated.

"Nick?"

"Annie. Go to sleep."

"But, Nick, just this one more thing."

"Okay. One more thing. What is it?"

Chapter Twenty-One

....

"That tears it."

Fred MacMurray, *Double Indemnity*, 1944

Returning home from the hospital turned out to be a community event. Zoey and Evan made food, and Evan propped a large card on the kitchen table with get-well wishes written inside. Deke and Jenny filled the living room and kitchen with bouquets of helium balloons, and Jenny sent word that she would be stopping by later in the day. Tyra baked a cake, and Merideth decorated it.

And Nick? Well, he stocked the refrigerator with bottled water, fruit juice, and, miraculously, a few cans of Diet Coke.

Sherman could hardly contain himself when he saw Annie, and he nearly knocked himself over with his own wagging tail when Nick brought him through the front door. Murphy trotted close behind, and Annie noted that the little thing had grown since she'd seen him last.

"Hey, buddy!" She smiled at Sherman, and he took a flying leap at the couch and landed on Annie with a *thump*. Murphy quickly followed, and the two of them began arguing over which of them would get to greet Annie first.

"All right, enough," Nick told them, and he picked Murphy up, took him to the wingback chair, and sat down. "Let Sherman welcome her home first."

Murphy whined before reluctantly settling in next to him while Sherman panted at Annie's face, not the graceful victor.

"You look awful," Merideth stated. "What do you need?"

"I already know what she needs," Zoey announced, a tall glass of soda over ice in her hand.

"Whaddya know? She really did know what I needed."

"No, she didn't," Nick interjected with a laugh.

"I feel just terrible about what happened," Tyra told her, sitting down on the other end of the couch.

"I keep telling her it wasn't her fault," Deke said. "But she just wants to own it."

"Come on, Ty," Annie told her. "You know better."

"I just wish I hadn't brought him into your life."

"It's a black eye," she replied. "I'm not blind. I didn't need surgery. He thumped me with my own stapler. I'll live."

"This girl has all kinds of guardian angels watching over her," Zoey told them. "You wouldn't believe the kind of messes they get her out of."

They laughed, and Tyra joined in at the last. Annie reached over and squeezed her hand to reassure her.

"How about some cake for everyone?" Tyra suggested.

"I'll help you," Zoey said.

"Me too." And Merideth followed them to the kitchen.

"So, Deke. Tell me about your meeting with Franklin Usher on Monday. Nick hasn't spilled a single bean, and I'm ready to burst with curiosity. Are we movin' on up?"

"We are indeed."

Annie found herself growing weary once the cake had been served and conversation began to wane. When she made a move to get up, one might have thought she'd started a project like painting a room or building an addition.

"I'm just going to the kitchen," she told them. "I can still walk."

Various shapes and colors of plasticware filled an entire shelf in the refrigerator, and Zoey explained as Annie inspected them.

"The red ones are single servings of vegetable lasagna, and the blue is chicken orzo with spinach, mushrooms, and snap peas. There's salad in the big bowl, and Evan's rice pudding is in the yellow container in the back. It's fantastic, by the way."

"Good grief. Did someone die?"

"You know me. This is just what I do."

"Thank you, Zo."

"You're welcome. Just don't go getting yourself all banged up anymore. You scared me to death."

"I'll do my best."

Annie tried to smile at her, but only half of her face complied. Zoey cringed.

"You look like a raccoon."

"Better than a skunk."

"Not by much."

"Well, thank you."

"Anytime."

Sherman waddled into the kitchen, Murphy impatient at his tail, and they both plopped down beneath the table and leaned into one another.

"How cute are they!" Zoey commented.

"I know."

As she sat down at the table, Annie happened to notice her five-point plan that used to hang on the door of the refrigerator now standing against the lazy Susan on the tabletop.

"What's this doing here?"

"What is it?" Zoey asked.

"My plan for change."

"Dunno. I thought it was on the fridge."

"Me too."

Annie pushed out of the chair and swept the paper with her. She replaced it on the fridge with the Christmas magnet then stood before it and read it over.

ANNIE'S FIVE-POINT PLAN FOR CHANGE

1. Get a really cool job. Something fun and exciting!

2. Get some great hair.

3. Move back to Monterey.

4. Work on smiling more to attract racecar drivers or international spies. (Get teeth whitened!)

5. A new car. Something sporty. Maybe a convertible?

It occurred to her that the only thing on the list she'd managed to accomplish was point number one. She did have a very cool job.

Her hair—just the same as on the night she wrote the list. And the days of a Monterey mailing address were now far behind her.

I do smile more, she thought. *And my teeth are pretty white, despite the fact that no racecar drivers or spies have shown any interest in dating me.*

Her car could use a tune-up, but the hope still twinkled on the horizon that she might go out and buy a convertible at a moment's notice, especially now that they would be working for Franklin Usher.

"Still thinking you want to be a character in a classic film?" Zoey asked from beside her.

"Doesn't everyone?"

"No."

She turned and looked at her, and Zoey smiled. "You are an exceptional *you*. Ask anyone in that room."

Zoey combed Annie's hair with her fingers and smoothed it down lovingly. "Well, maybe on this particular day you could use some better hair."

They shared a laugh and a hug, and Annie found herself feeling immense gratitude for her current life, the one without a convertible or a racecar-driver boyfriend.

* * * * *

Everyone had gone, and it was just Sherman and Annie as she heated up one of the plastic boxes of lasagna.

There's nothing like Zoey's lasagna.

Yellow squash, zucchini, mushrooms, broccoli. Just the smell of it nearly enticed Annie to eat it cold, but she decided to hold out for the microwave to do its stuff.

She removed some salad from the big bowl and drizzled Italian dressing on it before setting it on the table. As the microwave dinged, Sherman rushed to the living room for the hundredth time since Nick had taken Murphy home. Once again, he took a flying leap at the window seat and leaned forward to peer outside. No sign of Murphy, but he seemed determined to keep on watching.

He made the trip three more times while Annie ate her dinner.

At least he's getting some exercise.

When she headed upstairs to her bedroom, Sherman didn't

follow. He just remained in the window, keeping vigil and hoping for the return of his new best friend.

"Sherman," Annie called down to him, and she patted the mattress firmly. "Come on, buddy."

His reply: the most mournful howl Annie had ever heard out of him.

This is going to be a very long night.

Deciding that a walk might do them both some good, Annie pulled on a pair of sweatpants and an oversized T-shirt. When the shoes came out of the closet and Annie returned downstairs, Sherman revived and excitedly dashed out in search of his leash.

His short-lived enthusiasm melted to disappointment when realization dawned: *A walk. Not a ride in the car.*

He pulled and struggled until he got Annie to follow his lead toward Taurie, and he stood next to the back door of the car in expectation.

"Nothing doing," she told him. "Forget it."

He shifted from his right paw to his left and back again, still looking confidently at the car door.

"Are you kidding me with this, Sherman?"

One more shift, and another hopeful glance.

"No, Sherman. We're going inside. Come on."

She had to really pull to get him to go along, and he took the three stairs at the back door as if marching to his own execution.

"Sherman, be a good boy," she suggested to him, and his tail wagged just one time. A noble effort, at least.

There were two more howling sessions at the window overnight, but by morning Sherman seemed to have come to terms with the fact that life had rolled back in time.

It felt strange to stay home from work, and by ten thirty Annie felt restless. She even considered visiting her parents but thought better of it when she remembered the huge black eye she sported. Not something she wanted to share with her mother.

She watched some television and flipped through one of the magazines Zoey had left, eventually finding her way to the computer to check e-mail.

An e-greeting from Evan wished her a speedy recovery, as did one from Merideth, and a few items of spam invited deletion. Then she spotted the e-mail from Ted and Linda. Just your basic update on the pregnancy, but it lit a fire under her that she deemed long overdue.

Annie dialed their number and propped her feet on the desk while she waited for an answer.

"Linda? It's Annie."

"Hey, what are you doing home in the middle of the day?"

"Playing hooky," she told her. "Listen, I was wondering if anyone has made any plans for a baby shower."

"Not yet, that I know of."

"Good. Because I'd really like to give you one."

A long moment of silence preceded her reply. "You would?"

"Yes. I thought we could have it here at Gram's. But if you'd rather have it at your house or your favorite restaurant, we can do that too."

"Annie, are you serious?"

"Of course I am."

"I'm so…touched. Thank you."

"So do you have time to talk about it right now?" Annie asked her. "I thought I could get some idea of what you'd like."

"Well, yes. I have time."

"Great. So what do you think about location? Gram's house is good. Or I was thinking we could have it at this great little place in the village. It's called the Tuck Box—a real English tearoom."

"Oh, Annie, I've been there. It's lovely, like a little fairy-tale cottage. And their scones are the size of your fist! I love that idea."

"Great. I'll call them today. What about the date? We don't want to wait too long so you can still be comfortable and enjoy it. Of course, it will depend on availability, but how about the last Saturday of next month?"

"Okay."

"Will you make up a list of names and addresses?"

"I can e-mail it to you tomorrow."

"Awesome, Linda. This is going to be so much fun." And what a nice surprise it was that she meant it.

"Annie, thank you so much."

"You're family," she reminded her. "I want to do this for you and Ted."

"I just don't know what to say. It's very unexpected."

"Oh, and are you registered anywhere yet?"

"Babies R Us. I just finished it last night."

"Great! I'll look up the link and add it to the invitations, then."

"Seriously. I don't know what to say."

"Just say…'Yay! We're having a baby shower!'"

"Yay," Linda replied. "We're having a baby shower."

"Good."

As Annie surfed the Net for invitation ideas, she made the call to the Tuck Box to nail down the date and talk about the menu. After a few minutes, she gave the woman her credit card number for the deposit on the room as she opened a Notepad file on her screen and typed in the tearoom's Web address. Completely energized, and surprisingly excited about the whole idea, Annie's heart felt lighter. She should have done this weeks ago.

Sherman chose that moment to resume his half-howl-half-bark routine at the back door. Annie opened her mouth to reprimand him when someone knocked.

Evan peered at her through the window as she approached, and he waved.

"You look awful!" he said as soon as she opened the door. "Does it hurt?"

"Not too much. Come on in."

He held up a white bag and smiled. "I brought coffee."

Evan loved coffee, even considered himself a sort of coffee gourmet, and he continued to bring it over to Annie as if she might appreciate it as much as he did. But Annie's taste buds craved something cold and bubbly rather than bitter and hot.

"It's French vanilla."

Well, that might help.

He greeted Sherman, and they sat down at the kitchen table while he creamed and sweetened the coffee.

"So tell me how you're feeling."

"Honestly, I'm fine. I could have worked today."

"So I hope you're getting some rest while you can."

"Well, I tried. But I ended up planning a baby shower instead."

"You're joking. For Ted and Linda?"

Annie shrugged. "It seems like the right thing to do."

He regarded her seriously overtop his round wire glasses, and he grinned at her. "I'm proud of you, Annie."

"Thanks."

"I hope you won't get sick of planning showers, though."

"I won't. It's just the one."

"Well, I'm sure you'll want to get involved in arranging one for Jenny, too."

She considered his words then gasped. "Evan, what have you—"

"Oh! No!" he exclaimed. "Not a baby shower. A wedding shower."

"Oh," she sighed. Then the weight of his words fell on her. "Evan. Really?"

He nodded, beaming. "I asked her last night, and she said yes."

"Isn't it…a little soon, Ev? Are you sure?"

"We're both sure, Annie."

She fell speechless, and Evan peered at her in expectation, waiting for her to say…something. Then he broke the silence.

"I love her, Annie. And I think it was Ben Franklin who said—"

She smacked his arm and shook her head as she rose from her chair. Putting her arms around Evan's neck, Annie gave him a firm kiss on the cheek.

"Then I'm happy for you, Evan. You deserve this."

Chapter Twenty-Two
....

"Why, you speak treason!"
"Fluently."
Olivia deHavilland / Errol Flynn,
The Adventures of Robin Hood, 1938

Evan is getting married.

"I'm happy for you," Annie had told him. And at the moment that she said it, she almost thought she might mean it. But now, a few hours later, without the influence of his beaming, dopey face to reason with her...

Evan. Is. Getting. Married.

The announcement prompted a tailspin of photo-viewing, chocolate-craving, pizza-needing nostalgia. She'd only just come to terms with the burgeoning relationship between Jenny and Evan; now there was an impending marriage to reconcile?

If she had to be honest about it, despite the fact that this was no time for it, she did spend a few afternoons once upon a time dreaming about the wedding dress she would seek out once Evan finally asked her to marry him. If only in the first years of knowing him, Annie guessed she always just assumed he would eventually ask.

Evan didn't fit the mold of the future husband Annie had constructed, and in the beginning the very thought of them together seemed almost absurd. But as time wore on and she came to see the man he was inside, the attraction became gradually more intense. His best qualities just gravitated to the forefront, and the others simply drifted into a sort of blender-variety background that no longer seemed so important.

So before she even knew what had happened, Annie felt certain she had fallen in love with Evan, or was pretty close to it anyway. She'd often wondered if her feelings had initiated the demise of their coupledom. Perhaps he'd looked into her eyes one day and recognized her absolute surrender, jet-propelling him to go a little nutty about it. Fear of commitment burst from the waters like that shark in *Jaws*, and the dumb thing had quickly gnawed away at any possibility they ever might have had of moving forward. Annie had always just assumed it was Evan's problem. *Can't commit, period. Write him off for womankind.*

She'd begun suspecting it as Jenny and Evan grew closer, but now she knew the truth for certain, and she'd found it in a most unexpected place: at the bottom of the third miniature Snickers she'd consumed over the last hour. Try as she might, Annie couldn't deny it. She and Evan had never been able to get on track because his train belonged somewhere else.

A rap at the back door drew her attention. Nick peered at her through the window.

Annie gazed at her surroundings: the kitchen tabletop obliterated by Snickers wrappers and the full contents of her Evan box. A messy ponytail, wrinkled sweats, and Diet Coke dribbled down the front of her T-shirt created a total package; but the swollen black-blue eye smeared with remnants of salty, just-rejected tears put the cherry on the top of her humiliation.

"Hang on a minute," she called to him, knowing full well that he watched her gather up the hodgepodge and stuff it into the flowered hatbox where it belonged before she opened the door. "Be right there."

Nick turned the knob and poked his head inside before she completed her task. "No need to clean up," he said. "I'm just checking on you."

Sherman didn't bother to bark; he just waddled over to Nick and nuzzled a greeting against his leg with his nose.

"Hey, Sherm."

"I'm just hiding the wreckage," Annie told him, scurrying to toss the last of the photos and cards back into the box. "This is what happens when you make me stay home from work. I create messes."

"Well, what's *supposed* to be happening is some rest-and-recovery action."

He slid several photos toward her across the tabletop then picked up one of them to take a look. Evan, Sherman, and Annie in front of the Christmas tree, dated on the back.

"I guess you've heard the news," he speculated.

"News?"

"Evan and Jenny."

"Oh, that. Yes. It's…wonderful, isn't it?"

Nick didn't reply, but the lock of their eyes said what he didn't.

The doorbell rang, and Sherman woofed a couple of sharp barks without bothering to check it out.

"Are you expecting someone?" Nick asked.

"Pizza," she replied, embarrassed.

"With all that food Zoey and Evan loaded into your refrigerator?"

"Some days just call for pizza."

He grinned and reached for his wallet. "I'll get it."

While he paid the delivery guy with Sherman at his heel, Annie picked out the Snickers wrappers from inside the Evan box and pushed down the lid, sliding the box to the seat of one of the kitchen chairs.

"Is this lunch or dinner?" he asked before placing the pizza box on the table and glancing at Dog-clock for confirmation. A three o'clock pizza delivery.

"I'm not sure. Dinner, I think."

He produced two bottles of water from the refrigerator and grabbed the roll of paper towels, bringing everything to the table. He tore off a couple of paper towels from the roll.

"Mind if I join you?"

"It's your nickel."

They faced each other awkwardly, both of them eating their slices in complete silence. When he finished it, Nick wiped his mouth with the paper towel and tossed it to the table.

"I think I'll hit the road, Annie," he declared.

"After one slice?"

"Not really hungry. Is there anything you need?"

Annie looked up at him, fully intending to tell him that things were just peachy, doing fine, nothing to worry about. Instead, however, tears spouted from her eyes like a dam that had suddenly burst. Some traitorous thumb had been yanked from a dike somewhere, and there didn't appear to be any way to stop the flood that followed.

He leaned back in his chair for a moment, regarding her thoughtfully but saying nothing. Finally Nick sighed, stood up, and scuffed his chair next to her and sat down.

"Do you want to talk about it?"

"Not at all."

"Okay, then."

And with that, he placed an arm around Annie's shoulder, pulled her toward him, and let her cry for a few minutes. Unrolling another paper towel, he tore it off and handed it to her. Annie wiped her face and blew her nose.

"Doesn't it get a little old for you, Annie Gray?"

"What?"

"This bumpy road of lamenting the loss of a relationship that never came to fruition?"

She groaned. "I don't know why it's hitting me like this," she told him. "It's ridiculous. Evan and I have been over for...*ever.*"

"Are you sure?"

"Yes."

"All evidence to the contrary."

"Well, I know. But it's true. And Jenny is such a great girl, Nick. I mean it. I really like her, and she's perfect for Evan."

"And yet here you are, crying over him."

"Not over him," she admitted, almost on a whisper.

"Over what, then?"

I wish I knew.

"Fear?" she suggested, not sure at all.

"Of?"

"Of never being loved, maybe. Of never having anyone look at me the way Evan looks at Jenny. Of never truly knowing what that feels like."

Nick's silence provoked Annie's mind to wander around like a pinball, bouncing from one thought to another until she forgot what was last said.

"You know what your problem is, don't you?"

No, but it sounds like you do.

He stood up and crossed to the refrigerator, pulling off her five-point plan and waving it at her. "This is your problem."

"Hey!" she exclaimed.

"You're spending your whole life trying to build a life you saw in a movie."

"Put it back. That's none of your business."

"Maybe not, but I'm not blind, Annie. I can see the forest for the trees, even if you can't. If Evan hadn't met and fallen in love with Jenny, do you think you'd be sitting in your kitchen crying over him? Would you even give him another thought beyond what movie you're going to see together on Friday night?"

Annie looked up at him with wide-open, tear-filled eyes.

"No. You wouldn't. He's been your excuse to avoid something real for so long that now—"

"Stop it, Nick."

He tossed the paper to the tabletop and stared at it for several beats. "I'll stop, Annie. I'll be glad to stop. But just hear this one thing. Life does not have to be huge and over-the-top to be fulfilling. Every day doesn't have to be out-of-the-ordinary spectacular to be inspiring."

Annie thought of Gram and the Scripture verse about the gentle whisper of God. A pattern seemed to be forming.

"There is a—a *joy* in sharing simple things with someone special, in finding your own way and following the path that was laid out for you. There is a joy in the journey that you are totally missing. That list won't—" He paused, and Annie looked up at him. "Oh, forget it."

And with that, Nick walked out the back door and closed it behind him.

Sherman stood there looking at it, as if wondering if it would open again. Then, with an irritated glance at Annie over his shoulder, he plunked down to the floor to take a nap.

She wondered if he might have taken note of the fact that she always seemed to drive men away.

Looks like it's getting a little old for Sherman too.

* * * * *

"Nicky, it's beautiful!"

"I can't believe it's taken me so long to bring you out to see it."

Nick leaned against the lookout railing as Jenny snapped a few pictures to send to Tess. The Lone Cypress tree had been perched out upon that bluff for more than two centuries, now supported from plummeting into the Pacific Ocean by a sturdy line of cable.

Before Nick made the move to Carmel, he'd been a tourist to the area like everyone else, and 17-Mile Drive was just another bullet point on the list of sights worth seeing. It started in Pacific Grove at Esplanade, and for a small fee, excursionists could rubberneck past manicured lawns, mansions, and pristine golf courses, most notably the pinnacle: world-renowned Pebble Beach golf course.

The seventeen-mile trek could take anywhere from twenty minutes to a couple of hours, depending on the number of stops made at the various turnouts. Nick hadn't planned to make any stops at all that first afternoon until he felt the call of the Lone Cypress tree, and standing there above it he'd made the decision to leave Chicago behind and accept the job offer from the Monterey Police Department. That cypress had been calling his name ever since.

"Do you think Aunt Tess will be able to make the trip for my wedding?" Jenny asked him, still snapping digital photos of the scenery. "It wouldn't be the same without her."

"I can't imagine her missing it," Nick commented.

"I can hardly wait to introduce her to Evan. Aren't you excited for her to meet Annie? You two are becoming quite a couple, aren't you?"

Nick smiled. "I wouldn't call us much of a couple, Jen."

"No?"

He shook his head. "No."

"Well, what are you going to do about that?"

Nick turned toward Jenny and lowered his sunglasses to the bridge of his nose. "It takes two to tango, and Annie doesn't appear to have much interest in finishing the dance with me."

"Don't be ridiculous," she replied, letting her camera flop to the end of the strap around her neck. "She's crazy about you."

"Annie's very complicated."

"And you're not?"

Nick chuckled. "She's got issues."

"This, from the Issue King."

Shaking his head, he turned back toward his friend the cypress and wondered why it hadn't been until that very moment that he realized the reasoning behind his connection with the *solitude* of that tree.

"If you want Annie, Nicky, go get her."

He nodded dismissively.

"I'm not kidding. Get off your big tush and do something."

Nick pushed his sunglasses back into place and turned around. "Let's just see how it plays out, kiddo. Are you ready to head back?"

* * * * *

Annie couldn't bear the thought of another day at home, alone with her thoughts, and returning to work seemed like the perfect solution. Several new cases awaited processing, arrangements for the move needed to be made, there were files to box up, and (best of all!) not much time for self-analysis or pity parties.

Deke informed her that Nick would no longer come to the office. He'd report back to his duties as a police officer before the end of the week. His curtness on the subject told Annie that they had talked, adding to her humiliation. She chose to give that reality the cold shoulder, though. Ignoring everything about her own life outside of work, at least for that one day, would act like the makeup she'd applied over her black eye. Still there, but hopefully not as noticeable.

Deke and Annie ordered sandwiches from the deli around the corner, and they shared them at his desk at noon while discussing the details of the upcoming move.

"We'll want to be sure to keep the files separate as we pack them," he pointed out. "Closed cases; those in progress; and consults. That way getting settled in the new place will move quickly."

"Have you seen the office yet?" she asked him, taking a bite of her turkey sub.

"Offices," he corrected. "Plural. It's four rooms."

"Oooh," she nodded. "We'll actually have space for a conference room. I'll need to start dressing up every day. Maybe you should wear a tie."

"The day that happens…" He trailed off with a laugh. "Listen, Annie, I want to talk to you about your future plans."

Her heart thumped. "What do you mean?"

"I'd like to see about getting you licensed."

She considered his words. "Really?"

"Assuming that's something that still interests you."

"Yes!" she exclaimed. "Very much, Deke."

"Good. There are a couple of ways to go about it. The state requires three years or six thousand hours of compensated experience before you can apply—unless you acquire a degree in either criminal law or criminal justice, which can be subbed for a portion of your time in the field. Now, I'd be willing to pay for your schooling in order to speed up the process, if you think you'd like to go that route."

"Yes!"

"Then do some research today. Find out which school you want, and if you have to attend in person or can do online course work. You let me know what works best for you, and we'll sort that out."

"Deke, thank you."

"You've really proven yourself in these months, Annie. I'll tell you the truth; when I hired you, I figured you would just be a passable receptionist who might be able to fill in with some grunt work now and then. But you've got a future in the business, Annie. Nick says you were indispensable to him while he kept things going for me. He says you've got what it takes, and I agree with him."

"I'm glad to know he said that," she admitted. "I won't let either of you down."

"I know you won't," he told her. "And with your taking classes and gearing up for licensing, we'll want to hire someone for the front-office stuff. You can't be spending your time filing and answering the phones too, and I'd like to have someone in place by the time we move into the new offices."

"I'll place an ad."

"Well," he said, pausing for a moment, "actually, I have someone in mind."

"Really? Who?"

"Your friend Tyra."

Annie looked at him curiously. She almost thought he might be blushing beneath that dark skin of his.

"I had the chance to get to know her a little when you were in the hospital, and I was thinking she has a very nice presence. She'd be very good in the front office."

"I think so too," she told him, grinning. The idea of helping Tyra out of the Equity Now tangle of headsets set Annie's smile muscles to quivering.

"She has those two little ones to think about, so we can offer her something a little more substantial than what she's making over at that place where you used to work."

"That would be awesome! Tyra will be excellent for what you have in mind."

"I'll leave all of that to you," he said with a wave of his hand. "You call her and make the offer. Take care of training her. Make sure she feels right at home."

"Are you sure? I thought maybe you'd like an excuse to call her yourself."

Deke narrowed his eyes and stared her down. Then, with a shrug, he shook his head. "Nah. You take care of it. I have too many other fish to fry."

"Okay. I'll call her after her shift this afternoon."

"Good."

"Great."

He finished up his sandwich and tossed the remnants into the trash. Out of nowhere, he looked up at Annie and asked, "Now what are we going to do about you and Bench?"

"What about us?"

"You're on the outs. And there's no need for it. You need to nip it in the bud before it gets out of hand."

Nick never struck Annie as a big communicator, but at that moment she realized he'd apparently been *sharing* with Deke.

"You told him you love him, didn't you? So act like it. This reaction to Evan and Jenny is natural, but it doesn't mean anything to—"

"I'm sorry," she interrupted. "What? I told him *what*?"

"That you love him."

"Who?"

"Bench."

"No, I didn't."

"Sure you did."

"I didn't. When?"

"At the hospital."

"I told him no such thing."

"Annie, you told him you love him. That's not something you toss around lightly with a guy like Nick."

"I agree, and I wouldn't. Toss it around lightly, I mean. I didn't tell him that, Deke."

"Well, he says you did."

"Why would he say something like that?"

"You'd better ask him."

"Are you sure you didn't misunderstand, Deke? He told you that I said I was *in love with him*?"

"Yep."

"He's the one who's interested in me. Penélope Cruz told me so."

"Penélope Cr— Oh, never mind. You said you love him. Bench told me."

"Well, he lied."

"Not likely."

"Then I'm lying?" she challenged.

"Not likely either."

"What, then? Somebody has amnesia?"

Deke shrugged, and he drained the last of his drink before tossing the paper cup into the trash. "Better talk to him, don't you think?"

Talk to him? Where does a girl start a conversation like that one?

"Now, you've got lots to do this afternoon. Skedaddle."

Annie wished she could skedaddle all the way to Montana just then.

Nick said I told him I'm in love with him??

There had to be some mistake.

Chapter Twenty-Three
....

"What we've got here
is a failure to communicate."
Strother Martin, *Cool Hand Luke,* 1967

Tyra took the job offer with full-on celebration. Annie recognized the relief and joy in her declaration about presenting her resignation the very next morning. Tyra had been one of the longtimers whose number hadn't come up with the layoffs. But wouldn't Jasmine be surprised when another Equity Now employee hit the road, this time by choice and for greener pastures? It did Annie's heart good to be the one who blazed that trail for Tyra.

After their conversation, she called Nick to see about getting together for a discussion. It had been several hours since Deke broke the news, but Annie's brain still buzzed with it. Nick Benchley thought she loved him! And better yet, he thought she had told him so.

"Hi, Nick," she said into the voice mail on his cell phone. "It's Annie. Can you give me a call? I'd like to see you tonight if it's possible. Give me a call?"

She tried his home phone just afterward, and Jenny picked up.

"Annie, how are you?"

"I'm doing all right. And by the way, congratulations. Evan told me the news."

"Thank you. I never could have imagined being this happy."

"I'm glad to hear it. Listen, is Nick around?"

"No, this is his night for YMOE."

"What's that?"

"Young Men of Excellence. He teaches a workshop the first Wednesday night of the month down at the center."

"Really."

"Evan's been going. He says he gets a lot out of it. They're usually out by eight thirty. I can have him give you a call."

"I'd appreciate that."

"You know, Annie, Evan's been joking about wanting you as his best man at the wedding."

A pop of laughter burst out of Annie.

"And I guess if you were, I'd have to have Nicky as my maid of honor."

The visual summoned a whole stream of chuckles.

"So we thought we'd just reverse things. Evan is going to ask Nick to be his best man, and I was wondering if you would be willing to be my maid of honor."

Maid of honor at Evan's wedding.

The irony felt so heavy that Annie had to sit down.

"I know you and Evan have something very special," Jenny told her. "And I want you to know I'm in awe of it. I would never do anything to change it or come between you."

"Oh, Jenny."

"Seriously, we both want you to be a part of our day. Not just Evan, but me too."

"Thank you."

"So, will you?"

Annie knew there was only one possible reply. "Of course."

Jenny let out a squeal that hurt Annie's ear. "Oh, thank you. I'm so happy. Evan will be just thrilled."

"If there's anything I can do as the plans firm up," Annie said, "just let me know."

"Maybe we could go dress shopping in a couple of weeks?"

Really. What else is there to do but embrace it?

"We'll make a day of it."

Evan and Jenny equaled a force of nature now, sort of like an approaching hurricane. In that moment, Annie realized it wouldn't disappear just because she pretended it wasn't coming. She would board up the windows, buy water and batteries and lots of canned food, and just get over herself, hunker down, and make the best of it. In Deke's words, she had bigger fish to fry.

She stopped at home to walk Sherman and change clothes, and by 7:45 she'd followed her inclination and reached Santa Cruz in less than an hour. When she walked through the hall at the center, she could hear Nick's voice carrying down the corridor and right to her. She took a seat at one of the dozen tables on the cracked linoleum floor to wait for him to finish. A gush of laughter popped out of the room, and she listened as Nick told them to simmer down.

"Seriously, do you know what I mean?" he asked them. "Do you see how your word really means something, how you have to be man enough to stand by it?"

A hum of comments followed.

"Ask yourself this: what ever happened to honor? Look back to a time before us, when honor was something a man was willing to die for. A man's word was what designed his entire reputation, how he was known to the community around him. Today it's another thing entirely. We make commitments, but then the time comes and it's not convenient anymore. So what do we do? We make excuses. We back out. We let people down."

Nick's voice rang clear, confident and resolute. It pinched her heart a little to listen to him. When he joined the flow of young men leaving the room afterward, she curbed the urge to run over and hug him.

"Annie, what are you doing here?"

"Can we talk?"

"I have to clean up, but we've got some coffee made. Want to sit down and have a cup?"

"I'll skip the coffee," she told him. "But if we could have a few minutes, I'd appreciate it."

He led her back toward the room he'd just vacated, saying his good-byes to the dozen or so men still trickling out the door.

"G'night, Raymond," he said to one of them, before smacking another on the shoulder. "See ya, Jamal."

When they reached the doorway, Evan headed out as they went in.

"Hey, Annie. What are you doing here?"

"I came to talk to Nick."

"Let's go get coffee or something," he suggested, but then he read the look on Annie's face. "Or not. You talk. I'll see you both later."

"Thanks for coming, Evan," Nick called after him, and Evan waved before heading out the door.

Nick piled several stacks of handouts and pounded them cleanly together. Without looking up at Annie, he asked, "So what's so important that you had to come all the way out here?"

"Deke told me something today," she began—and she paused to question the wisdom in addressing it with him before she'd thought it all the way through.

"And?"

"Well, he said that you told him something…surprising."

"Do you want to share it with me?"

"He says you told him…that…well, that I…love you."

"And?"

"And why did you tell him that?"

"Uh, because it was rather stunning, and I chose to share it with my best friend."

"Nick, why did you tell him I said that?"

"I just told you."

"No, I mean, I didn't say that. Why are you saying that I did?"

He set down the paperwork and casually sat on the corner of the table.

"You don't remember," he stated.

"Remember what?"

"Telling me that you love me."

"This is what I'm saying, yes. I think I would recall something as monumental as that, and I don't have any recollection of it whatsoever. How do you explain that?"

"Oh, probably…*morphine*?"

"Pardon?"

"Your IV had some kind of pain medication in the drip, Annie. But you clearly said, 'I love you.'"

"No, I didn't." She'd meant the statement to be more forceful than it emerged.

"Yes, you did. You were going on about wanting to know this and that, and then you said, 'Just one more thing, Nick,' and I said, 'Okay, just one more,' and you said, 'I really and truly love you.' And then you went to sleep."

It was the strangest thing. Until she heard him tell the story, she'd have bet the farm she never said such a thing. But as he told it, it began to seem…*familiar*.

"Is it all coming back to you?" he asked her.

"No." *Liar.*

"Annie, what's the big deal?"

"Well, you must have thought it was a big deal, Nick, if you told Deke about it. And you remember it with such…clarity."

"I didn't have an IV, Annie. Things are pretty clear for me."

"Well, I shouldn't have said that to you."

"No?"

"No. Because it's just not…entirely…you know…true."

"Yeah, I got that when I found you mooning over my sister's fiancé the other day."

"I wasn't—" Annie stopped herself mid-word and let out an unintelligible groan instead. "You are so frustrating."

"But you are the picture of peace and calm for me."

Annie dropped to one of the nearest chairs and massaged her temples. After a minute or two, she inhaled slowly and blew it out in a long puff.

"So who do you love, Annie?"

She looked up at him, as he leaned back against the table with his arms folded and looked as if he had asked a random, legitimate question.

"What?"

"Your heart. What does it tell you?"

He straightened and closed the gap between them. Taking her by both arms, he guided Annie to her feet and tugged her toward him. "Right here, right now. What is your heart telling you?"

To run like the wind.

"Who ever knows what my stupid heart is saying," she muttered. "It's always wrong anyway."

"Do you want to know what I think?"

"No."

"Well, I'm going to tell you."

"Figured."

"I think you have been so busy thinking and planning and wondering that your heart can't be heard over all that construction."

"Oh, really."

"And I think the minute you managed to shut up long enough to relax—okay, it took medication to do it—but your heart uttered the words you've been carrying around all along."

"That I love you."

"Exactly."

"Arrogant much, Nick?"

"Not too much. Just enough."

Nick still held Annie by the arms, his face a mere few inches from hers, his eyes holding hers with an invisible grip.

"Are you ready to ask me?"

"Ask you what?" she asked. But she knew what. In fact, they both knew.

"Ask me already," he exclaimed. "Ask me to kiss you."

"No."

"Ask me to kiss you, Annie."

"No."

"Ask me."

"No."

And just like that, Nick released her, leaving Annie feeling like a withered petal fallen from a flower, and she nearly lost her balance.

"I guess I was mistaken, then," he told her, gathering his stacks of paperwork and heading for the door. "Consider yourself absolved from your words, Annie. We'll chalk it up to medication and put it behind us."

"Do you mean that?"

"Of course I do." He gave her a sweet, albeit disarming, smile. "I'm not the kind of guy who spends much time wanting someone who doesn't want me."

"It's not that I—"

He raised his hand, and Annie fell immediately silent.

"Let's stop talking now, all right?"

"Okay."

"Come on. I'll walk you to your car."

The moment he closed Annie's door and waved good-bye, she turned over the ignition, shifted into DRIVE, and headed straight for Zoey's.

* * * * *

"Didn't you want him to kiss you?"

"Well, yeah," Annie admitted. "I kinda did."

"Then why didn't you say it?"

"I don't know."

"Maybe because you didn't want him to win?"

"Maybe."

Zoey handed her a short, wide glass of water with perfectly formed cubes that clinked around in it.

"What's this?"

"Water."

"Are you out of Diet Coke?"

"I've been thinking Nick might be right. We consume too much of it."

"Nick's not right!" Annie exclaimed before sinking into a sigh.

"I can tell you this," Zoey told her. "Your meltdown over Evan and Jenny getting married is just plain ridiculous. You've known for years that things were never going that direction between you and Evan."

"I know."

"And his falling for Jenny is not a personal affront to you. Rather, it's just a natural thing between two people who *were* meant for one another."

"Yes. I know."

"Evan wasn't right for you, and Colby wasn't right for you. But I've never seen you look at a man the way you look at Nick."

Annie's heart skipped a beat. "What are you saying?"

"It's true. When I saw the two of you together at the festival that day, it just hit me like a ton of bricks. Nick's *The One*, Annie. And you know it too, or you never would have told him you were in love with him."

"But I was under the influence of—"

"I don't care," she interrupted with confidence. "You said it, and you meant it. All these years, Evan was a great excuse for you to not face the truth. What was that guy's name?"

"What guy?"

"The guy you adored in college. The one who attacked you."

"Danny." Annie clamped her eyes shut and shook her head. "Danny Radcliff."

"Danny. He let you down, and he scared the wits out of you, and he got you all mixed up about your feelings about love. You've been running from men ever since, Annie. As soon as something even started to develop, you sprinted like a marathon runner."

Just what I accused Evan of doing.

"But it's time to face it and make a change. Now you've got to just swallow your fear of pledging yourself to someone and wrap your brain around the whole idea of trusting someone enough to become part of a twosome."

"Zoey, I—"

"It's not easy, Annie. Opening up your life to another human being is hard. And some days you're probably going to wish he'd just disappear for a couple of weeks. Or a year. But the right relationship is worth the trouble, I promise you."

She thought about interrupting her again, but Zoey seemed to be on a roll. Annie suppressed the smile and just allowed her friend to continue.

"You need to ask yourself all the important questions. Then just be quiet and listen to how your heart will lead you. And then follow, Annie."

Without a word, Annie stood up and went to Zoey, embracing her vehemently. Then she turned around and headed for the door.

"Where are you going?"

"Home."

"Are you mad?"

"No."

"Scared?"

"Spitless."

"Okay, then. Drive carefully."

Chapter Twenty-Four

....

"I believe. I believe.
It's silly, but I believe!"
Natalie Wood, *Miracle on 34ʰ Street*, 1947

At the risk of messing up her life with yet another list, Annie grabbed a few mini Snickers, a bottle of water, and a pad and pen before heading for the kitchen table. The spot where all the madness began.

At the top of the page, she wrote, THE ONE. Then she began making a detailed list of the qualities he would have.

1. *Strong faith and sense of self.*
2. *Honest and trustworthy. Sincerity and integrity.*
3. *Self-contained. Doesn't rely on someone else to complete him.*
4. *Secure enough to trust me. No jealous rages.*
5. *Similar ideals and hopes for the future.*
6. *Someone I can be myself with. Someone I can trust.*
7. *Someone I respect, who can also respect me.*
8. *Someone who gets that the Lakers rule all sports.*
9. *Lovers of rap and hip-hop music need not apply.*

She read the list over a couple of times before setting down the pad of paper. Without intending to do it, Annie knew she'd painted a full and complete portrait of Nick. Of course, she had no idea whatsoever how he felt about rap and hip-hop, but she could hope.

"Life does not have to be huge and over-the-top to be fulfilling. Every day doesn't have to be out-of-the-ordinary spectacular to be inspiring. There is a—a joy in sharing simple things with someone special, in finding your own way and following the path that was laid out for you. There is a joy in the journey that you are totally missing."

Nick's words brought both comfort and a stinging sensation to Annie's heart.

And then Zoey's words fell down on her like rain.

"You need to ask yourself all the important questions. Then just be quiet and listen to how your heart will lead you. And then follow, Annie."

* * * * *

Nick punched "Veldon Smith" into the search box on his computer, and a massive list of priors appeared.

Smitty's nothing if not consistent, he thought.

With his leave of absence to cover Deke's, Nick had been pulled away from a case he'd been building against the guy for months. Now, as he prepared to return to the force, Smitty's case file showed little if any progress, despite Thorton's commitment to see it through.

"Did you follow up on any of the leads I gave you?" he asked Thorton when he and Chief Sheldon marched through the squad room toward Sheldon's office.

"It's a dead end, Bench," Thorton returned before they closed the office door behind them. "Let it go."

Letting go—not one of Nick's strong suits. Most of the guys he knew were only too happy to let go of an idea when it didn't pan out. If no evidence could be found to prove one theory, then move on to the next one until the proof sat well in hand. If the television program didn't hold interest, just click the remote to access eight hundred other channels that might. A dead-end relationship? Just walk out the door and find the next possibility.

Nick, however, tended to be more of a dog-with-a-bone variety, and he'd always figured that quality made him a better cop. But when applied to his friendship with Annie, he feared it rang out with a bit of Colby Barnes. The guy just couldn't take no for an answer, and it colored him a putrid shade of "Loser" in Nick's eyes.

He wondered if he'd crossed over that line himself, the one that divided "Interested Party" from "Stalker." The thought of it poked him in the throat. He'd felt so sincerely convicted that destiny had led them together, but now he surmised that most stalkers likely started out feeling that way too.

Letting go. Not his strong suit. But clearly, the time had come to make the stretch.

Okay, he prayed. *I get it. I won't pursue her anymore. Ship sailed. Now I hope You'll force the message from my brain down into my spirit because I'm not sure I know how to let go of the idea that Annie and I—*

They belonged together. He'd been so certain. But now he couldn't even form the words in his mind.

* * * * *

The sun had barely risen, but Annie sped across town in her car, Sherman standing at attention in the back seat. He seemed to sense this was more than a sunrise ride in the car. The radio DJ announced 7:30 a.m. as she pulled into Nick's driveway and shut off the motor.

"Oh, God, please don't let me mess this up."

Sherman's tail wagged double time. "Stay, boy," she told him, and he groaned at her in response. "I'm serious too. You stay!"

With firm resolve, Annie crossed the drive and headed up to the door. It took a couple of minutes for Jenny to open it; she held her robe shut with one hand, shielding her squinted eyes with the other.

"Annie. Is everything all right?"

"I'm sorry to be so early, Jenny. Is Nick up yet?"

"He's up and out by now, I'm sure. He runs almost every morning." She glanced at the hall tree and nodded. "His running shoes are gone—and Murphy's leash too. That means Nicky's gone."

"Do you know where?"

"Of course," she said with a smile, pointing down the hill. "Two miles to the beach and two miles back."

"Thank you, Jenny!" she exclaimed, and she took off at a full sprint toward the car.

"You're welcome," Jenny called after her.

"Okay, Shermie. We're cookin' with gas now."

He poked his head over the car seat and tried to rest his chin on Annie's shoulder. He didn't quite make it, so she reached back and gave his head a quick rub as she drove down the hill slowly, checking for any paths that might break away from the street.

Just a few yards from the beach she spotted him, running at an even pace, attached to Murphy by a long, red leash. They looked like two peas in a pod jogging side by side, a sudden reminder of Evan and Sherman. Murphy even lifted his little paws at much the same rhythm as Nick.

She pulled up beside them and rolled down the passenger window. Nick leaned down, looked inside, but kept on jogging.

"Good morning," she called out to him.

"Morning."

"Can we talk?"

"Is this a replay?"

"Come on, Nick. Stop so I can talk to you."

"Sorry. Murphy and I are occupied at the moment. I'll call you later in the day." Then he just continued toward the sand, this ridiculous man and his silly little dog.

Annie stopped the car, threw the gear into PARK, and opened the door. She pulled herself out and stood next to the car, watching him move farther away.

"Nick!" she called out, but he didn't turn back. "Nick! Come back here...and *kiss me*."

He stopped, but he didn't turn around. Murphy, on the other hand, seemed quite astonished, and he looked back at her over his furry little shoulder.

"I'm sorry," Nick shouted, his back still facing her. "I don't think I heard you."

"You heard me, you mule. I'm asking you to come back here and kiss me."

He turned slowly, letting second after second tick by before he finally sauntered back up the hill toward her.

There's going to be no living with him now.

"Are you sure?" he asked as he reached her. "Because you know, you can't take something like that back once you've done it. Can't unring that bell, Annie Gray."

"Oh, just hush up and kiss me."

And he did. He rounded the car and took Annie into his arms and kissed her half senseless. Her head began to spin, her heart raced, and beads of perspiration popped up on the back of her neck and all along her spine.

When they parted, she wobbled on her feet.

"Wow."

She hadn't meant to say it out loud, but—

"Wow!" she repeated.

"I tried to tell you," Nick said with a shrug. "And you almost missed out on it altogether. Not too smart, Annie Gray. You're a little slow on the uptake."

Annie grabbed him by the front of his shirt and dragged him toward her, wrapping her arms around his neck and diving headfirst into another kiss. This time, Nick's arms slid around her waist, and he lifted her up off the ground as he returned the kiss. Annie's leg bent at the knee like a cinematic heroine, and a slight moan snaked up from the pit of her stomach and popped out of her throat.

"Take it back," he said when they parted and he'd set her back on the ground.

She shook her head and blinked at him. "Wh–what?"

"You said I wasn't kiss-worthy. Take it back."

"Oh, I take it back," she said, and she couldn't stop herself. She actually swooned as she fell toward him and kissed him for a third time.

The sun had made its full arrival, squatting low in the sky at a full-on shine. After that last amazing kiss, the two of them just stood there, locked in one another's arms.

"You can trust me," Nick said on a whisper. "You have my word."

Annie noticed just then that Murphy had climbed into the car and sacked out on the backseat with his head buried in Annie's purse like some sort of broken pillow, one of his long velvety ears draped over Sherman's happy face.

"He looks right at home," Nick said.

"I kinda think we're all home now, Nick," Annie told him. "Home at last."

Fade out.

About the Author

....

 Sandra D. Bricker has been publishing in both the Christian and general markets for years with novels for women and teens, magazine articles, Christian devotionals, and short stories. With eleven novels in print and four more slated for publication through 2012, she has carved out a niche for herself as an award-winning author of laugh-out-loud comedy for the inspirational market. Sandie was an aspiring screenwriter as well as an entertainment publicist in Hollywood for fifteen-plus years for some of daytime television's hottest stars. When her mother became ill in Florida, she left Los Angeles to provide care…and begin a new phase of her life as a novelist. Those Hollywood dreams aren't yet buried, and Sandie hopes to see her books gracing movie and television screens one day very soon.

Keep up with Sandie via her Web site (www.sandradbricker.com) or her popular weekly blog (www.sandradbricker.blogspot.com).

Want a peek into local American life—past and present?
The *Love Finds You*™ series published by Summerside Press
features real towns and combines travel, romance,
and faith in one irresistible package!

The novels in the series—uniquely titled after American towns with romantic or intriguing names—inspire romance and fun. Each fictional story draws on the compelling history or the unique character of a real place. Stories center on romances kindled in small towns, old loves lost and found again on the high plains, and new loves discovered at exciting vacation getaways. Summerside Press plans to publish at least one novel set in each of the fifty states. Be sure to catch them all!

Now Available

Love Finds You in Miracle, Kentucky
by Andrea Boeshaar
ISBN: 978-1-934770-37-5

Love Finds You in Snowball, Arkansas
by Sandra D. Bricker
ISBN: 978-1-934770-45-0

Love Finds You in Romeo, Colorado
by Gwen Ford Faulkenberry
ISBN: 978-1-934770-46-7

Love Finds You in Valentine, Nebraska
by Irene Brand
ISBN: 978-1-934770-38-2

Love Finds You in Humble, Texas
by Anita Higman
ISBN: 978-1-934770-61-0

Love Finds You in Last Chance, California
by Miralee Ferrell
ISBN: 978-1-934770-39-9

Love Finds You in Maiden, North Carolina
by Tamela Hancock Murray
ISBN: 978-1-934770-65-8

Love Finds You in Paradise, Pennsylvania
by Loree Lough
ISBN: 978-1-934770-66-5

Love Finds You in Treasure Island, Florida
by Debby Mayne
ISBN: 978-1-934770-80-1

Love Finds You in Liberty, Indiana
by Melanie Dobson
ISBN: 978-1-934770-74-0

Love Finds You in Revenge, Ohio
by Lisa Harris
ISBN: 978-1-934770-81-8

Love Finds You in Poetry, Texas
by Janice Hanna
ISBN: 978-1-935416-16-6

Love Finds You in Sisters, Oregon
by Melody Carlson
ISBN: 978-1-935416-18-0

Love Finds You in Charm, Ohio
by Annalisa Daughety
ISBN: 978-1-935416-17-3

Love Finds You in
Bethlehem, New Hampshire
by Lauralee Bliss
ISBN: 978-1-935416-20-3

Love Finds You in North Pole, Alaska
by Loree Lough
ISBN: 978-1-935416-19-7

Love Finds You in Holiday, Florida
by Sandra D. Bricker
ISBN: 978-1-935416-25-8

Love Finds You in
Lonesome Prairie, Montana
by Tricia Goyer and Ocieanna Fleiss
ISBN: 978-1-935416-29-6

Love Finds You in Bridal Veil, Oregon
by Miralee Ferrell
ISBN: 978-1-935416-63-0

Love Finds You in
Hershey, Pennsylvania
by Cerella D. Sechrist
ISBN: 978-1-935416-64-7

Love Finds You in Homestead, Iowa
by Melanie Dobson
ISBN: 978-1-935416-66-1

Love Finds You in Pendleton, Oregon
by Melody Carlson
ISBN: 978-1-935416-84-5

Love Finds You in Golden, New Mexico
by Lena Nelson Dooley
ISBN: 978-1-935416-74-6

Love Finds You in Lahaina, Hawaii
by Bodie Thoene
ISBN: 978-1-935416-78-4

Love Finds You in
Victory Heights, Washington
by Tricia Goyer and Ocieanna Fleiss
ISBN: 978-1-60936-000-9

Love Finds You in
Calico, California
by Elizabeth Ludwig
ISBN: 978-1-60936-001-6

Love Finds You in
Sugarcreek, Ohio
by Serena B. Miller
ISBN: 978-1-60936-002-3

Love Finds You in
Deadwood, South Dakota
by Tracey Cross
ISBN: 978-1-60936-003-0

Love Finds You in
Silver City, Idaho
by Janelle Mowery
ISBN: 978-1-60936-005-4

COMING SOON

Love Finds You Under the Mistletoe
by Irene Brand and Anita Higman
ISBN: 978-1-60936-004-7

Love Finds You in Hope, Kansas
by Pamela Griffin
ISBN: 978-1-60936-007-8

Love Finds You in Sun Valley, Idaho
by Angela Ruth
ISBN: 978-1-60936-008-5

Love Finds You in Camelot, Tennessee
by Janice Hanna
ISBN: 978-1-935416-65-4

Love Finds You in Tombstone, Arizona
by Miralee Ferrell
ISBN: 978-1-60936-104-4

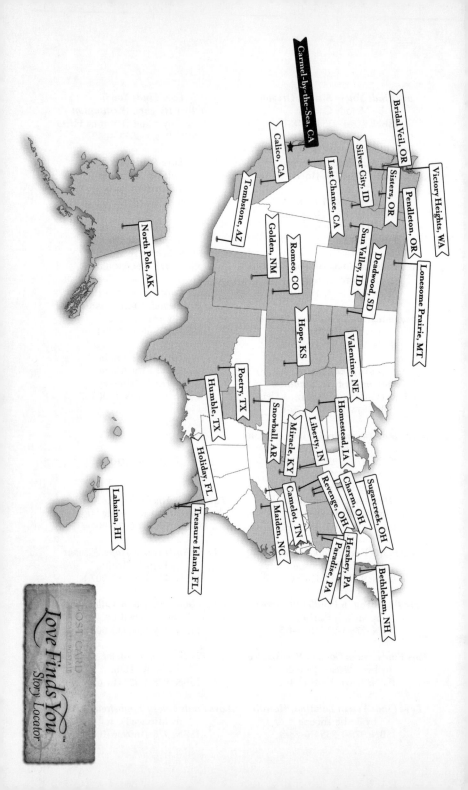